Hoopla Under the Huppah

To Aiva, Liv, Emme, & Chloe —

L'hayim !

Enjoy,
Dani Weinst

:)

Books in the
YaYa & YoYo Series

Praise for *Hoopla Under the Huppah*
(YaYa & YoYo, Book 3)

"The energy of the characters jumps off the page as you see the world through their eyes—the humor and challenges of daily living and family life all brought together by emerging understandings of Jewish ritual. YaYa's and YoYo's questions and observations about Jewish weddings offer wonderful springboards for lively discussion in school and informal educational settings. *L'hayim!*"

Ray Levi, Ph.D.
Director, Day School Leadership Training Institute
William Davidson Graduate School of Jewish Education
The Jewish Theological Seminary

"*Hoopla Under the Huppah* is an engaging story, written from the perspective of a precocious pre-teen, about the preparations for her aunt's upcoming wedding. Author Dori Weinstein captures her heroine's thoughts, concerns, and emotions as we share YaYa's confusion as well as her complex experiences which encompass a broken arm, a splattered ketubah, and more. Throughout the story readers are introduced to the beautiful and meaningful customs and traditions surrounding a Jewish wedding just as YaYa begins to learn more about her family and herself. This delightful book is appropriate for every young reader!"

Rabbi Jeffrey Wohlberg
Senior Rabbi Emeritus
Adas Israel Congregation
Washington, DC

"Oh, how I love YaYa and YoYo! As a Lutheran pastor, I learned and laughed much in this third book around these charming and hilarious twins. Beautiful, creative, and authentic explanations—so accessible, even for those of us who are not Jewish. The joy and beauty of this wedding, and all of the rituals and traditions around it, are tremendous fun. I adore this sweet family and am so glad there is another book about their adventures in faith and love."

Melanie Heuiser Hill
Author of *Giant Pumpkin Suite*

"In *Hoopla Under the Huppah*, YaYa and YoYo are invited to be in their favorite aunt's wedding. YaYa gets caught up in the excitement and wants everything to be perfect! When her well-meaning actions don't go as planned, YaYa turns to Jewish tradition to help her make things right. YaYa is a lovable main character with relatable flaws and lots of charm. Readers will ultimately root for open hearted YaYa as she learns about the true meaning of family and friendship."

Barbara Bietz
Author of *Like a Maccabee*
and *The Sundown Kid—A Southwestern Shabbat*

"*Hoopla Under the Huppah* is just the kind of book I would've loved to be able to recommend to kids when I was a Jewish Day School librarian! YaYa and YoYo and their family are charming and believable characters, and the book artfully interweaves a wealth of information about Jewish wedding ritual and tradition into the engaging story of Aunt Rachel's wedding. I loved the touches of humor and goofiness, and the way the family, like so many real-life families I know, integrates Jewish observance into their contemporary lives with joy and playfulness."

Elisabeth Kushner
Author of *The Purim Superhero*

Jewish Educators Love *YaYa & YoYo!*

"I feel like I just began the journey of YaYa and YoYo and am looking forward to their next adventures. I found myself smiling while I read. YaYa's voice as a Jewish fifth-grader gives many children an opportunity to see themselves in the characters of this book and feel a sense of belonging. We have waited a long time for a series like this one!"

Jane Taubenfeld Cohen
Former Head of School,
South Area Solomon Schechter Day School
Author of *We Can Make It Happen!*

"*YaYa & YoYo: Sliding into the New Year* is not only a pleasure to read, but also paves the way for a captivating Jewish journey for kids and pre-teens. Dori Weinstein uses humor, wisdom and warmth to address the challenges that every Jewish family faces in raising committed, knowledgeable Jews in the 21st century. I am sure that YaYa and YoYo are going to become household names in the vital enterprise of strengthening Jewish identity and commitment. My kids and I can't wait to hear about their next adventures!"

Rabbi Charles Savenor
Director of Congregational Education
Park Avenue Synagogue
New York, New York

"Our students have been waiting in line to check out [Dori's] books from the library and cannot wait to read more. Our teachers are using her books as mentor texts for developing characters and using details in writing."

Nancy Penchev
Lower School Media and Instructional Tech Coordinator
Scheck Hillel Community School
North Miami Beach, Florida

"In the book, *Sliding into the New Year*, we gain a wonderful new author of children's Jewish literature in Dori Weinstein. She brings a modern, human tone to a story that is both timely and engaging. Many books geared toward Jewish children focus purely on the meaning of the holidays or on telling stories with didactic preachiness. Ms. Weinstein instead creates a nuanced child, who has believable conflicts and who resolves them in believable ways. And she does so within the context of a fun and entertaining story as well.

Lydia Schultz
School Librarian
Talmud Torah of Saint Paul
Saint Paul, Minnesota

"In a genre largely dominated by historical fiction and characters dealing with extreme adversity, it is very refreshing and appreciated to have an author who provides characters that our students can relate to and enjoy. Since her visit, [Dori's] books have been in constant circulation!"

Michelle Epstein
Media Director
The Epstein School
Atlanta, Georgia

"Dori is not just another author, her messages are positive and powerful. Her books are meant to reach children in grades three through six but her messages are enjoyable for those hard to reach preteens/tweens as well...a great new strong voice in literature for the tween audience."

Laura Weissman-Rothschild
Librarian
Gerrard Berman Day School
Oakland, New Jersey

"[Weinstein is] a master educator and brilliant author."

Rabbi Joseph Robinson
Director of Congregational Learning
Temple Beth-El, Birmingham, Alabama

"The kids loved [Dori's] books so much that they were laughing out loud reading them for hours after classes ended!"

Rabbi Suzanne Brody
Director of Education and Youth Programming
Temple Beth-El
Ithaca, New York

"Our students are looking forward to devouring a new series—especially one that incorporates Jewish life!"

Rebecca Butcher
Library Media Specialist
Atlanta Jewish Academy
Atlanta, Georgia

"As a librarian in a Jewish Day School, I am grateful for [this] series as it fills this gap in fiction for middle grade students, and I eagerly anticipate the subsequent adventures of YaYa and YoYo."

Beryl Bresgi
Librarian
Solomon Schechter Day School of Bergen County
New Milford, New Jersey

Hoopla Under the Huppah

Dori Weinstein

Five Flames Press

YaYa & YoYo: Hoopla Under the Huppah
First edition— October 2017
Five Flames Press

www.yayayoyo.com

Cover illustration by © Ann D. Koffsky
Cover design by Ilana Weinstein
Cover graphics by Ward Barnett
Editors: Leslie Martin and Judy Cohen

ISBN-10: 0-9890193-2-2
ISBN-13: 978-0-9890193-2-3

For our parents

Martin and Susan Margolin

Shelly and Joan Weinstein

*who led us to, and stood
with us, under the huppah.*

And in memory of my mom

Sandra Margolin

*whose spirit was felt deeply
under the huppah that day
and who is missed every day.*

And of course for

Gary

*my b'shert, my huppah-mate,
life-mate, and best friend.*

Here's to the next twenty-five years together!

CONTENTS

1

Growing Pencil Trees

I could feel the bumps, grooves and smooth parts against my tongue. And even though my mom constantly bugs me about it, I still always seem to end up with a pencil between my top and bottom teeth when I'm concentrating. If I'm lucky and I'm having a good day, it's just the eraser that winds up on my tongue and not the pointy writing tip.

I was focusing on my math homework, plugging away at fractions and percents.

...Okay, so if I divide four by seven, it will be a little bit more than half, so it has to be more than fifty percent....

My train of thought was interrupted by a knock on the door, which I could barely hear over the Corey McDonald song I was listening to. My parents can't understand how I can do homework with music playing but I think everything works a little better when Corey, my all-time favorite musician, is singing to me in the background.

There was a second knock, a bit louder.

It was then that I realized I had chewed my pencil so much that it had more dents in it than a golf ball. I wiped the slimy, yellow writing stick on my jeans and tossed it into a cup I had on my desk so Mom wouldn't see I had been biting on it. I grabbed a different, unchewed one from the floor near my desk, and called, "Come in," over my favorite song, *Love You Like a Sno-*

Cone.

Mom popped her head into my room and with a strangely goofy grin on her face, announced, "YaYa, phone call for you."

Everyone in my family calls me YaYa, but my name is actually Ellie Silver. YaYa is my family nickname because my Hebrew name is Yael, which I often like to point out rhymes with such lovely things as "la belle." In French that means "the beautiful one." My twin brother Joel's Hebrew name is Yoel, which I often like to point out rhymes with such lovely things as "toe smell." In English that means "stinky toes."

When we were babies and first learning how to speak, Joel tried to call me Yael but it came out as YaYa and his own name came out as YoYo so that's how we're known in our family. We don't mind at home, but once we're out the door, we're Ellie and Joel, plain and simple. After all, now that we're eleven years old we don't want the world to know that we're still called by our toddler nicknames. How embarrassing would that be?

Mom held out the phone. I nodded and gave her the "wait a second" signal with my pointer finger in the air, but didn't look up. I finished writing "57%" in my math workbook.

"Come on, YaYa, she's waiting," Mom said, stepping into my room and trying to figure out how to forge a path through the maze of my prized possessions on the floor. After she almost tripped over my open flute case by the door, she gave up trying to enter any farther.

"Who is it? Maybe I should call her back," I suggested. "I want to get through these problems first. I'm on a roll." Mom looked at me, as shocked as if I told her I'd just earned a seat on the next mission to Mars.

She spoke into the phone, "Can she call you back in a few minutes? She's just finishing up some homework." Then Mom seemed to be listening to the voice on the other end because she was nodding her head as if the caller could see her. "Okay, so you're going to call her? Great. It'll probably be just ten more minutes." Without looking up from the page, I held up my hand to indicate that I'd probably only need five. "Maybe five minutes," she said into the phone. "Yep, okay, bye." And she hung up.

"You're doing your math homework? Without a reminder?"

I looked up from my work. I saw Mom through my hair, which at the moment hung like a veil of long, light-brown, blonde-streaked, stringy tangles in front of my face. I reached for a little black elastic band that dangled from the knob on my desk drawer and quickly pulled my hair back into a messy ponytail. Now I could actually see her just beyond the mound of clean and dirty laundry that was jumbled into one big pile on the floor.

"Mom, I like math. It's fun, and I especially love the way Ms. Webster explains everything. She's probably the best teacher I've ever had!" I understood why Mom was so surprised. Along with my messiness, time management is one of my weaker areas. I tend to wait until the last minute to get my homework done, and sometimes that means doing it on the bus on the way to school in the morning. I'm working hard on keeping up with my assignments. Plus, I really am enjoying math this year, so it's not like it's torture or anything to get it done. I can't say the same for my social studies homework. Blech. That's the worst.

"That's fantastic, YaYa. I'm so happy to hear that

and I'm very proud of you!" she said from the doorway. "I'd come over and give you a big hug, but I can't seem to make it across this minefield of yours." She shook her head and gave me one of her famous Mom looks, complete with mouth scrunched to the side and eyebrows raised. She can't stand that I keep my room like this. She must have realized that I had cleaned up a bit, seeing that I was doing my homework at my just-recently-cleared-off desk. This was a big deal. I mean, I was working AT MY DESK! She remained standing there with a strange look on her face. I wanted to finish up before the phone rang again so I bent back over my book and continued my calculating and writing.

After about a minute, I looked up at her. "Done!" I said victoriously, dropping the unchewed, smooth yellow pencil to add a little drama.

"YaYa," Mom said.

"Yep?" I answered, expecting that she'd toss me the phone so I would be able to answer it when the mystery caller called back.

Instead, she pointed at my desk. "Just out of curiosity, why is there a pencil in your cup of water?"

Oh no! I had tossed the first pencil into the wrong cup! It landed in the cup I was drinking from, which happened to be right next to the one full of pens and pencils. Oh well, at least she didn't notice how chewed up it was.

I giggled and said, "I'm trying to grow a pencil tree!" I learned from Joel that humor, even really, really bad humor, is a great distraction and can be a good way to get out of a sticky situation. Joel tends to tell fairly awful jokes, and believe me, I wouldn't normally want to imitate him, but I so very much did not want to have to sit through yet another one of Mom's lectures on how everything has its proper place and why I should put things back where they belong.

"A pencil tree, huh? Good luck with that, goofball," she said with a laugh. "Anyway, that was Aunt Rachel. She's going to call back in a few minutes. She really wants to talk to you. I think it's important."

"Oh, I didn't realize it was Aunt Rachel! Yay!" I exclaimed.

Then Mom said, "And YaYa, I've told you a thousand times, you need to stop chewing on your pencils!"

How does she do that? I mused, staring at the bite-marked pencil sitting in the water cup. *It's like moms have amazing superpowers!* I wondered if I'd automatically get those powers if I ever became a mom someday. Or do you have to go to Mom school to learn that stuff?

I took the pencil out of my cup, took a sip of water and looked around. My desk was clean and there I was, getting my homework done the night before it was due and not waiting until the last minute in the morning. Maybe I'd even get to the bus stop on time. Maybe I'd even get there early! It seemed like I was right on track and everything was going smoothly. What I didn't know then was that once I answered that phone call, my life would feel as if it was spinning out of control like the Tilt-a-Whirl at the State Fair. And even I, the girl who lives for thrill rides, had no idea how chaotic the ride was about to become.

2

TVs, TP, and Roller Coaster Hills

Jeremy, my annoying almost-thirteen-year-old brother, barged into my room and said, "I heard the phone ring before. Is it for me?"

"What do you think, Jay? Would Mom be standing in *my* room, handing *me* the phone, if it was for *you*?" I have to admit that came out much snottier than I meant it. He brings out the worst in me.

He mocked me in a high-pitched, whiny voice, "*Would Mom be standing in my room...?*" Then he turned to Mom, "See what I have to put up with?" Oh, like he's so innocent all the time!

We used to get along. In fact, we call him Jay because when he was about three years old and Joel and I were toddlers, Jeremy wanted to be the third twin—not that "three twins" makes any sense since twins only come in pairs! But since we were called YaYa and YoYo based on our Hebrew names, he wanted to be called YerYer because his Hebrew name is Yeremiyahu. My parents thought YerYer sounded kind of ridiculous so they suggested JayJay or just Jay. He goes by Jay all the time now.

Mom replied, "It wasn't for you, Jay. It was Aunt Rachel calling for YaYa and she's about to call back." Then she turned and pointed at me. "And there's no need for you to be so nasty." She was right, I know, but he's so obnoxious all the time that whenever he says anything to me, my mouth automatically reacts without my brain having time to think about it.

"Well, don't take too long on the phone," he practically snarled at me. "I'm waiting for an important call."

Unbelievable! I looked at the cell phone in his hand that was a pre-bar mitzvah gift from our parents. Once he started seventh grade he began biking to school on his own, so Mom and Dad wanted him to have a phone for safety reasons. Now he and his phone are inseparable.

"Use your own phone, Jay! That's why you have it." All I can say is that if he'd be nicer to me, I'd be nicer to him.

Right on cue, the phone in Mom's hand rang and I kangaroo-hopped over Laundry Mountain to take it from her.

"Hi," I said into the phone. "Can you hang on for just one sec?" I waved to Mom and Jeremy as a signal that it was time for them to leave.

"Come on, Jay," Mom said, directing him out of the room and back into the hallway. "Let's leave YaYa to have her conversation."

He turned and stuck his tongue out at me without Mom seeing. I stuck my tongue out right back at him, accompanied by a good, solid eye-roll, but called out sweetly, "Mom, can you close the door behind you, please?"

With the click of the door, the two of them were gone and I was finally available to talk with Aunt Rachel.

"I'm sorry, are you still there? Hello?" I asked into the phone. It occurred to me that she might be calling to discuss something about the wedding. She and Uncle David were getting married in only a couple of weeks (eighteen days to be exact) and I could hardly wait. I'd started a countdown on my calendar until the big event, crossing off each day as it passed, ending with a big giant heart around November 22. I was positive that it was going to be one of the best days of my life. I think maybe I was even more excited than the bride and groom. I suddenly felt tingly all over, anticipating what she wanted to talk about.

"Hey, YaYa!" Her cheerful voice came through loud and clear.

"Hi, Aunt Rachel!" She is so cool. She's my dad's younger sister and one of my favorite people in the world. "Sorry I couldn't answer right away. I wanted to finish up my math homework. And guess what? I was working AT MY DESK!" I added excitedly.

"Does that mean you're sharing the desk in YoYo's room?" She knows us so well.

"No, I'm actually in my own room at my very own desk! Can you believe it? I'm working on keeping my room neat," I said with a silent, guilty shrug, eyeing the empty bag of M&Ms on the floor, the crumpled-up tissue on my bed, the half-full water bottle on my bookshelf, and a random sock hanging from my lamp that hasn't lit up for three months (and would probably work just fine if I would simply put in a new lightbulb).

"So you've managed to find your desk. That's terrific!" She paused. "Hold on, you're not trying to play a YoYo-style trick on me, are you?"

I giggled. "No, not at all," I said. Aside from telling his really bad jokes, Joel loves to play tricks on everyone, especially me. Every now and then I get him back, but he's the one who has truly earned the reputation as family prankster. The original Silver family practical joker, however, is Aunt Rachel.

TVs, TP, and Roll Coaster Hills • 9

"Well, good for you! Keep up the great work," she said. "Okay, listen, I don't want to keep you from the rest of your homework, so I'll make this quick. I have an important question for you."

"Okay," I said, eager to hear what she wanted. My heart began to race a little bit. *This is it!* I thought to myself. *I'm finally going to find out what I'm doing in the wedding!*

Rollercoaster going up...chains clankety-clanking. The world below getting smaller and smaller. Anticipation building!

"Can you still get to your bicycle or did your parents put them all away for the winter already?" she asked.

Rollercoaster car sitting on top of the very steep hill, teetering.

"My bicycle?" I asked. I wasn't sure I heard her correctly.

"Yeah, can you get to your bike?"

Huh. Well that was *not* what I was expecting. I was pretty sure that a bike was not part of the wedding planning. Not unless she was going to ask me to bike down the aisle!

"Yes, I can still get to it," I answered feeling curious, confused, and discouraged all at once. This was beginning to seem like a huge letdown.

Rollercoaster breaking down, 400 feet in the air....

"Great. I need you to do me a favor. Are you allowed to ride to the store by yourself?" she asked.

"I'd have to ask my mom. Why?"

"Well, it's kind of important. If you could, I need you to please bike down there and pick up some toilet paper for me. I'm all out and I don't have time to get any."

FOR REAL? This is what she called me for? That's why Mom had a goofy look on her face when she came to my room? This is what she waited for all that time while I finished my math problems? If she had enough time to wait and even call me back, why didn't she just get up herself and go to the store?

Rollercoaster hurtling to the ground at 190 miles per hour, completely out of control, impending doom awaiting.

"Yeah, I guess I can ask her," I answered, not even trying to hide my disappointment. Then another thought occurred to me. *Maybe she's hurt and can't go. Maybe something's wrong!* "Are you all right?" I asked.

"Oh, yeah, yeah, I'm fine. Are you sure you don't mind?" she asked.

Am I sure I don't mind? Actually, I'm pretty sure that I DO mind. But I wasn't going to say that out loud.

"No, it's okay," I said glumly. "I'll see if I can do it." For the life of me I couldn't understand why she needed someone to run out and buy toilet paper right away. I mean, how much of an emergency could it have been? Then I thought about it for a second and decided that I really didn't want to know.

"You would do that for me? It's pretty chilly out. You don't mind?"

"I'll do it if Mom says it's okay." Our parents had told me and Joel that in the spring we'd be allowed to ride our bikes around on our own as long as we stayed on the bike path. But maybe they'd say it was all right if it was for something important. But then I questioned inside my head, *Is this something important?*

"Thanks, YaYa. And hey, if she says yes, while you're at it, I could use a gallon of milk. Oh, and a TV. Like a nice 50-inch flat screen. Could you pick up one of those for me too?"

WHAT? Okay, seriously, what IS this woman doing in her bathroom? I wondered.

"And maybe a watermelon...and a pack of gum," she threw in as an afterthought.

I was tongue tied. I started to ask, "You want me to—" But then she cut me off.

"And the milk. Don't forget the milk. I know you can do it. You're such a strong girl. You okay with that?"

"Uh. Um. Uh," I stammered.

"Oh, YaYa, you are the best!" she gushed, without actually waiting for me to say yes. "But actually, you know what? I don't really need any toilet paper."

I didn't know what to do with this. I was dumb-founded. I was speechless. I was wondering if maybe she was losing her mind.

Rollercoaster doing a loop-de-loop.

"To tell you the truth, I don't need any of that stuff. I was just pulling your leg. Do you want to know the real reason why I was calling you?"

I should have guessed it was a joke! Joel would have been proud of her. I exhaled loudly. What a relief!

And back up the hill we go.

"Okay," I said, not knowing if the next thing out of her mouth was going to be serious or not.

"Have you heard that Uncle David and I are getting married in a few weeks?" she asked playfully.

"Yeah, I think I heard something about that!" Now it was my turn to be funny. In all honesty, it's all I'd been thinking about for almost a year since they an-nounced their engagement. It was like asking me if I knew that we need air to breathe. Or that lakes are full of water. Or that Corey McDonald is the best singer on earth. Duh!

"...And that we want you and your brothers to be in the wedding, but still weren't sure what we wanted you to do?"

"Of course!" I answered breathlessly. How could I not remember! Finally, we were getting to the real reason for the call. This is what I had been hoping she was calling about. *This better not be a joke,* I thought, *because I don't think I could handle it.* I could not possibly be more excited for this wedding even if I tried! I'd never been to a wedding before, and I didn't care if I was going to be the one hanging the decorations, or serving the food, or greeting the guests.

"Well, we've been discussing it for a while, going back and forth about what you guys should do and we finally came to a decision."

"Please don't tell me that we're in charge of the toilet paper!" I quipped.

"Ooh, good idea!" I could practically see her smiling through the phone. She's so much fun.

"You can put Jay in charge of that job," I said, giggling, showing that I have a sense of humor too.

"I'll think about it," she said almost sounding serious, but I knew she wasn't. "So go ahead, guess."

"Are we passing out the programs?" I jumped in.

"Nope."

"Am I a flower girl?"

"No, I think you're a bit too old for that job now," she said. I thought so too, but honestly, if she wanted me to wear a clown suit and do cartwheels down the aisle, I would have agreed. "We're giving the flower girl job to Uncle David's niece Anna. She's five."

That makes sense, I thought. *That's about the right age to be a flower girl.*

"Okay, then. Am I taking pictures?"

"No, we've hired a photographer for that."

"Do you need a musician? I can play the flute! I'm getting pretty good at it."

"That wasn't what I was going to suggest, but what can you play?" she asked.

"Well, I just started in September and I already know three songs: *Twinkle, Twinkle, Little Star*, *The ABC Song*, and *Baa, Baa, Black Sheep*."

Aunt Rachel laughed. "Oh, Yaya! You're adorable! You know those are all the same song, don't you?"

Hmm, no wonder they all seemed so easy and familiar to play!

I tried to cover up. "Um, yeah, yeah, I knew that!"

"Anyway, we're all set with the musicians. Keep guessing," she said.

"Okay. Are we showing people to their tables? Cleaning up the confetti? Sampling the food ahead of time?"

"Mmm, food sampler, now that's a great job!" Aunt Rachel said with a snicker. "YaYa, you crack me up! No, none of those things. Would you like me to tell you?"

"Yes, please!" I said, my heart beating a little faster.

And there we were, sitting on the very tippy-top of the highest roller coaster hill, anticipating the excitement and stomach-tingling drop about to happen.

"Are you ready?"

"Yes!"

"Are you sure?"

"Yes!"

"You're going to love it!"

"Tell me, tell me, tell me!" I sang out anxiously.

After a long, dramatic pause, she finally said it. And I was speechless.

My roller coaster car just dangled there, stuck on the top of the hill, not moving.

3

Hold up!

I held my breath as she told me about their decision.
"Uncle David and I would like you and your brothers, along with his niece Samantha, to be the huppah holders," she shrieked excitedly, like a kid tasting cotton candy at the circus for the very first time. "How great is that?"

I had absolutely no idea how to react. Seriously, I didn't know what to say. I tried to respond but the only sound that came out of me was one weird squeak. I was actually, quite literally, speechless.

"Hello?" Aunt Rachel asked. "Are you still there?"

I cleared my throat. "Yes, I'm here. Can you repeat that, please?"

"We want you guys to be our huppah holders!" she said again with even more enthusiasm than the first time.

That's what I thought she said.

"I thought you'd be so excited about this. I was expecting you to start screaming and doing your happy dance."

"I don't get it. What does it mean?"

"What do you mean, 'what does it mean?' You don't know what it means to be a huppah holder?" she asked, sounding surprised. "Well, that explains why you're so quiet. I assumed you'd know."

I sat down on the floor (okay, I actually sat down

on top of my stuffed hippopotamus, which was sitting on top of last month's *Tween Bee* magazine, which was sitting on the floor) and braced myself for a possible letdown. Even though I'd said I wanted to have some sort of a role in the wedding, anything at all, this didn't sound so good. It sounded like I was going to be holding something for them, and not something important either, like the rings or the wine cup. For all I knew, it might be something I'd hold from my seat—like their car keys. Maybe I'd even be sitting way in the back, using binoculars to see the ceremony.

"Well, you know what the huppah is, don't you?" she asked.

"Not really," I answered.

"Yes you do!"

"I do?"

"Yes! You know how the couple stands under a canopy?"

"Yeah, of course. So is it something that goes under the canopy?"

"No, it doesn't go under the canopy—"

I cut her off. "Oh, it doesn't?" I couldn't hide the disappointment in my voice.

"No, silly. It *IS* the canopy!" she replied. "You guys will be the huppah holders. You'll hold up the huppah, the canopy."

Whoa!

"Time out! The huppah *IS* the canopy?"

"Yes!"

"And we'll get to be up there with you when you're getting married? Right up front?"

"Yes!"

"On the *bimah*? We get to see it all up close?"

"Yes!"

"On the bimah?" I repeated, not believing what I was hearing, thinking that maybe I was getting something mixed up. "Right up there on the bimah—the stage-like thing at the front of the synagogue?"

"Yes!"

"Right up on the bimah—where they keep the Torahs in the ark? At the very front of the sanctuary?"

"Yes!"

"For real?"

"YES!"

"AAAAAAAAAHHHHHHHHH!" I shouted. "NO WAY! THIS IS AMAZING!" This was better than anything I had hoped for! Even better than front row seats at the wedding! Never mind that, this was even better than front row seats at a Corey McDonald concert! Well...wait...maybe I shouldn't get too carried away....

"There it is!" Aunt Rachel said with a delighted chuckle. "That's the YaYa I was expecting to hear! Are you doing your happy dance?"

"Yes!" I answered, doing a jig right on top of Laundry Mountain. But right in the middle of my celebration dance I thought of something, stopped, and jumped off the pile of clothes. "But wait, hold up. Won't our arms get tired? And you guys are so much taller than me and YoYo. How are we supposed to hold it over your heads?"

"There are poles. There's one on each corner. You don't have to hold up the canopy with your hands, you just hold on to the poles and we'll stand under it."

"Oh, that...is...AWESOME!" I exclaimed. "So, we'll be up there the whole time and we'll get to watch you come down the aisle from up there?

"We're still working on the details." Her voice dropped a little bit when she said that as if something was bothering her, but then she picked right up again. "We might have you stand on the bimah holding the huppah in place before the guests come into the sanctuary or we might have all four of you carry it down the aisle as the first part of the procession. In any case we'd be honored if you guys would be up there with us. What do you think?" As if she needed to ask!

"Are you kidding me? That would be AMAZING!"

"So it's a 'yes?'" she joked.

"Yes, yes, yes, yes, yes, yes, yes, yes, yes!" I giggled. "Thank you! This is the best phone call ever!"

"Wait, is it truly the best or are you just relieved now that you know that you don't have to carry a TV on your back while biking?" Aunt Rachel asked with a little laugh.

"No, it's actually the best phone call I ever got in my whole entire life!" I replied.

"I'm so glad you're happy about it," she said. "Can I speak with YoYo next?"

I walked over to Joel's room where he was sitting at his clean, uncluttered desk doing his homework. I extended my hand with the phone in it.

"Your turn."

He looked up at me with his freckly face and asked, "Who is it?" while taking the phone.

"Aunt Rachel," I said with the same goofy grin that Mom had on her face before. I wondered if she was going to ask Joel to run to the store to get toilet paper too, but I didn't stick around to find out.

I went back to my bedroom to pack up my homework so I wouldn't forget to bring it to school in the morning. I couldn't have been in my room for more than two minutes. I stepped into the hallway in time to see Joel walking out of his room and saying into the phone, "Okay, here's Jay. Thanks, Aunt Rachel."

Well, that was fast, I thought. I didn't hear any screaming. I didn't hear a single, "No way!" or "That's awesome!" How could that be?

He passed the phone to Jay who listened for a few seconds and said, "Okay. Cool. Thanks."

Okay? Cool? Thanks? That's his reaction to possibly the single greatest thing that's ever happened to us? I'm pretty sure I will never understand those brothers of mine!

Curiosity drew me into Mom and Dad's room. I examined the big framed picture of the two of them standing under the huppah at their wedding. They looked so young and so happy. In the picture, Mom wore a beautiful white dress that went all the way down to the floor and a veil that was pulled back over her hair. She was holding a huge bouquet of pink and white flowers and Dad had a matching pink flower pinned to his black tuxedo jacket. He had his arm wrapped around her waist and their smiles were so big I bet their cheeks hurt. I wondered what made them smile so much. Did the photographer say something funny to them? Were they thinking about all their wedding presents? Were they imagining they'd someday have awesome twins named YaYa and YoYo?

I studied the picture carefully. The huppah was connected to four poles just as Aunt Rachel had described, but no one was holding them. Every inch of each pole was covered with white flowers, and the huppah stood there all on its own. There wasn't room for anyone to hold on to the poles without crushing the flowers. A feeling of dread rushed through me.

What if Aunt Rachel was wrong? What if they didn't need us to hold the huppah after all? What if I misunderstood what she was saying? Or what if it was Aunt Rachel who misunderstood how the whole thing worked?

Before I allowed myself to get any more excited about the possibility of being in the wedding, I had to get the facts. I didn't want to squeeze all of my hopes into this bubble just to have it popped.

I raced out of the room because I needed answers. I had to find Mom.

4

A Cold Fall

Hey, Mom?" I called out.

"I'm down here," she answered from the foyer. "I'm just about to take LuLu out for a walk." *Oops! We're* supposed to be the ones walking her. LuLu, the most adorable dog in the world, had joined our family a few weeks earlier, and part of the deal with our parents was our promise to take care of her. "You guys were all busy doing your homework, so I didn't want to bother you."

Sometimes I think Mom looks for excuses to walk her even though it's our responsibility because she loves LuLu like she's her fourth kid.

"Can I come with you?" I asked as I came down the stairs.

"You can. Or you could walk LuLu yourself and I'll get dinner ready."

"I want to talk to you about something. Can we go together?"

"Sure," Mom said, looking a bit concerned. "Everything okay, honey?"

"Oh yeah, everything's fine. I just wanted to ask you some questions about the wedding."

"Right! The wedding! I didn't even ask you. What do you think about the job that Aunt Rachel and Uncle David are giving you? Isn't that great? Being a huppah holder is a big responsibility!" she said, slipping her arms through her jacket sleeves. Meanwhile, LuLu was jumping as if someone was holding a treat over her head and she was trying to snatch it. The little metal tag attached to her collar clinked every time she sprang up and down.

"Yeah, I think so," I said zipping up my own jacket. I tried to grab LuLu's leash, which was fastened to her collar and which followed her almost obediently as she leaped all over the foyer. "But I'm a little bit confused." Finally I caught the leash.

Mom opened the door. I couldn't believe how dark it was already. Even though it gets this way every November, I'm always surprised when we turn the clocks back and it feels like nighttime even before we have dinner. LuLu, not caring about the dark or the cold, practically yanked my arm off—she couldn't wait to get outside. We stepped out into the brisk air and Mom closed the door behind us. The cold bit into me. I should have worn gloves and a hat, but didn't feel like going back in to get them.

"What are you confused about, YaYa?" We settled into a comfortable pace, walking side by side with LuLu taking the lead and stopping to sniff the ground approximately every three steps.

"Well, I just went into your room to check out your wedding picture, and I noticed that the huppah stood there all by itself. No one was holding it. How come nobody held your huppah? Why would she ask us to do a job that doesn't need to be done? How can we hold something covered in flowers? Won't we squish them?"

Mom laughed.

"Slow down, YaYa! I think I can answer all your questions," she said in her reassuring voice.

"First of all, the huppah itself is the covering that creates almost a ceiling or a roof over the couple. It represents their new home, but it's open on all sides to be welcoming to others."

"Wait a second. That sounds just like Abraham's tent in the Torah," I jumped in. "Rabbi Green talked about that in Shul School." (Shul School is what my brothers and I call our synagogue's religious school.)

"Exactly," Mom said looking at me with a proud grin. Then she continued, "Believe it or not, we have lots of different huppah traditions. Some people use a *tallit*—"

"A tallit? For real? Like a prayer shawl that people wear in synagogue?" I asked.

"Uh-huh," Mom answered, "Some people take a tallit and attach it to four poles. Some use a huppah that's already made, like the one they have at the synagogue. A huppah like that one would have poles with stands, so no one has to hold them. Some people like to decorate the huppah by draping it with cloth and hanging lights or putting flowers on it. Dad and I made ours a little differently. You know that big painted canvas hanging on the wall behind our bed?"

"Yeah," I answered.

"Well, that was the huppah that I designed and painted. We attached it to the poles and the stands that the synagogue had. We simply took off their top and added our own. Then the florist covered the poles with lots of flowers."

"Yeah, that's what I saw in the picture," I said.

"Aunt Rachel and Uncle David decided to have a homemade one like Dad and I did. But theirs is going to be a bit different."

"How?" I asked.

"First of all, they're going to attach the huppah to poles that you guys are going to hold for them."

"That's a relief!" I said trying to keep my teeth from chattering.

"Also, remember when the five of us worked on that art project a few months ago? The square cloth we painted for their wedding?" Mom asked.

"Of course I do. That was so much fun!"

"Well, they gave fabric to twenty-four other friends and relatives and asked everyone to design a unique square. They had a quilter sew all the pieces together to make one big covering. They want it to feel like all of their friends and family are under the huppah with them."

"But I'm *really* actually going to be under there with them, right?"

"You sure will!"

"I can't believe it! That's so cool!"

"I thought you might like that," Mom said with a warm smile.

I felt so much better. I let out a loud sigh, but it came out kind of shivery because of the frigid temperature.

"Are you okay, YaYa?" Mom asked.

"I'm fine. Just kind of cold, that's all. No biggie," I said, trying to hide the fact that I was beginning to understand how the ice cubes in our freezer would feel if they had any feelings. I got this funny image in my head of ice cubes with faces wearing earmuffs and rubbing their little ice arms with their little mittened ice hands, trying to warm up. For a moment, I actually felt bad for the little guys. Then I remembered that ice cubes don't have feelings...or arms...or earmuffs.

Yeah, earmuffs might have been a good idea....

"YaYa, why didn't you wear your gloves? Or a hat?" Mom asked sounding both annoyed and sorry for me.

"I wasn't paying attention. I was in a hurry to come out here with you to find out about my huppah holding job," I answered honestly.

"You need to take care of yourself," she gently reminded me, "because the last thing we need is for you to get sick right before the wedding."

"Oh come on, Mom," I said, "is there ever a good time to get sick?"

"Fair point, YaYa, but I want you to be especially careful over the next couple of weeks. Wash your hands often with warm water and soap, go to bed on time so you get plenty of rest, drink lots of water, and by all means, stay away from anyone who is coughing or sneezing!" She said all this as if it was the first time she was imparting this wisdom on me. I guarantee it was not. She'd been repeating this advice to my brothers and me for weeks.

"Ok-k-k-kie dok-k-k-kie," I answered, my teeth shivering and clacking together.

"Here, give me LuLu's leash. I'll finish walking her. You go inside and warm up."

"You sure?" I asked.

"Yes, go."

"Okay, thanks," I said and passed her the leash, then super-speedily sprinted toward home. I've gotten pretty good at this running business because I do it almost every morning to catch the school bus, which, I'm proud to say, I hardly ever miss anymore. In a matter of seconds I was almost at our front door.

Just my luck, right as I was about to turn onto the walkway to our house, I tripped over something on the sidewalk. As I was falling, I felt my body moving downward almost as if in slow motion. I knew I was going to end up flat on the pavement, and there was nothing I could do about it other than putting my arms out in front of me to try and block the fall. Sure enough, before long, I was face down on the cold concrete with my left arm twisted under my body, a shooting pain racing through it like a fire burning inside my skin.

This—

OW!

...was not...

OUCH!

...good.

ARGHHH!!!

5

Breaking News

My arm hurt so much I couldn't even cry. I couldn't yell for help. I couldn't make a single sound because I wasn't able to breathe. I've heard of people having the wind knocked out of them, and that's precisely how I felt—like someone was stepping on my chest and my throat and I couldn't take any air in or let any out. I couldn't do anything but lie there in unbelievable agony. Then suddenly, as if the big foot lifted from my airway, it all came out.

"Mommy!" I wailed. I haven't called her "Mommy" since I was a baby. My crying turned into sobbing until I had more trouble breathing. Finally, I managed to let out a roaring "OW!" I'm not sure how such a loud noise came out of my little body.

I curled myself into a ball right there on the cold sidewalk and kept my eyes closed as I howled. I don't remember anything ever hurting so much. In an instant, I could feel my mom hovering over me, stroking my hair, trying to get me to calm down. LuLu must have thought I was playing around because she started jumping on my legs. Mom snatched her up and yelled for someone in the house to come out and help.

All at once I was crying, LuLu was barking, and Mom was calling someone (I assumed it was Dad) on her cell phone. Joel and Jeremy's feet thudded as they rushed outside.

"Why is YaYa on the ground?"
"What happened?"
"Is she okay?"
"I bet she's faking it."

I heard Mom telling my brothers to bring LuLu into the house then come back out with their jackets on.

It sounded like some of our neighbors came out to see what was going on. I guess I was screaming pretty loudly. Someone must have called or run to Dr. Conover's house, which is down the street, because when I opened my eyes he was on the ground next to me. I don't know how much time passed but it felt like an eternity, which is exactly how long I thought the pain was going to last.

In a calm, soothing voice Dr. Conover talked to me but I don't remember what he said. I don't even know if I was able to hear him over my own crying. I do remember that he asked Mom if he could pick me up and then he carried me into the house. I also remember feeling my body begin to thaw out once we were inside.

As he gently placed me on the couch, he said something about taking a look at my arm.

I overheard Jeremy quietly remark to Joel, "Isn't Dr. Conover the kind of doctor that delivers babies? What does he know about arms?"

I was kind of wondering the same thing.

"We'll need to get that jacket off so I can get a better look," Dr. Conover said. *At least he sounds like he knows what he's doing,* I thought.

I nodded but couldn't speak.

Mom held the sleeve of my jacket and I slid my right arm out without any problems, but then it was time to slip my left arm out. I couldn't even lift it. Mom carefully pulled the sleeve while the doctor held my arm up. Even though they tried so hard not to hurt me, it felt like someone dug a pitchfork into my arm. I screamed right in Dr. Conover's ear. He jumped back a little, probably worried I'd busted his eardrum. I didn't mean to but I couldn't help it. Once the jacket was off, he slowly pulled my shirtsleeve up to the elbow to take a good look at my arm.

"OW!" I howled again.

The pain was so intense that I felt dizzy and like I might faint. I can't remember most of what Dr. Conover and Mom talked about but a few key words leaped out at me from the blur: "...fracture...swelling...dislocated...."

I don't recall hearing Dad come in but all of a sudden he was right there with me too. His store, a small book shop called The Silver Lining, is so close to our house that he can be home on a moment's notice if he needed to be. Clearly this was one of those times.

"Could we get some ice and a small towel, please?" Dr. Conover asked without looking up. For a flash of a second I pictured my little ice cube friends in the freezer and imagined that someone was about to rescue a few. Although, if you really think about it, pulling an ice cube out of the freezer would be worse for it than having it stay inside...but whatever. My mind was loopy from all the pain. I wasn't thinking clearly.

Jeremy ran to the kitchen and came back with a dish towel and a plastic sandwich bag filled with ice cubes. *I guess he can be nice when he wants to be*, I thought. I looked up at him to say "thanks" with my eyes, since I couldn't utter a single word, but I don't think he understood my silent message. With Joel, I can just give him a certain look and he'll know exactly what I'm getting at. Maybe it's a twin thing, I don't know, but Jeremy and I don't seem to be able to connect like that.

Dr. Conover wrapped the bag of ice in the towel and tried to gently lay it on my arm, which was so swollen it looked like someone had taken a bike pump and filled it with air. He placed the bag just above my wrist, the most swollen part. The cold and the pain made me jump off the couch for a moment.

"Ow, ow, ow, ow, ow!" I cried out as I sat back down, remembering Jeremy's earlier comment about Dr. Conover delivering babies and wondering if this guy really knew what he was doing.

"Do you have any pain relief medication like Tylenol?" he asked Mom.

"Yes, I'll go—"

But before she could finish her sentence, Jeremy called out, "I'm on it!" and bolted up the stairs. Within seconds I could hear his enormous feet thumping BOOM! BOOM! BOOM! as they flew down the staircase, ending with a giant thud, skipping the last few steps, just like he always does. He ran into the living room with three different bottles of medicine.

Mom had already gone to the kitchen and returned with a glass of water. I took a few deep breaths and managed to stop crying long enough to take a sip. Then I took another deep breath followed by another sip of water. Once I calmed down enough, Mom handed me a pill. As I swallowed it, the doctor asked, "Do any of you kids play soccer?"

Huh? I thought in disbelief. *This is a mighty strange time for him to be making small talk with us while I'm suffering. If his next question is "What's your favorite position to play?" I might have to gather all of my strength, find my voice and shout for Mom to find a "real" doctor.*

Both boys nodded.

"We all do," Joel said. *Why on earth does Dr. Conover care about what we do for fun?* My confidence in this man was draining like water from a bathtub.

"I assume you guys play with shin guards, right?" *Why not talk about the weather or maybe how the stock exchange is doing this week?*

"Yeah, of course. We're not allowed to play without them," Joel answered.

"Great," Dr. Conover said. "Can you please bring me one of your shin guards?"

"Do you want to see our cleats too?" Jeremy asked, sounding confused, but also eager to show off our sports equipment for some strange reason.

Dr. Conover laughed out loud. "Maybe some other time, Jeremy. For now, just one shin guard will do. I want to use it as a splint to stabilize Ellie's arm. I'm pretty sure she's got a big ol' fracture here."

Aha! Now he's starting to sound like a real doctor!

Once again, it was Jeremy who ran out of the room, this time to fetch the shin guard.

"Wh-wh-what's a fracture? What does that mean?" I managed to ask now that I had finally stopped crying.

"It means you may have broken your arm, my dear," he replied quietly.

It took a moment for me to process the words that Dr. Conover said, but once they sank in, I started crying all over again, even harder than before.

Dr. Conover looked surprised. "What's going on? You haven't moved and I didn't touch you. What set you off again?"

"I...I...I...," I stammered. "Supposed...t-t-t-to...Aunt...

R-R-R-achel's...wed-d-d-ding...," and then I out and out bawled.

"Oh, honey." Mom rushed over to sit next to me on the couch. She put her arms around me, clearly understanding my blubbering message. "Don't worry about that. You'll still be in the wedding. Let's take care of your arm now and figure all of that out later."

Joel, always trying to make us laugh, broke in, "But hey, at least you didn't catch a cold! Mom's been bugging us for weeks not to get sick."

Mom gave him a "Not now, Joel!" sort of look. Then she stroked my hair and said, "Don't think about the wedding. Let's focus on getting you to feel better."

Don't think about the wedding? How could I not think about it? Within less than one hour, I received the greatest news ever, and then it was all whisked away from me, like Joel pulling one of his pranks and yanking the chair out from under me as I was about to sit down. How was I supposed to stand up on the bimah and hold the huppah with a broken arm? My arm hurt so much, I didn't know if it would ever feel better. I couldn't imagine being able to hold my arm up, let alone the huppah.

This was supposed to be one of the greatest events of my life. I had to be a huppah holder. I had to.

How could I possibly *not* think about it?

6

A Real Pain

I guess Dr. Conover actually did know what he was talking about because when Mom and Dad took me to Urgent Care we found out that I had, in fact, broken my arm. I got a big cast that went all the way to my elbow and I was even allowed to choose the color. I went with neon green because that's one of my favorites. People were allowed to sign it, so at least that was something cool that came from the disaster.

Mom used her permanent markers to draw a colorful bouquet of flowers on the cast. Everyone wrote nice things like, "Feel better!" or "Get well soon!" and stuff like that. Joel wrote, "Break a leg!" which seemed kind of mean until he explained that's how they say "good luck" in showbiz. My darling older brother Jeremy wrote, "Nice going, Klutz!" Isn't he just the sweetest? Oh, and did I mention that he wrote that on my other arm? The one without the cast? In permanent marker? Boy did that take forever to wash off, especially since I couldn't do it myself with a broken arm!

After a few days I kind of got used to the cast and the pain started to go away. Sleeping was hard, though, because I couldn't roll over easily without my arm getting in the way. Showering was tricky, too, because I wasn't supposed to get the cast wet, so I took baths and kept my arm out of the tub the whole time.

"Boy, breaking your arm, is a real pain...in the

neck!" Joel joked one Sunday afternoon as he saw me in the kitchen trying to open a jelly jar. I tried to hold the jar in place with my bad arm and twist off the cap with my right hand. I'm a righty, so this shouldn't have been all that difficult, but I couldn't get a good grip on the jar. It kept slipping around. Joel came over and easily popped it open. It was a cross between being helpful and showing off.

"Thanks," I said.

"Hey, YaYa," he remarked, "Did you know that before George Washington was the President he was an army general?"

"Yeah, I know that," I answered. "Why?"

"Do you know where he kept his armies?"

This is so random. Why is he asking me about General Washington? I wondered.

"I don't know, maybe like Valley Forge? If you need to do research on him, just look him up yourself," I said.

"I don't need to look it up, I know the answer. So come on, let's try this again. Where did General Washington keep his armies?"

"If you know the answer then why are you asking me?"

"I just want you to try to answer the question. Come on! Where did Washington keep his armies?"

"I told you, I don't know exactly."

Joel said pointing at my arm in the cast and said, "In his sleevies!" He waited for my reaction. "Get it? He kept his *armies* in his *sleevies!*" Then he cracked up, pleased with his little joke. He does that a lot.

"Oh my goodness, you are such a nerd," I said. Secretly though, I did laugh a little to myself. I much prefer the corny jokes to having tricks played on me.

"Hey, it was funny!" he said, defending himself.

"On a scale of one to ten, I'd give it a three," I said, feeling generous.

"Oh come on, it was at least a six!" he insisted. Then he asked, "So, how is your arm, anyway?"

"Mostly okay, I guess," I said. "If I turn it the wrong way or bang it, it hurts a lot, but for the most part it's not too bad. It's just annoying when I try to do regular things, like buttoning a shirt or opening a jar." I gestured toward the jelly jar on the counter.

"Yeah, I see that," he said.

"But the wedding is my biggest worry. Mom and Aunt Rachel promised I'd still be able to hold the huppah, but what if I can't? What if my good arm gets tired of holding the pole? What if my good arm falls asleep and I drop the pole? The wedding would be ruined!"

"I'm sure it won't be a problem, YaYa," Joel said calmly, "and look, if it's keeping you awake at night, they can always give you something different to do—"

"NO! No, no, no, no, no!" I cried out, "No way! This is the best job in the wedding—except for maybe being one of the people getting married! Unless they're thinking about letting me be the rabbi so I can perform the ceremony, I do NOT want a different job."

"Okay, okay, don't bite my head off!" Joel said taking a step backwards. "Sheesh, I was just trying to help."

"Sorry," I said, "but this is a big deal for me. Breaking my arm two and a half weeks before the big event is bad enough. The thought of not being a huppah holder is more than I can handle."

"I get it. Look, I'm excited to be in the wedding, too. Why don't you try lifting weights with your right arm so that it's good and strong in time for the wedding?"

"Nuh-uh! If I lift weights with only one arm, then when they take this cast off, I'll have one arm that looks like a steel beam and one that looks like a string bean! No way!" I huffed.

"Ha! A bean and a beam!" Joel laughed. "That sounds like something I'd come up with! Okay, well, I'm sure you'll figure something out. Good luck." And with that he shrugged and left the kitchen.

I replayed our discussion in my head as I continued making and eating my peanut butter and jelly sandwich. On my way to the fridge to put away the jelly, I held the jar in my right hand and pumped it like I was lifting weights. Then I did a few reps with the peanut butter jar. Because, you know, just in case....

7

Checking out the Kid's Tuba

To take my mind off of all this huppah-holding business, I went to see what Mom was up to. Dad told me she was in her studio. I climbed the stairs to the top floor and knocked on the door.

"Come in," Mom sang out cheerfully.

I opened the door and stepped in. Mom's studio is just like her—it's warm, comforting, and cheery. Light floods the room through windows on all four walls. When Mom and Dad turned our attic into a studio, she designed it that way—with lots and lots of natural light, because Mom says that's how she works best. She's told us a million times at least.

The walls glow a cozy, dark, golden yellow. Every-where you look, colors jump out—from the easels, the completed pictures on the walls and even from the paint cups. When I was much younger I used to love spinning around the center of the room with my eyes wide open, watching all the colors mix together right in front of me. It was my own version of Spin-Art. That room is simply magical.

"Hi, sweetie," Mom said with a paintbrush in her hand (and an accidental streak of pink paint in her brown wavy hair). Her red t-shirt was peeking out from under her favorite painting shirt—one of Dad's old white button-down shirts, about two sizes too big for her. It hung down to just over her knees and was covered with paint stains and splatters.

"Hi, Mom. Whatcha working on?" I looked up at the painting of a carousel with blue, yellow, and pink pastel-colored horses, right above her. It used to live in my room until I decided that I didn't want it anymore because it felt too babyish, but I'm glad she didn't get rid of it. Now it stays in the studio along with other favorites that we couldn't bear to say goodbye to, which hang in the spaces between the windows.

I love looking at all the art Mom's made. Of course, she doesn't get to keep all the things she creates since she often makes them for other people. I don't know if I could do that. If I worked so hard on something for so long and felt incredibly proud of it, I don't know if I would be able to hand it off to someone else. But Mom seems to be okay with it. She has a huge scrapbook filled with pictures of every piece she's ever completed since she started working as a professional artist, so at least she gets to keep her work that way. She once told me that her pieces of art are like her "other kids," and just as she has photo albums filled with pictures of us, she also has them for those "kids." And just as she couldn't hold on to us as babies forever, she had to let go of her other "babies" too.

"I'm just putting the final touches on Aunt Rachel and Uncle David's ketubah. Come around and take a look. I'm really happy with how it's coming out." She backed her chair away from the easel to make room for me.

Mom has been making ketubahs for almost as long as I can remember. (In Hebrew, you'd call more than one ketubah "ketubot," but I like to say ketubahs). Ketubahs are traditional, artistic Jewish marriage contracts. When I was a little kid, like in kindergarten,

Mom took her first class on how to make a ketubah. I was so excited about it that one night after she returned home from her class, I asked if she would make one for me. I cried and cried when she said I had to wait until I was a grown-up to get one. It didn't make any sense to me. "Why do I have to be a grown-up to get my very own *kid tuba*? Isn't it supposed to be for children?" I asked feeling confused and hurt. "How come you're making tubas for other kids, but I can't get one?"

Mom explained that she wasn't learning how to make musical instruments for children but rather works of art for grown-up couples getting married. It was such a sad day for me when I finally understood that I wasn't going to be getting a Mom-made brass instrument for my birthday. Although honestly, it's just as well. I can only imagine how much I would have butchered the tuba, which seems to be even harder to play than the flute, especially back then when I was so small. It probably would have sounded like a dying whale.

I stepped carefully over the tarps and cloths spread around to protect the shiny wood floor from paint spills. I always feel at home in the studio, where it's kind of cluttered. Every bit of space is filled with paintbrushes, smocks, different kinds of ink, colored pencils and pastel crayons. Unlike in my room, where you might find a random t-shirt on the bookshelf or a toothbrush in the sock drawer, Mom has stuff everywhere but it's all organized in labeled bins, baskets, and boxes.

"What do you think?" she asked, pointing to the work in progress and looking as proud as a preschooler presenting her macaroni-covered picture frame. It was the most beautiful "kid tuba" I'd ever seen.

"Wow, Mom! It's amazing! It's perfect! I love the colors!" I exclaimed as I examined it. The ketubah had all the words written in dark black ink in the middle part of the paper. The words on the right side were in Hebrew letters and to the left was English writing. Mom did all the calligraphy herself. That means that she made the letters look very fancy. I wouldn't have the patience to work so carefully on all those letters. But she sure did and it showed. If it was up to me, I'd find a super cool font on the computer and use that. But not Mom! She does each and every letter by hand with her special calligraphy pen.

"What does the Hebrew say?" I inquired.

"Actually, the letters are the same as Hebrew but this text is an ancient language called Aramaic."

"I don't get it. It's Hebrew but it's not Hebrew?"

As usual, she had an answer that made sense. "It's kind of like how French and Spanish are written with the same alphabet as English, but the languages are different. Some people do have their ketubot written in the Hebrew language but Aunt Rachel and Uncle David wanted theirs to be more traditional, so they chose to have the words written in Aramaic. That's how ketubot and other legal documents were written when the custom first began over two thousand years ago."

"I didn't know that you knew a whole other language," I remarked. "How is it that I've known you for eleven years and I'm still finding out new things about you?"

Mom smiled. "I don't really know it that well. But I can read it and since it's very similar to Hebrew, I can understand a lot of it. I bet you could too. Wanna give it a whirl?" She backed her chair up a bit more and I stepped a little closer.

"Do you see any words that you recognize?" she asked.

I studied the writing. It was difficult to read because unlike the Hebrew words that I can read, it didn't have the dots and lines around the letters that tell you which vowel sounds to attach to the consonants. "No, I can't read that."

"Look harder," Mom said. "I think you'll find some familiar words in there."

I kept looking. "Oh wait! Does that say that 'Rachel' and 'David' right there?" I asked. Mom nodded. Oh, this was fun! It was like putting together a tricky puzzle.

"Can you read this word?" She pointed at a string of letters toward the top.

I tried sounding it out.

"Em...Emrik...Imrock...Amark...Amreek...Amreka...." I struggled with it for a while and then all of a sudden it clicked. "Oh! America! It says America!"

"Right!" Mom said with a big smile. "It does. The top part of the ketubah says the date and the place where the couple is getting married."

"That's pretty cool," I said. "So are all ketubahs the same other than the names and dates and design?"

"Some things are consistent. In a standard, traditional ketubah all of this text on the bottom is the same," she said pointing at the black Aramaic letters, "but some couples customize their ketubot to make them unique." She pointed at a phrase that was written within the artwork, not the text. "Take a look at these words up here. You'll find them in a lot of ketubot but not all," Mom said. She read the Hebrew, *"Ani L'dodi, V'dodi Li."* Then she pointed just below the Hebrew words and said, "Here it is in English."

"I am my beloved's and my beloved is mine," I read aloud.

Mom explained, "While this phrase isn't part of the traditional text, many people choose to include it somewhere on the ketubah because it's so lovely. Each couple decides what they want their ketubah to say. Some use the traditional text with no English at all while some ketubot are written completely in English."

"Huh, that's interesting," I said. "I didn't realize there are so many ways to write a 'kid tuba'."

Mom smiled when I said that.

"Would you like to see some of the other ones I've done?"

"Are you kidding? Of course I would!" I was really getting into this. She got up and walked over to the bookshelf on the other side of the room. She pulled out a big photo album and carried it back over to her chair by the easel. She opened it on her lap and turned the pages until she found what she was looking for.

"I've made ketubot for Orthodox couples, like this one," she said while pointing to one that had no English on it at all. She turned the page.

"Here's one I did for a Reform wedding. This couple chose to have theirs written in Hebrew and English, but no Aramaic." She opened to another page and then to another as she continued.

"Look at this one," she said sounding excited. I could tell she was having fun showing off her accomplishments.

The next one had a big bright rainbow across the top with a red heart on each end. "This is Danny Garner-Blum's parents' ketubah. His moms hired me to create one that was unique to them." She turned to another page. "This is the one I made for Caroline Levy's parents. They wanted theirs to be written entirely in English. Plus the text of theirs was different from the others because Caroline's dad is Jewish and her mom is not. It was important to them to have a ketubah, so I made it for them as they requested."

"Wow, Mom. I knew that you made these pretty, artistic things that people have at their weddings and then hang up in their houses, but I never actually knew what it all meant."

Mom got up and walked across the room again to slide the photo album back into the empty space on the shelf.

"I love that you're interested in learning about it, YaYa," Mom said looking proudly at me as she returned to her seat.

Meanwhile, I leaned in and took a good look at the ketubah on the easel and said to Mom without looking away from the piece, "I think it's kind of funny that there's all this serious, business stuff going on in the middle and then beautiful, colorful artwork all around it."

"You know, there's actually a term in Hebrew for that. Have you ever heard of *hiddur mitzvah*?" Mom asked.

I shook my head no.

"Well, all I can say is thank goodness for hiddur mitzvah! It's how I make a living! Hiddur mitzvah is all about taking something that's a Jewish commandment or tradition and making it look pretty and special. Hiddur mitzvah is the reason we decorate the sukkah. It's why we have a hand-stitched challah cover and a gorgeous seder plate. Making the things we use beautiful makes them even more enjoyable, meaningful, and pleasant to look at."

"Maybe that's why Aunt Rachel will be wearing a fancy dress to her wedding," I added.

Mom nodded. "I never thought of it that way, but yeah, I suppose so. I mean, she could get married in jeans and sneakers, there's no law against it, but let's face it, that wouldn't feel very special would it?"

I shook my head as an answer to Mom's question. I still hadn't taken my eyes off of the ketubah. Suddenly I noticed something that didn't look right.

"Uh oh," I said. I think I kind of meant to just say that in my head but no, I definitely said it out loud. Like a worm at the end of a fishing pole, it was just dangling uncomfortably in the air between the two of us.

"What do you mean 'uh oh'? What? What?" Mom sounded a bit panicky. "What's wrong?"

I could understand her nervousness. It was obvious she'd spent hours and hours on the ketubah. I was a little afraid to tell her and was sorry I'd said anything at all.

"What, YaYa? Tell me what you see!" she said with an even more urgent tone in her voice. "What is it?" I could see her eyes scanning the page, looking it over so carefully, trying to see what I could see.

A million thoughts ran through my head at once: *If I had worked on a project for days and days and someone saw a mistake, would I want to know about it? Or would I rather just be proud of my work and not know about the mess-up? What about Aunt Rachel and Uncle David? How would they feel if their beautiful ketubah had a mistake on it? What if they found out I knew about it and didn't say anything?*

Mom was practically breaking into a sweat next to

me. I was starting to sweat too.

Ugh. Me and my big mouth.

8

Searching for Hidden Treasures

There was a terrible, uncomfortable silence in the room. Mom held her breath, urgently trying to find the mistake, her eyes moving wildly as she searched every centimeter of space in front of her.

"I don't see it! YaYa, I really need to know if there's an error. Please tell me," she said trying to sound calm, but not doing a very good job of hiding the quiver in her voice. I felt so awful. I wished I had never seen it. It would have been so much better if she had noticed it on her own or even not at all.

I pointed at the bottom part of the text, "Look down here," I said very quickly, hoping that if I said it fast enough it would hurt less, like when you pull a band-aid off really quickly. It stings for a minute but then it goes away. "It looks like you were saving this space and meant to come back to it but you made a bunch of blank lines. So now you have these weird, empty lines on the bottom which you probably can't erase since you made them in ink." I cringed, expecting Mom to freak out.

To my surprise, she let out a huge, enormous, loud sigh. It reminded me of the sound you hear when they let the air out of those big blow-up jumpy houses. WHOOSH....

"Oh, honey, you had me so worried!" She wiped the sweat off her forehead with her sleeve. "Those blank spaces are there for a reason. It's not a mistake at all. Before the wedding ceremony, the ketubah will be signed by two witnesses. Those spaces are for the witnesses to write their names." Her whole body melted into her chair.

"Oh! Well, that's good news!" I said, feeling just as relieved as Mom. Thank goodness! Mom and I both sighed at the same time. Then we looked at each other and laughed. What a relief!

I went back to admiring all the artwork she had created around the text of the ketubah. Across the top were mountains. The ones on the left were green and across the page they blended into white, snow-covered peaks. Green vines with lots of colorful flowers cascaded down the sides. The bottom looked like a landscape view of Jerusalem with golden buildings, some with domes for their roofs. But as I looked closer I noticed that two buildings had nothing to do with Jerusalem at all.

"Hey, Mom," I said, pointing, "That looks like a New York City skyscraper in the bottom left-hand corner and there on the right it looks like the Eiffel Tower in Paris. Isn't that supposed to be Jerusalem though? Those buildings aren't even in Israel! Did you do that on purpose?"

"Good eye, YaYa! I did put them there on purpose. Aunt Rachel and Uncle David gave me a list of all the things they wanted to include so the ketubah would tell their personal story. It's like a hidden picture game. I put in symbols that reflect who they are as a couple but you might not see them at first unless you're looking for them. Of course the couple knows they're in there but someone visiting their home and looking at the framed ketubah hanging on a wall wouldn't necessarily see it all."

"No way! That's so cool!" I said. "So what are some of the hidden things?"

"Well," Mom said, pointing at the bottom left corner, "they met when they were in college in New York, so the Empire State Building represents the beginning of their story." Then she swooped over to the Eiffel Tower. "They hope to travel to Paris together someday, so they asked me to include a landmark from there symbolizing a dream for their future. And, as you know, they both love Israel and have each spent time there, so that's why the Jerusalem skyline is included. This whole bottom part is like an illustrated view of their story together through geography."

"I love it!" I exclaimed as I studied the picture even closer.

"Keep looking," Mom said. "Let me know if you find anything else."

I moved in to really examine it and the more I looked, the more I saw. "Yes! I see a tennis racket over here and a pair of ice skates on this side." Each one was hidden among the golden buildings on the bottom. You'd never see them if you weren't looking for them, but they were definitely in there. What a cool idea!

"Look closely at the mountains."

I scanned the top left hand side of the picture and finally saw it. "Hikers!" I called out. Two tiny figures with backpacks walked along a thin brown trail on the side of the green mountain.

"Right! That's Aunt Rachel and Uncle David hiking. And on the other side?" Mom encouraged.

I pointed excitedly as I found them. "There they are, skiing!" This was so much fun.

"Anything else?" she asked with a sly grin.

"Should I be looking for something in particular?" I asked.

"Something you'll really like. You'll know it when you see it," she said, seeming to enjoy this little game of hide and seek.

I concentrated, carefully examining each and every inch of the artwork. Suddenly I saw it. "O.M.G.!" I called out.

"You found it?" Mom asked with a huge smile on her face.

"It's US!" I exclaimed, bursting with excitement. "I see our whole family!" Hidden in the flowers going up the vines were tiny faces! And they looked just like cartoon images of us. "There's Aunt Rachel and Uncle David...." My elation grew with each face that I found. "You and Dad, Grandma Ruth and Grandpa Jack, YoYo, Jay, and me. Are those other people Uncle David's relatives?"

"Yup, you got it!" Mom beamed.

"Oh, this is the coolest thing ever! We made it onto their ketubah!" I cheered. I was so excited that I jumped up and down and started dancing and singing, "We're in the ketubah, we're in the ketubah...."

"YaYa! Calm down! I'm so glad you like it, honey," Mom said from her seat, "but please stop jumping around. I don't want you to bang into it. Some parts still need to dry. And there are open paint cups and unwashed paintbrushes all over the place."

"No worries, Mom," I said. "I'll be careful." I stopped jumping.

I stood still and marveled at Mom's brilliant creation for a little while longer. I leaned over and gave her a big hug. I felt like saying "I'm proud of you" the way she would say it to me, but that would sound weird coming from me to her. So instead, with my arms wrapped around her neck I said, "Seriously, Mom, this is super cool! I really, really love it. And I know that Aunt Rachel and Uncle David will too."

"Thanks, sweetie," she replied.

And then it happened—an awful, horrible, stomach-turning nightmare. Not because I was jumping around, not because I was being wild, but simply because I hugged my mother in an attempt to show her my admiration. As I unwrapped myself from Mom's neck, the cast around my arm banged into a small, uncovered cup full of black paint, knocking it off the little ledge that holds the paint cups.

We watched, frozen and horrified, as the cup bumped against the ketubah. The brush that had been sitting inside it hit the edge of the easel. As the paint cup fell to the floor, it felt like it was happening in terrible, detailed, slow motion, just as everything seemed to be in slow motion when I fell onto the concrete and broke my arm. All we could do was watch helplessly as black droplets rained and splattered everywhere.

"OH NO!" Mom and I screamed in horror together. And this time, it was for real.

9

Paint Drops on Roses...

"OH MY GOD! Is it ruined?" I gasped and covered my mouth. I stood in front of the splattered ketubah, frantic. My heart was racing. I could hardly catch my breath. Never in my life had I been such a klutz. Now I'd gone and broken my arm and possibly destroyed Mom's greatest masterpiece.

Mom's face became almost as pale as the paper she used for the ketubah. She sat there frozen in her spot, as if she'd turned into a bug-eyed, open-mouthed statue.

I removed my trembling hand from my mouth and put it on her shoulder. "Mom?" I asked shakily. "Mom?"

I looked at the easel. The paint had splattered all over the artwork, and even on some of the writing in the middle. It left little, tiny, black dots all over the place—on the mountains, on the Jerusalem skyline, on the flowers—pretty much everywhere. And there was one particularly bad splotch on the bottom, near a domed building in Jerusalem. It was bad. It was really, really bad, and I felt ten times worse than I ever had in my whole life. I wished I could hit a rewind button, go back in time and get a do-over.

What a disaster. Not just for Mom but for my aunt and uncle who were so excited about their ketubah. How on earth could I have done this to them? Sure, it was a mistake but that didn't make me feel any better. *What's wrong with me?* I wanted to scream. Thinking about the two of them made my stomach hurt. It was a different kind of pain but it was as bad, if not worse, than when I was lying on the pavement the other night with my arm twisted beneath me like a garden hose.

Finally, as if the spell that had turned her into a lifeless statue was lifted, Mom began to move slowly in her chair. She started whispering to herself. At first she mumbled over and over again, "Ohmygod, ohmygod, ohmygod...." Then she stood up quickly, pulling her hair away from her face, saying, "What am I going to do?" I wanted to evaporate and disappear into the golden yellow walls of the studio. Funny how only moments before, that room felt like a magical fairyland but now it felt like a dark dungeon.

I didn't hit rock bottom, though, until I saw tears well up in her eyes. The pain of a broken arm was nothing compared to making my mom cry.

After the longest few moments of my life, in which I aged two hundred years, and in which the only sound I could hear was the second hand of the clock on the wall ticking away rhythmically, Mom stepped back and started talking directly to the easel, "Okay, okay, I can fix this. I'm not going to panic." (She was already panicking.) "I can fix this. I can do it."

I've seen Mom under the stress of deadlines before. I've seen her get mad at my brothers and me when we argue. But it was kind of scary to see her like this, talking to the easel. However, I did like the sound of her saying, "*I can fix this.*" I hoped she was right about that.

"Mom," I repeated quietly, a little afraid that she'd suddenly grow fangs and claws and attack me, the evil ketubah destroyer. I shrank in my place and waited for her to respond.

She turned toward me, and fortunately, did not turn into a werewolf.

Trying to speak calmly, I got all choked up. Tears rolled down my cheeks and my voice cracked. "Mom, I am so, so, so sorry."

Mom took a deep breath and looked at me with her eyes all teary. She started to say something but took another deep breath instead and closed her eyes. Finally she opened them, looked directly at me and said, "I'm going to fix this."

Hope started to elbow its way into my stomach, and was doing a tango with the nausea that had taken up residence in there.

"I don't know how, but somehow I will fix this. It has taken me so many weeks to get to this point and I know I can't start from scratch. I'll need to come up with a clever way to make this right without starting over. You're very creative, YaYa. If you come up with any ideas, let me know. Between the two of us, we'll make this right."

I nodded without making a sound. I appreciated that she had confidence in me and didn't write me off as a useless destroyer of things.

"What needs to happen right now is that you need to go change your clothes and bring the ones you're wearing down to the laundry," she said.

I didn't realize it until she pointed it out. I looked down at my clothes and saw that the paint didn't just hit the artwork. It was on my shirt, my pants and even my socks.

"Okay, I'm going," I said as I tiptoed toward the door. I slipped off the paint-splattered socks. "I really am sorry. All I wanted to do was give you a hug because I love the ketubah so much. I'm sorry I messed everything up."

Even though it was looking like she was going to forgive me, it still felt like my whole life was ruined and that my best bet was to run off to a tropical island like Guam or Tahiti and live off of coconuts for the rest of my days.

"I know it was an accident, YaYa," Mom said. "And I did appreciate the hug." She stood up, walked over to where I was standing and hugged me. I hugged her back with all my might. I was so grateful that she didn't hate me. And she tightened her squeeze too. I think she needed the hug as much as I did.

After a few seconds she let go of me, took a step back and said, "Go change. I'm going to try to dab and scrape some of the specks off before it all dries and the color soaks in. Then I'm going to need to walk away from this and figure things out. We'll come back to it together later, okay?"

I nodded and turned to leave as she went back to her seat by the easel. I held my messy socks at arm's-length from my body, like I was carrying a stinky diaper to the garbage pail, trying not to get any more paint on me.

All of a sudden, Mom got panicky again. "Oh my goodness, is it really one-twenty-five already? I completely lost track of the time," she said looking up at the clock directly over my head above the doorway. "Aunt Rachel is coming over this afternoon at two." Mom started talking really fast. "You absolutely can't tell her about what happened! I already told her that she can't see the ketubah until it's all done because I want to surprise the two of them together with the final piece, so she knows better than to ask to come upstairs and see it. But under no circumstances is she to know about this. Do you understand?"

I nodded once more, now feeling a full-on macarena going on in my stomach.

"She and Uncle David will never know about this mishap. I plan to present them with a perfect, beautiful ketubah. There's no reason to upset them."

"I won't say anything." I promised.

Why would I? I was already miserable enough for the two of them, their future children and grandchildren. No need to drag them into my conga line of doom.

10

...And Whispers in Kitchens

After putting my clothes in the laundry and taking a shower (I even found paint in my eyebrows), I headed to the kitchen to say hi to Aunt Rachel, who had already arrived. She and Mom were sitting together at the table, talking and sipping coffee. Mom was cool as a cucumber, as if an epic disaster hadn't just taken place in her studio.

LuLu was cozied up in Aunt Rachel's lap, and judging by her happy tail wags, seemed extremely content as my aunt petted her gently and rhythmically. LuLu looked up at her and I bet that if she could talk she would have said, "You're my favorite human!" For sure, she's one of mine, so I totally get that. I get it so much that I'm not even insulted to think my own dog likes my aunt better than she likes me. I know LuLu loves me, but she never stays with me the way she does with Aunt Rachel. The amazing thing is that we'd only had LuLu a few weeks, but like a magnet to metal, when Aunt Rachel visits LuLu zips right over to her, nuzzles up and doesn't leave her side until it's time for her to go. When I was little I did the same thing whenever I saw my favorite aunt. I still kind of do!

Just as I was about to step into the kitchen I heard something that made me freeze in my spot. It sounded like Aunt Rachel was crying. I stood motionless against the wall to the left of the entryway and peered in with just my right eye, the rest of me hidden behind the wall. I didn't want to interrupt, and Aunt Rachel probably didn't want me to see her crying. I certainly didn't want to embarrass her. *Did Mom tell her about the ketubah? Even after she made me promise not to breathe a word about it?*

I listened in.

"It's just so frustrating. Sometimes it feels like we can't agree on anything!"

"Do you want to tell me about it?" I heard Mom ask in a quiet voice, almost a whisper, clearly trying to keep this conversation between the two of them.

Okay, not about the ketubah....

"I don't want to bother you with my problems." Aunt Rachel sniffled while stroking LuLu's fur.

"What are you talking about? We're family! Your problems are my problems," Mom said softly. "Tell me, maybe I can help."

Problems? Aunt Rachel is having problems? Why is she crying? Who can't she agree with? Someone at work? Grandma? Uncle David? Oh, I sure hoped it wasn't Uncle David. I knew that I probably shouldn't have been listening in, but my curiosity got the best of me and I couldn't bear to walk away. It's not nice to be nosy and I should have minded my own business, but I care about Aunt Rachel. I leaned in and listened some more.

"It's as if we've been arguing over every single detail. It's horrible. I love him so much, but planning this wedding has been extremely difficult for us."

What? They're fighting? This is terrible! I thought as the muscles in my stomach tensed up. I really wished she had been talking about someone from work.

Next I heard Mom's voice, "You know, Mark and I had a hard time agreeing on parts of our wedding too.

It's easy to get caught up in the details about bouquets, caterers, and who makes it onto the guest list."

Aunt Rachel nodded.

"I'm sure you know that people who love each other can argue and disagree," Mom continued. "It feels terrible now, but trust me, you'll get through this and your wedding day will be beautiful and magical. I'm sure of it."

Beautiful and magical? Good thing we're not telling her about the ruined ketubah, I thought.

Aunt Rachel blew her nose into a tissue. "I mean, we're two weeks out! By now everything should be set and we should just be getting ready. Instead, we're still quarreling. We've argued about every single detail from silly things like what type of flowers to use in the centerpieces, and who's going to sit at the table with wacky Uncle Joe—"

Mom cut her off. "Nobody should have to sit next to Uncle Joe," she said with a wink. "You really have to appreciate his sense of humor. The last time we saw him was at the family reunion picnic. He had asked if he could bring a pet and he showed up with a can of sardines in a fishbowl."

Aunt Rachel allowed herself a little giggle but then continued. "But we're also arguing over big things, like whether or not David should wear a *kittel* under the huppah."

There was silence.

"You know what a kittel is don't you?" Aunt Rachel asked.

"Sure," Mom answered, "it's the white robe that the rabbi and the cantor wear on the High Holidays over their clothes."

"Precisely! It's what the *rabbi* and the *cantor* wear.

But now *he* wants to wear one under the huppah. He's been reading up on Jewish wedding rituals and likes how the kittel represents starting fresh and clean."

"Like on Yom Kippur," Mom said.

I never knew that people wear kittels under the huppah.

"That sounds kind of nice. I think the description of both of you wearing white and starting fresh is a lovely idea," Mom said. "So, what's the problem with the kittel?"

"I don't know, it just makes me feel kind of uncomfortable. Aren't people buried in a kittel when they die?" Aunt Rachel asked.

"Yeah, but some people also wear them when they're leading a Passover seder. And in some synagogues it's not only the rabbi and the cantor, but even the congregants wear them on the High Holidays," Mom offered.

Aunt Rachel sniffled. "You guys didn't have one at your wedding. I've never seen this done before and it feels foreign and strange to me. Does that make me a terrible person?"

As if she actually understood what was going on, and to assure her that she's not a bad person, LuLu licked Aunt Rachel's hand. Aunt Rachel scratched LuLu behind her ears.

Mom said, "Of course you're not a terrible person. You want things to be the way you imagined them to be. I get that. But I understand why he wants to wear it, too. Maybe don't worry so much about it feeling strange and try to see if the meaning behind it speaks to you. I have no doubt that you two will figure this out, but I also know that it's painful to fight with someone you love." She paused then continued with a little smile. "If you're afraid that people will get the two of you mixed up because you're both wearing white, I think you can relax about that," she joked Joel-style, trying to break the tension. Aunt Rachel let out a soft chuckle.

And speaking of Joel, guess who happened to walk by just as I was eavesdropping? Mr. Corny Jokes himself. I put my finger up to my lips to shush him before he could say anything. Then I whispered, "I'm listening in on Mom and Aunt Rachel's conversation." I quickly added, "Don't judge me."

"Judge you? Are you kidding me? I'll go get my spy gear and listen in with you!"

Before I could even respond, Joel had taken off, sprinting up the steps to his room. Of course he knew where all of his gear was and would have no problem finding it. Had it been me, I would probably have been in my room looking for over an hour. But Joel knows exactly where everything is at every moment. Well, I guess I know where everything is in my room too: no matter what it is, it's most likely somewhere on my floor.

Within a few seconds Joel came bounding back down with two sets of wireless headphones, some sort of listening device, and an armful of other spying equipment including night goggles, mirrors, binoculars, and even a lightsaber from his Star Wars collection. I had no idea what he had in mind for that thing!

"What's all that for?" I asked with a look indicating I thought he was perhaps turning into Wacky Uncle Joe.

"A good spy, like a boy scout, is always prepared. You never know what you might need," he answered very seriously.

Give me a break!

"I think the listening stuff will be more than enough," I told him.

I already felt weird listening in on the conversation. Using Joel's spy gear made it feel worse. It's one thing to happen to be standing nearby. It's another thing to put a device in the room and listen in from afar.

I wasn't sure what to do. Should I spy and quench my curiosity or should I walk away? I imagined a little red devil and a little white angel on each of my shoulders, just like you see in cartoons, whispering in opposite ears. *Do it! Don't do it! Do it! Don't do it!*

The little red devil won.

11

Circular Arguments

Joel motioned to me to follow him. We tiptoed over to the living room, out of earshot of Mom and Aunt Rachel.

In a hushed voice, Joel said, "So, what are we listening to, anyway?"

"Why were you so quick to get your spying equipment if you didn't even know what I was listening to?"

"Well," he answered shrugging his shoulders, "I love spying! If it's interesting enough for you to listen in, then I figure it's gotta be pretty juicy, and I'd want to hear it too."

"What if they were talking about seating arrangements for the dinner, or what kind of cake they're going to serve, or how much to tip the caterer? Would you be interested in listening in then?"

Joel looked up at the ceiling as he thought about it and replied, ticking each item off on his fingers. "Seating, nope; cake, absolutely; tips, not at all. Are they talking about the cake?" he asked eagerly.

"No," I said. Then I lowered my voice even more. "It's actually kind of serious. Aunt Rachel was crying."

"Crying? Aunt Rachel doesn't cry. She's the perkiest person I know."

"YoYo, everyone cries sometimes. And yes, she really was. It sounds like she and Uncle David are arguing a lot about wedding stuff."

"What do you mean? What kind of stuff?"

"I don't know all the details yet. I had just started listening in when you came by. So far all I heard was that Uncle David wants to wear a kittel under the huppah and Aunt Rachel doesn't want him to. She says it makes her uncomfortable."

"Why does he want to wear a kittel? Isn't that what the rabbi wears? And why does she care?" he asked.

"I'm not exactly sure but I get the impression she thinks it's kind of weird."

Joel considered this. "Okay, but if you think about it, at the end of the wedding, they're going to stomp on a glass! That's kind of strange too. It seems normal to us because we're used to that idea, but I bet someone who doesn't know about Jewish weddings might think that's a completely weird thing to do."

"Good point," I agreed.

"Come on," he said, putting the headphones on, "Let's see what else they're talking about in there."

Listening in felt so wrong but I didn't want to miss out either. Maybe I was even a little bit worried. Would Aunt Rachel and Uncle David fight so much that they would call off the wedding? That would be horrible! I didn't want to consider that possibility. I picked up the headphones and was about to put them on. Instead, I tapped Joel on the shoulder and motioned for him to take his off.

"YoYo," I said, "you're really good at being sneaky, right?" Dad taught me that sometimes it's a good idea to put a compliment out there first before you ask something of someone.

Joel definitely seemed pleased that I'd noticed his skills. "Yeah, I'm pretty good at it." He sat up a little taller, looking proud and taking the bait.

"Well, anyone can spy using technology like this," I said holding out my headset, "but I think it takes even more sneakiness to do it old-school, without the equipment. I think I want to go back by the kitchen and listen in from there. It's more of a challenge that way, don't you think?"

"I guess," Joel said, looking longingly at his night-vision goggles. He sure likes his spy toys.

"How about if we act like real spies and have a stakeout. We can pretend to be playing cards so at least if someone walks by we won't look too suspicious. If we sit in just the right spot they won't see us at all but we should be able to see them," I suggested.

"Hey! You're pretty good at this spying business yourself," he said, complimenting me back. Not that I care all that much about whether or not I'm a good spy but coming from Joel, that was a pretty big deal. "Playing cards sounds good. I'd love to get my Grand Canyon souvenir deck, but I don't think you ever gave me back the cards you lost when you last borrowed them," he said, reminding me once again, for the thousandth time, that I'd misplaced a few of his cards. I'm sure they're somewhere in my room. Maybe I'll find them sometime before I graduate from high school.

"I think we have a deck in the game closet downstairs. I'll go look for it," I offered and zipped down to the basement to find the cards. Sure enough, they were right where they were supposed to be. I guess there is something to be said for putting things back where they belong.

I sprinted back upstairs and sat on the floor right outside the kitchen. Joel started shuffling the deck.

"Shhh! You're making too much noise, they'll hear us!" I whisper-barked at him. "Plus, I can't hear what they're saying when you do that! We don't have to play for real, you know. Our goal is to hear what Aunt Rachel is talking about," I reminded him. "The card playing is an act."

"We might as well play, though," he whispered back with a shrug. "Crazy Eights. Let's go." He dealt eight cards to each of us and then put one face up in the middle. It was the queen of hearts.

I picked up my pile using my right hand and organized the cards by suit, which was quite a challenge with one arm in a cast and only my fingers sticking out. Once I finally got things in order, I was able to concentrate on what was going on in the other room. I could see their legs under the table and LuLu still balled up contentedly in Aunt Rachel's lap.

"Then there's the whole circling thing," I heard Aunt Rachel say.

"What do you mean?" Mom asked.

I put the queen of spades down on top of the queen of hearts.

"Well, traditionally the bride circles the groom seven times, but nowadays people do it lots of other ways. Some people choose to do only three circles. Or the couple can circle each other or you can skip the whole circling thing altogether." I could hear sadness in her voice.

Joel put down the four of spades. I immediately slapped down the four of clubs.

"So what do you want and what does he want?" Mom asked.

I could see Aunt Rachel's hand still playing with the fluff of fur behind LuLu's neck. "I like the idea of maintaining the custom of me circling him seven times. That's how I assumed we'd do it. I mean, why change it if you don't need to? I guess I kind of assumed we'd have a fairly traditional wedding."

"Okay, so what does he want?" Mom asked.

"He thinks I should make three circles mostly because seven takes too long. He said that the important thing is that we do some circling and that three is as good as seven. The circles symbolize us making a new family unit, and we both really like that."

"So that's good," Mom said cheerfully. "You see? There's something you agree on."

Aunt Rachel added, "Once upon a time, they used to say that the bride made circles to protect the groom from evil spirits." She dismissed this idea with a wave of her hand. "As if! I'm not sure how much sway I'd have against the evil spirits! I guess it is kind of fun to think of it that way. But if that's the case, shouldn't he protect me too?" She waved her hand again as if shooing the problem away like a pesky fly. "This isn't one of our most serious arguments but it adds to the huge list of things we don't see eye to eye on," she said, sniffling again.

Joel glanced at me with a sudden look of alarm. His eyes got big and wide. Was he thinking the same thing that I was? We often find ourselves on the same wavelength. Sometimes it seems like we have a sort of twin telepathy where we can read each other's minds. We can't really, but it often feels that way.

I glanced right back at him with a look that meant, *Oh no! Do you think things are so bad that Aunt Rachel is going to give up on the whole idea of the wedding? Are they going to call it off?*

His glance turned into a look of sheer panic. I shot him the same look, sure that we were thinking alike.

Finally he whispered, "You put down the four of

clubs! Now I don't have anything to put down!" With a frustrated sigh, he picked up one card, then another, and another, his eyes growing wider with each additional card. It was then that I realized we were *not* on the same wavelength at all, and that he wasn't even paying any attention to what was going on in the kitchen. After picking up so many cards that he could hardly hold them in one hand, he triumphantly smacked down the eight of clubs and whispered, "Diamonds."

In the kitchen, Mom made a suggestion. "Maybe this will help. Let's go through the reasons for three versus seven circles. If we talk it through maybe you'll figure out what you want."

"Okay," Aunt Rachel agreed. "So, seven is a big number in Judaism. You know, the world was created in six days and on the seventh day God rested, we break up the Torah readings into seven portions when we read it each week, we recite seven blessings at a wedding. The list goes on and on for the number seven."

I didn't have any diamond cards to put down so I put my cards on the floor face down. With one arm in the dumb cast, it was too hard to hold them and pick from the deck. I took the top card from the stack and what was the first thing that came up? The seven of diamonds! Good timing, considering the conversation in the kitchen all about sevens! I put it down and kept listening. Joel glared at me, clearly annoyed that I got a good card in one try while he was holding practically half the deck.

Mom asked, "And what's the symbolism behind three circles?"

"It's not the official one but David says that he likes

to think of it as one for you, one for me and one for us and our future family together. Actually, I do kind of like that explanation."

"I think it's pretty great that Judaism allows us to dive in with different interpretations and ideas. It sounds like you both like the idea of three circles so why not go with that one?" Mom asked.

"I do like it but I also like the idea of doing it the traditional way. The number seven has so much meaning," Aunt Rachel said with a heavy sigh. "Oh, I don't know. It shouldn't be this hard, should it? I'm worried that if we're disagreeing so much now, what will happen once we're married?" A sad strain took over her voice. "Who's to say that this isn't what it's going to be like all the time?"

"Did you fight a lot before you got engaged?" Mom asked.

"No, never. Even when we broke up after college it wasn't because of a fight. We had decided to try going our separate ways and seeing where life took us. It was a very friendly parting. We never argued like this before." She stopped and considered for a moment. "Well, actually, our whole relationship started because we were arguing over books we'd read. Those weren't real fights though. They were just college-kid debates. It feels very different now and I hope this isn't our new normal. What if every time there's a decision to be made we argue about it?"

LuLu circled around on Aunt Rachel's lap and plopped down to a new sleeping position.

"I'm sure this isn't the way it's always going to be with you two. But you'll have to figure out how to keep *shalom bayit*...."

Shalom bayit? What did she mean by that? It was

obviously something in Hebrew. I knew both of those words but I'd never heard them together like that as an expression. Shalom means hello, goodbye or peace. Bayit means house. Hello house? Goodbye house? Neither of those made any sense. Peace house? I assumed that it must be something to do with that. Maybe it means a peaceful house?

Mom continued, "There's so much build-up about what should be and what's expected for the big day. Keep in mind there are so many things that won't be important a year from now, let alone ten or twenty years down the road. My best advice is to take a deep breath, do something else for a while—" *Just like she's doing with fixing their ketubah,* I thought, feeling a twinge of anxiety from bringing to mind that sore subject, "—and then sit down with David and calmly and rationally discuss things. If there's something that's extremely important to him and you don't care that much, don't be stubborn for the sake of being stubborn. And if there's something that you truly feel strongly about, explain it to him. There has to be give and take. Not just in the wedding planning, but throughout your marriage."

Now I was really feeling awful. Not only did I feel bad about listening in on a conversation that wasn't meant for my ears, I was actually dreading where all this was going. Sure, most people disagree and argue now and then when they're together all the time. In fact, I don't think a single day goes by that I'm not bickering about something with at least one of my brothers, but this didn't sound good. It almost sounded like Aunt Rachel was ready to give up.

Well, maybe she was ready to give up, but I sure wasn't. I knew right then and there that I had to do something. And I had to do it as soon as possible.

Or at least right after I beat my brother at Crazy Eights.

12

Fifty-Two Card Pile-Up

Let's play another round. You've got to give me a chance to get you back. It's only fair," Joel demanded quietly. I nodded.

Just as Joel was silently dealing the cards, making sure to place each one down ever so softly, Jeremy sauntered over to us. Joel put his finger to his lips and whispered, "Shhh. They don't know we're here," pointing into the kitchen. Jeremy flashed us one of his *I'm-definitely-up-to-something* grins.

He poked his head into the kitchen and said, "What's up, Aunt Rachel?"

"Hey, Jay! How're you doing, buddy?" Aunt Rachel asked, trying to hide the sadness in her voice. Her red, teary eyes may have given her away, but Jeremy didn't seem to notice.

"I'm okay." He gave a little wave of his hand and stepped back to stand over us.

"Please don't let them know we're here," I whispered looking up at him with pleading eyes from the floor. "Please, please, please! We want to hear what they're saying. They're talking about wedding stuff."

"Why do you care about wedding stuff?" Jeremy asked in a whisper, grimacing like he just bit into an extra-sour pickle. "Don't you have anything better to do?" He was eyeing the kitchen, undoubtedly scheming one thing or another to mess up our stakeout.

"Have you met me?" I asked incredulously. "This wedding is like, my life! No, I don't have anything better to do. I need to know each and every detail of this thing."

Jeremy looked over at Joel. "You too?"

"Have you met me?" he asked, clearly mocking me, but then added with a shrug, "I like spying. It doesn't matter all that much to me what we're listening to. Plus we're playing cards."

"Cards! I love cards! Wanna play some Fifty-Two Card Pick-Up?" Jay whispered with sudden enthusiasm.

I proceeded to actively ignore him and listen in on the conversation. I've learned over the years that this is usually the best policy with my older, obnoxious brother.

Aunt Rachel sighed and said something about choosing the song for their first dance but I couldn't concentrate on what she was saying because there was a finger jabbing me in my shoulder. I turned toward my pesky brother and scowled.

"YaYa, did you hear me? Did you hear me?" Jeremy asked, sitting down next to me.

"What?" I said in my most annoyed tone. I wanted to make it clear that I wished he'd leave.

"Fifty-Two Card Pick-Up? What do you say?"

In the kitchen, Mom was listing what I could only assume were names of songs, but I'd never heard of them. "How about *Wonderful Tonight*?" she suggested.

Jeremy poked me again, a little bit harder this time. "YaYa, come on, Fifty-Two Card Pick up!"

"Yes, I know! I heard about it. It was terrible," I said, still focusing on the kitchen. "Now, please be quiet!"

My two brothers looked at one another with confused expressions on their faces. "What do you mean it was terrible? It didn't happen yet," Jay whispered.

"Shhh! I'm trying to hear what they're saying!" This was so annoying. All I wanted to do was hear the conversation, and now he wanted to have a conversation of our own. I needed to get rid of him as soon as I could so I quickly replied, "Yeah, it was like, last Tuesday. It was awful. I think someone may have even died."

"What?! No one ever died from that!" Jeremy whispered gruffly. I appreciated that at least he was respecting our quiet space. "How could someone die from Fifty-Two Card Pick-Up?" He seemed like he was going to explode.

"Jay, it was a huge accident. I'm pretty sure I heard that someone died. And of course there were tons of injuries."

"A card accident? With injuries?" he hissed. Fortunately he didn't shout it out.

"Yes."

"What the heck are you talking about?" my older brother asked me, all of a sudden looking serious and confused.

"I'm talking about the big accident on Highway 10 last week. The huge pile-up," I answered. "Why'd you bring that up anyway? What does that have to do with anything? Why can't you just leave me alone?"

All of a sudden, he and Joel looked at each other and they both got up and ran away down the hall so that I couldn't see them anymore. Next I heard loud, roaring laughter coming from the two of them. They were out of sight, but not out of hearing range. I had no idea what was going on, but I didn't care. The good news was that they were gone.

I heard Aunt Rachel say, "...but aside from all that, our biggest argument is about the huppah. We had both agreed from the beginning that we'd have the kids hold up the huppah for us—"

I gasped. *No no, no! Don't tell me that's off the table!*

At that crucial moment Joel returned without Jay and said, "That was so funny! And good work getting Jay to go away."

"Shhh!" I waved my arms around like I was swatting mosquitoes. "Quiet! This is about us!" I pointed my thumb over my shoulder in the direction of the kitchen.

"Us?" he asked, looking confused. "Why are they talking about us?"

"I don't know. I just heard her say something about the huppah holders. That's us! Now be quiet so I can hear. This is important!" I whispered sharply at him.

I heard Mom say, "Oh, please don't tell me that you're going to take that away from them. The kids are so excited about being your huppah holders. Especially YaYa. You'll break her heart if you don't let her do it."

True! I held my breath as I waited to hear Aunt Rachel's response, as if keeping the air inside me would somehow steer her to giving the right answer.

"No, of course I'm not taking that away from the kids. They're absolutely going to be our huppah holders. We agree wholeheartedly about that. We can't wait to have them up there with us."

At the sound of that good news I let out all the air that I was holding in my chest. Unfortunately, I exhaled with a bit too much force, which caused me to cough, which made enough noise for them to hear me in the kitchen.

Suddenly the conversation stopped and Mom called out, "Is someone out there?"

I looked up at YoYo with petrified eyes.

Joel looked back at me and mouthed the words "*We're busted.*"

So much for our perfect stakeout.

13

The Misery Compromise

I had no choice. I gulped and responded as innocently as possible, "It's me."

"And me," Joel added.

"How long have you been out there?" Mom asked getting up, her voice sounding closer as she came toward us.

I stood up too and headed into the kitchen, feeling like I was walking right into oncoming traffic. LuLu jumped off Aunt Rachel's lap and followed Mom to meet me, her tail wagging furiously. No matter what's going on, she loves being right in the center of the action.

"I don't know. YoYo and I were just hanging out playing cards." *That was true.*

"Were you listening in on our conversation?" Mom asked, now looking me right in the eye. LuLu sat down on her hind legs and she, too, was looking up at me expectantly as if waiting to hear what I had to say.

"Um, I heard some things, but I wasn't totally paying attention. I was mostly focusing on our card game." *Not so much true.* I felt my ears getting hot. For some strange reason whenever I get embarrassed or upset, my ears get pink, then red, then really, really bright red like when you put metal into a fire. They almost feel that hot too.

Even if they had believed me, I think my ears and

my eyes must have given it away. My ears were burning up, and as for my eyes, I wouldn't even look directly at Aunt Rachel. I was too upset with what I had heard. I was worried, sad, and even a little bit mad at her. Obviously that wasn't fair or reasonable, but at that moment I didn't care. Just the thought that they might call off the wedding was beyond devastating. Although come to think of it, I don't remember if she ever actually said anything about calling it off or if that was all in my head.

"YaYa, come here, honey," Aunt Rachel said sweetly. At the sound of our favorite human's voice, LuLu bounded across the kitchen and leaped right back into Aunt Rachel's lap. Maybe she was afraid I was going to take her spot.

I walked over slowly as if there were poisonous snakes slithering all over the floor and I was trying to avoid stepping on them. If she was calling me over to tell me the worst possible news ever, I was in no hurry to hear it. When I got to the table, she motioned for me to sit down in the seat that Mom had been sitting in. I sat but still didn't look up at her. Instead, I stared at a birthmark on my wrist. It kind of looked like the shape of an alligator head.

"YaYa, listen to me." I looked up from the alligator head and my eyes met hers. "I'm sorry if you heard some things that may have been upsetting but I want you to know that Uncle David and I absolutely want you and the other kids to be our huppah holders. I can see you're upset and something tells me you're worried about that, right?"

I nodded.

"Is anything else bothering you?" she asked.

I shook my head to say no but as if my mouth had a

mind of its own I blurted out, "Are you guys going to break up? Please don't break up!"

While I was looking at Aunt Rachel, I saw the entryway to the kitchen out of the corner of my eye. I noticed my brothers' bodies filling up the space within the doorframe, both listening intently. Clearly there was no need to hide anymore. They stood there like a totem pole with Joel in front of Jay, who was a full head taller. Apparently he had returned from his laughing spot in time to hear the conversation that was about us. Those boys may have claimed not to care about all the wedding stuff, but they did care about Aunt Rachel.

"We're not breaking up, we're just going through a stressful time," Aunt Rachel said softly, stroking my hair. "We love each other very much and we can't wait to be married. In fact, did you by any chance hear us talking about how many times we're going to do the circles under the huppah?"

"Yeah, I heard that." I felt my cheeks and my ears get even hotter. How humiliating to get caught! Lucky for me, neither she nor Mom focused on the fact that I was eavesdropping. She just got to the point.

"Well, this is probably the sweetest thing that anyone could ever say—and this is why I love Uncle David so much. He said he wants to do three circles instead of seven because he doesn't want to waste a single second before we become husband and wife. He wants us to be married as soon as possible."

"No offense, Aunt Rachel," Jeremy said, "but that's the sappiest thing I've ever heard."

"It really is!" Mom said, laughing. "But it's sweet nonetheless."

"Oh, it is so goofy!" Aunt Rachel agreed, with a little chuckle. "But his real message is that while all the rituals and customs are important, the bottom line is that he can't wait for us to be a family." A tear fell down her cheek. She was back to crying again, but as she wiped it away with her hand, she didn't seem to be embarrassed about doing it in front of us like I thought she would be.

She continued. "I know Uncle David is really looking forward to officially becoming your uncle and being a part of this family. And I'm excited to be a part of his too. I'm not going to lie to you, it's been a hard few weeks, maybe even months, but we'll be okay. Sometimes people who love each other argue. It doesn't mean we don't love each other, it just means that we need to work things out. Do you and your brothers ever argue?" she asked without actually needing an answer since she knew it already.

I answered with my best "Are you kidding?" expression, thinking about all the things Joel and I bicker about and how Jeremy can be so mean sometimes. I looked over at the two of them. The truth is that I do love my brothers and even though it doesn't always seem like it, I know they love me too.

"Well, I'm glad to hear that you're not breaking up and I'm especially glad to hear that you're still planning to get married," I said, "but you started to say something about us being your huppah holders. What's the deal?"

"Right. That," Aunt Rachel said slowly. "I want to have all four of you guys walk down the aisle, bringing the huppah with you as you walk. I think it would be a cool way to start things off. You'd each hold one pole as you carry it down the aisle and then you'd position yourselves on the bimah when you get up there. Uncle

David wants you to be on the bimah already as the guests arrive. He thinks it would look much nicer to have the huppah up there, ready and waiting for us to walk in. He's also worried about you guys carrying the huppah down the aisle. He's afraid one of you could possibly trip. But I'm not concerned about that. Plus I really want you all to be a part of the procession."

She took a deep breath, then said, "It's true that all the details are making me a bit miserable but I realize that these are all just details about one day. I'm excited to marry him. It's just that the 'getting married' part has been challenging."

"Well, that's a shame, Mom said. "You two should enjoy every bit of your wedding day. I'm sure you'll work out some sort of compromise. Remember that whole shalom bayit idea we talked about?"

"What does that mean, anyway?" I asked. "I heard you mention it before. I know bayit means house and shalom means hello, goodbye and peace. I'm guessing this has to do with peace and not a greeting, but why do you keep saying that?" I figured there was no point in trying to hide the fact that I had been eavesdropping anymore.

Mom answered. "Shalom bayit is a Hebrew expression for 'peace in the home.' It means that sometimes when people live together in a family, they have to figure out ways to get along when they don't agree. That may mean one person not getting what they want and letting the other person have their way, or it may mean coming up with a compromise that both sides can live with, or finding a completely different solution altogether."

"So if we can come up with an idea that you guys both agree on, you'll have shalom bayit?" I asked.

"On this issue, at least," Aunt Rachel murmured softly while playing with LuLu's fur.

I took this as an invitation to help. "Okay, let's see what the real problem is here," I said feeling like a detective diving into a mystery. "You want us to walk down the aisle and be a part of the procession."

"Yes," Aunt Rachel said. I smiled a huge smile. Of course I liked that idea too.

"And Uncle David wants us holding the huppah on the bimah before the wedding begins, so the guests see it right away as they come into the sanctuary."

Aunt Rachel nodded and explained. "He says it sets the tone before the ceremony even begins. Without the huppah up on the bimah, he says it feels like any old day at the synagogue, but having it already up there, it's almost like it's calling out, 'Time for a wedding, people!'"

"Hmmmm," I said, leaning back in my chair, setting up a little suspense. I rested my hand on my chin and tried real hard to look like I was wracking my brain for a solution. All of a sudden I thought of Mom and Dad's picture in their bedroom, and an answer came to me in a flash.

"How about this?" I proposed. "What if you use the poles and weighted bases from the synagogue's huppah but replace their top with yours? That way the huppah can stand on its own on the bimah. The four of us can walk down the aisle first, and then we'll go up and each hold one of the poles."

It seemed like an obvious solution to me but for one reason or another neither Aunt Rachel nor Uncle David ever thought of it themselves. Maybe when you're right in the middle of something it's harder to see the big picture.

Judging from her reaction Aunt Rachel felt the same way. "YaYa, that is brilliant! I love it!" she yelled out loud. LuLu, who had fallen asleep and had been snoring like a Great Dane in her lap, was awakened by Aunt Rachel's sudden exclamation and jumped down to the floor. Poor LuLu! She looked so startled. She ran straight into her crate.

We had found LuLu in October in our synagogue's sukkah after she had run away from her owners, Mr. and Mrs. Browning. It's a long story but in the end, the Brownings decided they were too old to take care of or keep track of her anymore. They agreed to let us keep her, and she's super happy living with us. She still gets a little skittish when she hears loud or unexpected noises and often runs for cover. It must have been so scary for her being homeless for a little while out in the world on her own.

Aunt Rachel, now with an empty lap, jumped up from her seat and hugged me.

"YaYa, that is seriously a simply brilliant solution. I'm going to call Uncle David right now and tell him what you came up with. I don't know why we never thought of that!"

My thoughts exactly....

She practically skipped out of the kitchen with her cell phone in her hand. She went to another room but we could hear her excited squeals of happiness as she shared my idea with her future spouse.

A few minutes later she came back in, smiling like she'd just won the trillion dollar lottery. "YaYa, he loved your idea! Thank you!"

To say that I felt proud of myself would be as much of an understatement as saying that it's a bit chilly in Alaska in January. I was so happy I felt like I might pop. I was happy for the two of them and I was happy I was able to help. Now, if only I could help Mom figure out how to fix the ketubah, I would be the happiest kid alive.

I hugged Aunt Rachel and she kissed me on top of my head. "Love you, kiddo!" she said.

"Love you, too," I said back. I told her I had to go and walked out of the kitchen, stepping right over the cards that were strewn all over the floor.

"Heh, heh. Fifty-Two Card Pick-Up!" Jeremy laughed, pointing at the mess he had made. It seems that he hadn't been talking about a fifty-two-car pile-up before. Apparently, Fifty-Two Card Pick-Up is a "game" where one person throws all the cards in the air and makes the other person pick them up. It was all starting to make sense to me now. The mess looked fine to me, though, and it didn't even occur to me to pick the cards up. I got about halfway up the stairs when Joel yelled to me to come and help him clean up.

"Ugh," I moaned and came back down the stairs.

As YoYo and I picked up the cards, I thought about what had taken place in the kitchen. Then, as if someone flicked a light switch in my head, another brilliant idea popped into my brain. I was on a roll!

I bolted up the stairs to solve the next problem and, come to think of it, never did finish cleaning up the cards.

14

A Real Fixer-Upper

I stared at the ketubah on the easel and it almost felt as if it was staring right back at me. My eyes lasered in on the big splotch on the bottom and I felt certain my idea might actually work. I looked carefully at the text in the middle and could see that all of the little dots were gone already. I guess Mom was able to dab or scrape them off right away while I was in the shower and before Aunt Rachel came over. I could still see splatters on the flowers and the different scenes but I figured it was too hard to scrape the parts that were already painted. I wondered if she'd be able to paint over the dots with the matching colors. I realized this would make her work almost double but at least the ketubah wouldn't be ruined. It was definitely coming along but that that ugly blob on the bottom near Jerusalem still looked awful.

The more I looked at it, the more confident I was that I knew how to fix it. The more confident I became, the more my excitement and happiness felt like kids on the last day of school, barreling out of the classroom on their way to the exit doors. I couldn't hold it in anymore. I raced out of the room and flew down the stairs to tell Mom. Once downstairs I ran quickly yet quietly to the kitchen. I wanted to get Mom's attention without Aunt Rachel seeing me. I stopped at the entryway and tried to catch her eye. They were talking about boring stuff like the seating arrangements, (major snore), and for some reason Mom was quite engaged in the conversation. I couldn't get her to look up.

I tried waving my arms. Nope. Jumping up and down. Nothing. Jumping and waving simultaneously. Finally! She looked up.

"YaYa, what are you doing?" Aunt Rachel turned around too. So much for being subtle.

"Mom!" I shouted, still jumping up and down. "I figured it out!" I knew I couldn't say out loud what the "it" was, but I also knew that I couldn't wait until Aunt Rachel left to blab about my brilliant idea.

"Figured what out?" Mom asked.

"You know, the *thing*!" I said, pointing my head toward the attic and making my eyes pop out, hoping she'd get my secret message. She did not.

"What thing?" she asked looking confused.

I clenched my teeth as if not moving my lips too much might make it more obvious to her. "You know, the THING!"

"YaYa, what on earth are you talking about?" Mom said sounding both annoyed and curious. Now I was beginning to get frustrated.

"The thing! You know...the THING we talked about before. I figured it out!" I was now full-on bending my body, wriggling around trying to indicate that I came up with a solution for fixing the ketubah without actually saying it out loud.

"You've got to give me more to go on, YaYa," she said.

"Mom," I started, "just before Aunt Rachel came

over we were talking about the thing...you know, the thing...upstairs, that we were talking about...before. I figured it out!"

Finally, the last piece of the puzzle fit.

"OH! THE THING! UPSTAIRS!"

"Um, hi," Aunt Rachel said, waving her hand at us. "Do you guys need to talk about something privately because I'm getting the distinct feeling that this is a conversation I'm not supposed to be a part of."

"I'm sorry, Rachel," Mom said, "That was rude of us." She turned to me and said, "Let's talk about this later."

"No, Mom!" I insisted. "I don't think I can wait. Aunt Rachel, do you think you could excuse us for a few minutes so I can show my Mom something? It's very important."

"No problem," Aunt Rachel said pulling out her phone. "I need to make a call anyway. Go ahead."

"Are you sure?" Mom asked. Aunt Rachel nodded.

I grabbed Mom's hand and practically dragged her up the two flights to her studio. Once we were upstairs I told her my idea. I wasn't sure but I almost thought I detected a hint of a smile in the corners of her lips.

"I'll have to look at it to see if that's even possible," she said walking a tightrope over hopeful and doubtful. I think she didn't want to get her hopes up, or mine, but this time I definitely spotted a glimmer of something, maybe excitement, in her eyes. I had a feeling she loved my idea as much as I did.

Maybe I would be the happiest kid in the world after all!

15

It's Crazy Enough
That It Just Might Work

We studied the bad paint spot together. Mom sat down in front of the easel and measured it with her thumb.

"YaYa, I get why you were so excited. I think your idea is going to work." She looked over her shoulder at me. "I had a feeling you'd figure something out. I love it."

I was so happy that I was going to give Mom a hug but she put her hand up and said, "No hugs! Not here!" And we both shared a strained, knowing laugh. "I want to get to this right away," she said. "Do me a favor and go down and tell Aunt Rachel that I'm going to be a few minutes. If I can get this done right now we'll feel so much better."

"Okay," I said, but I didn't move.

"What are you doing? Aren't you going to go down to her?"

"I just want to see how you're going to do it. I'll go in a minute."

Mom started working on the spot and I couldn't take my eyes off the ketubah. I kept my fingers crossed under my chin, hoping with all my might that my idea would work and that everything would be okay.

Mom got lost in her work, and I guess I did too. It

was fascinating watching her carefully dab and scrape, wipe and cover, sketch and paint. I don't know how long I was standing there but I watched Mom magically turn an unformed blob of paint into the cutest little image of LuLu frolicking near a gold dome in Jerusalem.

"It's perfect!" I exclaimed. "I'll go down to Aunt Rachel now." But when I turned and faced the door, a pair of eyes met mine.

"Aunt Rachel! You're not supposed to be up here! It's supposed to be a big surprise for you and Uncle David."

"You were gone for so long! I wanted to make sure that nothing happened to you or that you didn't leave and ditch me!" she said as she stepped into the sunlit room. "And well, now that I'm here...." She moved closer to us.

I didn't realize we had been up there for so long, but considering how much fixing Mom did while I stood there mesmerized, I guess we lost track of time.

Aunt Rachel slowly made her way across the room until she stood directly behind Mom. She gasped and covered her face with both hands. She started crying again and this time I wasn't sure if she was crying because of all the splatters that hadn't yet been cleaned up, or if they were tears of joy. She stood there, tears flowing freely like rain down a gutter spout. She wiped the tears away and stared at the ketubah while Mom and I stared at her. It was strangely quiet for a few seconds except for Aunt Rachel's sniffles and shallow breaths. Finally she spoke.

"This...is...," she paused and inhaled, trying to catch her breath from all the crying, "...the...most—" She paused again and my mind began to race, filling in the next word. *Wonderful? Awful? Phenomenal? Disappointing?*

She took another breath and finally said, "...beautiful thing I've ever seen. It's exactly what I imagined. Even more." She focused on the ketubah. I could tell by the expression on her face that she was filled with admiration and awe. I know that feeling! It's exactly how I felt the first time I saw Terror Plummet, the mucho-scary slide with a five-story drop at Splash World Waterpark.

Mom and I exhaled together. I could feel the pride pouring out of her. She had worked so hard on this and filled it with colors and love.

"So, what was the 'thing' you kept talking about downstairs?" Aunt Rachel asked with a hint of concern in her voice.

"There was a teeny tiny mishap that needed to be fixed," I answered cautiously.

"A mishap?" Aunt Rachel asked sounding alarmed.

"There was a bad splotch that needed to be fixed," I explained carefully. I didn't want to share too much. Mom shot a warning glare at me as if to say, "Don't say anymore, YaYa!"

"I can't even see a splotch. Where is it?" Aunt Rachel asked, scrutinizing the picture.

"The splotch became LuLu!" I exclaimed, pointing at it. "That was my idea!"

Adding LuLu was just the icing on the cake. In the end, the splatter incident turned out to be a great thing because LuLu hadn't been included in the original picture and now, given how much of a love-fest was going on between my dog and my aunt, it totally made sense for her to be in it.

Aunt Rachel took out her cell phone and once again

called Uncle David. Unlike last time when she was squealing with joy, this time she was all choked up. He has a pretty loud voice so Aunt Rachel held the phone a little bit away from her ear, which made it possible for us to hear him too.

"David, I need you to come over to Deb and Mark's right away. Are you busy?"

"Hey. You okay? Are you crying?"

"I'm okay, but if you're not too busy, I'd like you to come over now."

"What's going on?" He sounded worried.

"It's just been a very emotional day for me. Come over when you can, okay?"

"I'll be right there. Love you."

"Love you too," she said and ended the call.

Mom went back to working her magic. She continued dabbing and painting, and as each moment passed, the ketubah grew closer and closer to looking perfect. Aunt Rachel and I stood behind Mom, giving her space to work but following along with our eyes.

Uncle David arrived about fifteen minutes later. He came racing up the stairs with my dad and my brothers behind him.

"Rach, what's going on?" he asked full of concern.

"Uncle David said that you called him crying," Joel said entering the room.

"David, come and look at this!" Aunt Rachel made room for him next to the easel.

"I thought we weren't going to see the ketubah until it's done. Is it finished? Did something happen?" he said from the other side of the room, trying to make sense of the urgent phone call.

Mom said, "It's not quite done yet, but we had a small incident along the way." I was surprised that

Mom was willing to share this. I guess she realized that since it was all good now it would be okay.

Uncle David cut her off. "What kind of incident?"

Mom cleared her throat in an effort, it seemed, to stall and come up with a good answer. At this point I saw no reason not to tell them. After all, the ketubah looked wonderful. All's well that ends well, right?

"Can I tell them now?" I asked Mom in a quiet voice in case she said "No." She gave a little shrug, which I took to mean that she was giving me permission. "I sort of knocked a whole cup of paint over and it splattered all over the ketubah," I revealed at last.

Uncle David's eyes grew wide and his face went pale. Aunt Rachel gasped and covered her mouth like she did when she first saw the ketubah. Mom looked straight ahead at the easel. I think Uncle David wanted to say something, but cleared his throat instead.

"Nice going, YaYa," Jeremy said sarcastically, patting me on the back.

"Don't worry!" Mom added quickly. "I just fixed it and Rachel came up to take a look. As soon as she saw it she wanted you to see it right away too."

Uncle David seemed like he didn't know what to make of this and was weighing whether it was good news or bad news. He stepped over a tarp, finally face to face with the ketubah. I followed his gaze as his eyes wandered slowly upward from the bottom, taking in each and every detail of the piece. The color that had drained out of his face moments ago started to come back with each inch he studied. By the time his eyes focused on the top part of the ketubah, his face took on a rosy glow. His eyes even got a little watery.

"It's not all cleaned up yet," I told him, "but the worst parts are gone. Look at LuLu on the bottom! Isn't she cute?" I pointed to show him where to look. "Until just a little while ago, that was the worst blotch on the whole thing. Now LuLu is part of your ketubah! It's perfect, isn't it?"

"No," he said simply, focusing on the LuLu spot.

Uh oh. My stomach clenched up for the hundredth time that day.

"No?" Mom, Aunt Rachel and I all said at once.

"No, it's not perfect," he said and we were left with an awkward silence in the room. I heard Mom swallow and I felt so bad for her.

Then Uncle David broke the silence. "It's not perfect. Which is why I love it. It's perfect because it isn't perfect," he said, staring at the artwork with a look of amazement, grabbing Aunt Rachel's hand.

The tension in the room broke.

"Huh? That doesn't make any sense!" Jeremy said.

"Yeah, what are you talking about, Uncle David?" Joel asked.

"The fact that it isn't perfect is exactly what makes it so perfect," he repeated. "You know how we break the glass at the end of the wedding?" he asked, looking at my brothers and me.

"Yeah?" we all said in unison.

"Do you know why?"

"Because it's a tradition," I answered.

"That's true, but it became a tradition for a reason. We do it to remember that even on the happiest day of our lives there's still sadness in the world. Originally it was a reminder of the destruction of the Temple in Jerusalem but now it also reminds us that the world isn't perfect; there's always something that's broken. It's our job to do *tikkun olam*, which means repairing the world. The imperfect ketubah, like a broken glass, will always remind us that even though our lives together are beautiful and wonderful, there's always more that needs to be done to make things even better—even things we can't see right away."

Aunt Rachel nodded in agreement.

"You know what, Deb?" Uncle David continued, turning to look at Mom, "don't fix it anymore. I think it's great the way it is."

"No, I should clean it up," Mom protested. "I can't let it go out the door like this."

Aunt Rachel chimed in. "How about if you continue covering up the really obvious splatters, but leave a few secret ones in for us?" She looked up at her tall soon-to-be-husband. "We'll know what the hidden message is even if other people won't see it. We already have so many secrets hidden inside this ketubah, why not add this too?"

I never saw this turn of events coming. They actually *want* the splatters?

"Yeah, leave a few in," Uncle David agreed. The two of them looked into each other's eyes. Honestly, it was a bit too sappy for me but I could see that they truly were in love. It was as if they were silently thinking, *Ani l'dodi v'dodi li*—I am my beloved's and my beloved is mine, just like it said on the ketubah.

At that moment it was hard to picture them not getting along, let alone arguing and fighting. All I could see was the two of them making mushy-gushy, lovey-dovey eyes at each other as Uncle David took a tissue from the nearby tissue box and dabbed under Aunt Rachel's puffy eyes to dry her tears. He kissed her softly on her forehead and pulled her in for a one-armed hug as she rested against his shoulder.

"Careful hugging in here," I cautioned. "That's how

this whole thing started."

They all looked at me expectantly, waiting for me to elaborate.

"Never mind," Mom said, waving my comment away and giving me a wink. "I'm okay with leaving in a few hidden spots if that's what you want. But since this is my gift to you and since my name is going on it, I want it to look as polished as possible. But I'll be sure to do as you request."

I couldn't believe that after the disastrous spill it turned out okay. Now the question was, would anything else go wrong or were we done with the jinxed wedding already? I looked down at my neon green cast full of marker signatures and smiled.

I was pretty sure we were done with all the mishaps and misfortunes.

I mean, what else could possibly go wrong?

16

Spit on It

A couple of days after the ketubah incident I went into the family room to chill out. I plopped down on the couch and pointed the remote at the TV. A commercial came on that showed a lady looking tired and frustrated as she chased after her toddler who was smearing his pudding-covered hands all over the white walls. The scene cut to a different woman sitting at a desk in an office tossing a pile of papers in the air, pulling on her hair and looking like she was going to lose it. Next was a man sitting in his car stuck in a traffic jam, honking the horn and spilling coffee on his suit and tie. Clearly they were all having the worst day ever.

"Do you need a break? A chance to get away? Come escape the stress of life and try your luck at Mount Pine Casino and Resort. Try your hand at our slot machines, play a round of poker, spin the roulette wheel. It's all right here at Mount Pine Casino and Resort. A short drive to a world away. Come stay and play with us. Luck is on your side!"

I considered this for a moment.

Luck, huh? Let's see...I broke my arm, my aunt and uncle are fighting, and then worst of all, I almost destroyed the ketubah. I'm beginning to feel like luck is NOT on my side. Maybe I'm like a bad luck charm. Is that a real thing?

I became extremely curious and decided to find

out.

Maybe if there's something I did to invite the bad luck in, there's also something I could do to make it go away.

I pointed the remote again to turn off the TV and went to the family computer. I jiggled the mouse to make the screen come back to life and typed the words "bad luck" in the search bar. So many results came in that I scrolled and scrolled and quickly became overwhelmed. I decided to try to narrow my search to make it relevant to me, so I typed in "Jewish bad luck." Plenty of suggestions with the word "superstition" popped up. I clicked on the first ten links, trying to learn whatever I could about a person being bad luck and bringing bad fortune to those around them.

By the time I was done clicking, reading and investigating I was convinced that somehow I had managed to draw the attention of the *ayin hara*, the "Evil Eye," and was now officially cursed with bad luck. I felt like I not only accidentally invited the evil eye into my life but it decided to buy a bus ticket, move in with me, make itself at home and bother everyone else in my world too.

Some of the articles I read said that it was nothing more than mere superstition while others said that it was absolutely real. Some said that people believed in the evil eye a long time ago but no one does anymore. Others said that it's not only very real today but there are ways to ward off the evil spirits and keep them away for good. It was hard to decide what to believe but the more I read, the more I was convinced that, even though I had no idea what I did exactly, I must have done something to anger the evil eye and I had to do something about it before I completely ruined the wedding—or anything else. I read on about some of the things I could do to solve the problem.

The first solution seemed pretty easy. The website said that the way to get rid of the evil eye once it's been provoked is to spit three times onto your fingers.

Well that's kind of weird, but what have I got to lose?

I tried to spit on my fingers but after the first spit I realized that I was making a mess and getting saliva everywhere. So I went to the bathroom, stood over the sink and did it again. I spat three times.

Am I allowed to rinse it off? Will that undo whatever the spitting's supposed to do?

I decided to rinse my fingers hoping that it was the act of spitting that would help regardless of what happened to the saliva after it was out of my mouth.

As I walked back to the office I wondered:

How often do I have to do this? Should I randomly walk around spitting on my fingers? Is there a special way to spit? Do I have to do it three times in a row really quickly?

So many questions!

I figured that the more I did it, the better, and that it wouldn't be very reasonable or practical to keep running to the bathroom every time I wanted to spit on my fingers. I had another idea. I grabbed a washcloth from the linen closet and I stuck it in my back pocket. As Joel mentioned when we were spying, it's always good to be prepared. Now I could wipe off the spit anywhere and anytime I wanted to.

According to the website, the spitting helped get rid of the evil spirits once they were already hanging around but there were also things I could do to keep them away in the first place. Based on what I read, I knew just what I had to do.

I ran up to Mom's studio, burst into the room and swung open the door to the closet that holds all of her crafting supplies.

Mom was at the easel still fixing the ketubah.

"Hey, honey. What's up? You startled me! Everything okay? Do you need something?" she asked from behind the easel.

"Nah, I'm good. I'm working on an art project." It was easier to leave it vague than to explain what I was doing. I just hoped I could get what I needed and get out of there before she started to ask too many questions. I wanted to get this taken care of as quickly as possible.

"I'm almost done here for the day," she said, "then I'm going to the store for a few things. Do you need anything?"

"No thanks," I said with my face in the closet, rummaging through the arts and crafts supplies.

After a few minutes Mom said, "Actually, I think I'm at a good stopping place right now. I'm going to take off. You'll be okay without me for a little while?" she asked.

"No problem," I answered, my voice muffled from inside the closet. "Joel and Jay are around. We'll be fine."

Mom cleaned off her paintbrush and slid out of the room with a quick, "Okay, see you soon."

"Bye," I called back without taking my head out of the closet.

I found a ball of red yarn and a pair of scissors. *Perfect!* I quickly snipped off a piece of the yarn and ran back downstairs, stopping only once at the top of the steps to spit three times onto my fingers. I chose to spit on the fingers that were not covered up by the cast. I figured the more spit-to-skin coverage the better.

I returned to the website to follow the instructions.

Place a red thread around your left wrist. This will ward off any evil spirits.

That's easy enough, I thought. *All I need to do is tie the string around my left wrist.*

I looked down, but as it turned out I couldn't see my left wrist. Why? BECAUSE THERE WAS A STUPID CAST COVERING IT, THAT'S WHY!

Of course, I chuckled ironically to myself. *Why would I have good luck trying to get rid of bad luck?*

I didn't know what to do. Should I put it on my right wrist or would that make things even worse? Would that possibly invite the ayin hara to find me even faster? Maybe I should I tie it around my left ankle? But what if I did that and then it got covered up by my socks or my pants? Would the red string still be able to keep the evil eye away if it was hidden from view?

I decided to tie it around my left wrist, but over the cast. I didn't know if that would work or not but I thought it was my best option. If that was the right place to put it in order to send the evil eye running, then that was where I was going to put it. Of course the piece of string that I had cut off was way too short to go all the way around the cast, so I ran back upstairs to the studio as quickly as I could—I didn't want to waste a single second.

Wouldn't you know it? I stubbed my toe on the top step. Of course I did! This was how my luck was going! It hurt so much but I tried my best not to scream and draw any attention to myself. If it weren't so painful and ridiculous I might have actually found it funny.

With tears in my eyes I held my breath and hobbled back to the studio. Thanks to my now-throbbing toe I was moving much slower than the last time I zipped into the room.

I picked up the yarn that I had left on the table and held the end of it in my left hand between my thumb and forefinger. I let the ball of yarn dangle and drop to the floor. Then, with my right hand, I snipped a nice long piece.

That should do it, I thought, feeling satisfied with myself.

I placed the scissors on the table and left the ball of yarn on the floor. (It didn't even occur to me to put it away.)

Then came the next challenge. How was I supposed to tie the string around my cast with only one hand?

I laid the string on the table, picked up one end with my good hand, then the other end, and managed to get the two ends up on top of the cast. Now what? There was no easy way for me to tie the two ends together. I needed some help.

I took the piece of string and went downstairs. I had my fist in the air about to knock on Joel's bedroom door when I stopped myself. I couldn't possibly explain this without him teasing me. I was sure of it. And of course Jeremy would only be worse. So instead, I picked up the phone in my parents' room and called my best friend Megan. She would never make fun of me. After a couple of rings she answered. I was glad that she picked up and not someone else in her family. I had no time to waste!

"Hello?"

"Hey, Megan. It's me, Ellie."

"Hey, what's up?"

"Are you busy right now? Any chance you could

come over and help me with something for just a few minutes?" I asked. I had decided to ask her to come to me instead of me going there because I was too afraid to venture out of the house. Who knows what could happen out there where there are cars, buses, and trucks. As it was, I already stubbed my toe in my own house!

"Let me check with my mom. Hold on a sec," she said. I love that she didn't even ask me what I needed. She was already getting permission from her mom, no questions asked. Now that's a great friend!

After a few seconds she came back to the phone. "Yeah, my mom said it was okay but she's busy right now so it's going to be a little while before she can bring me over. Can you wait a few minutes?"

"Yep, no problem," I said with great confidence. In reality I was nervous about having to wait any longer than necessary to ditch the bad luck. "Just come when you can, the sooner the better."

"Is everything okay?" she asked.

"Yeah, yeah," I answered. "Nothing for you to worry about. I'll explain when you get here." Of course once I said that I began to worry that maybe I had cast some bad luck on her over the phone. I didn't want her to get a flat tire or worse so I added, "Just be careful!"

"Be careful? You sound like my mom!" she laughed. "I'll be over as soon as she's ready to take me."

"Okay, great. See you soon. And thanks!" I said and hung up the phone.

I draped the red string over my cast and walked slowly and carefully toward my room. I kept it balanced there so that it was in the right place, even though it wasn't tied down. I figured I'd just sit on my bed and wait for her without moving a muscle to avoid any further mishaps. After sitting there for a few seconds I decided that maybe it would be a better idea to wait on the stairs by the front door. That way I wouldn't have to rush when the bell rang and possibly bang into something or stub another toe. And goodness knows there was plenty in my room for me to trip over.

I moved cautiously out of my bedroom and down the hallway. When I got to the staircase I held on to the banister and took one step at a time, putting both feet on each step as I went down, like a toddler learning how to walk. Then I sat and waited. And waited. And waited. I was beginning to worry that something bad had happened to Megan, when finally the doorbell rang.

I jumped up to answer the door but didn't see Lu-Lu's leash which had fallen off the hook. I slipped on it and fell right on my back.

"Are you kidding me?" I said out loud to no one in particular. "ARE YOU KIDDING ME?"

As I lay on the floor looking up at the light fixture hanging above me from the ceiling I couldn't help but imagine the whole thing breaking away and crashing on top of me. I quickly spat on my fingers. Because, you know, just in case....

17

String Theory

The good news is that the light fixture didn't fall on me. Maybe the spitting was working after all!

I got up off the floor and opened the door for Megan. The moment she stepped one foot into the foyer, without even saying hello, I blurted out, "Please tie this string around my cast. It's an emergency!" Then I spat three times into my other hand and wiped it off on the washcloth.

She stood there, staring at me with a look that I took to mean that she was simultaneously grossed out from my spitting, a little insulted by my lack of hospitality, and maybe even somewhat scared of me.

"Uh...hi...Ellie," she said haltingly. "I only have a little while. My mom is coming back for me in about twenty minutes. Ummm, what's going on?"

I realized I needed to use better manners. "Hi, Megan. Thanks for coming over. Come in," I said doing my best Mom imitation. And that was it for the niceties. I dove right into my request. "Can you please tie this red string onto my left arm? Directly over the cast. I'll explain after, I promise."

"Um...sure?" she said more as a question than a response. "Can I take off my coat first?"

"Nope, not yet."

She gave me another perplexed look but tied the string on me anyway and I immediately felt better, like a helium balloon lifted my problems right off my shoulders. I shut the door.

"Oh my goodness, thank you so much!" I hugged her. Unfortunately, I accidentally also clunked her in the head with my hard cast.

"Ow!" she exclaimed rubbing her head. "What the heck?"

"Ack! I'm so sorry!" I cried out, rubbing her head on the bad spot right along with her. "You see, this is why I needed the red string. Maybe it takes a little while to kick in."

"Ellie...," Megan began speaking very slowly while slipping out of her jacket. "You know that you're my best friend...." I nodded and held my good arm out for her to pass me her jacket. She continued, "And you know that I'm here for you no matter what...."

I nodded again while throwing her jacket on the floor by the coat closet.

"And even though sometimes you have some crazy ideas, I'm always on your side."

Still nodding.

"So, let's recap today's events so far," she said. "You called me to come over because you needed help as soon as possible. I had my mom rush me over because I didn't know if you were in trouble or anything. You greeted me with a request to tie a string around your cast and then you clunked me in the head. I have no idea what is going on here! Want to fill me in, please?"

"Okay, so first of all, clunking you in the head was not part of the plan at all. That was an accident. So sorry about that," I started. "As for the rest, come with me into the office. I want to explain this to you with pictures and illustrations."

"All right," Megan said a bit hesitantly as she followed me into the office. We stood in front of the computer. Once again I jiggled the mouse to bring the screen back to life. Waiting for us there was a picture of a wrist with a red string tied around it.

"See, right there, that's what we're doing!" I exclaimed as if everything was now going to be all cleared up for her.

"Huh? What are we doing?" she asked with a scrunched-up nose, looking even more confused now than she did before.

"There! The red string!" I said, pointing at the picture in front of us and holding up my cast, "You tied a red string on my left wrist, just like it says. Thank you so much!"

She waited patiently. After a moment or two I realized that this had not clarified the situation one bit. I continued, "I needed to ward off the evil eye, and you helped me do that by tying the string over my cast, which I couldn't do on my own, so thank you! You are my hero!" This all spilled out of me so quickly that I had to stop for a second to take a breath.

She looked at me blankly, without uttering a single word. She was still lost.

"Okay, from the beginning, here we go...." I took a deep breath and began spewing information.

"The evil eye has apparently found me and has been bringing me bad luck, so I had to tie a red string around my left wrist to keep it away, but I couldn't do it myself, so I needed someone to tie the string around my wrist for me, but I couldn't get the string around my wrist because the cast was in the way because I had broken my arm...because of the evil eye...and I needed two hands to do it. I didn't want to bother my mom with the string because she was busy fixing up the ketubah for my aunt and uncle who are getting married but are fighting all the time...because of the evil eye. She was fixing the ketubah because I ruined it...because of the evil eye...so I tried to tie the string on by myself, but I couldn't do it and I wasn't about to ask my brothers to help. So I called you and I slipped on LuLu's leash ...because of the evil eye...and now you're here and the string is on me and I'm already feeling better."

I looked at her to be sure she understood. She just blinked at me.

"Plus I stubbed my toe."

After a long, long silent pause Megan put her hands on her hips and said, "WHAT?"

"Because of the evil eye," I finished.

"What?" she repeated, sounding not only confused but exasperated with me. "What?" She said one last time. She seemed to be at a loss for other words.

"Do you want me to repeat all that?" I asked.

"No!" she said, "Just explain it to me. In English. At half the speed."

And so I did. I explained every last detail of every single unfortunate event that had happened to me in the past several days. I told her that I didn't know how or why the evil eye had found me, but that I was trying everything I could to get rid of it and keep it away.

"You actually believe in that? It seems like a silly superstition to me," she said.

"I don't know what to believe anymore. All I know is that all this bad stuff is happening to me and to the people around me and I'm willing to try anything to make things better."

"Okay, so what else does it say we should do?"

This is why Megan is my best friend. She so gets

me!

"I was in the middle of looking into it when I found the red string idea, so I stopped reading. Here, let's take a look together."

We studied the computer screen side by side, scrolling around at all the different pictures of red strings tied on people's wrists, on baby carriages, and cribs. There were even pictures of famous celebrities wearing red string bracelets.

"What's with that weird hand thing?" Megan asked, pointing at a hand with a blue eyeball smack in the middle of it.

I read the description underneath the picture: "*The* hamsa *is a five-fingered hand-shaped amulet—*"

"Hold on," Megan interrupted me, "What's an amulet?"

"I don't know. Let's look it up," I replied. I opened a new tab, went to a dictionary website and typed the word *amulet* in the search box. I read the definition out loud. "It says that it's a small object worn to ward off evil, harm, or illness, or to bring good fortune."

"Oh," Megan said, "Like a good luck charm, or at least a keeping-bad-stuff-away charm."

"That makes sense," I said with a nod and started reading the description under the picture of the hand again. "*The* hamsa *is a five-fingered hand-shaped amulet that is supposed to keep away the ayin hara or evil eye. The name comes from the Hebrew word hamesh and the Arabic word hamsa, both meaning five, referring to the symmetrical digits on the hand. A symbol of an eye can often be found in the center of the hand.*"

"I guess I also need a hamsa!" I exclaimed. "I thought I was all set with the red string, but maybe not."

"Where are you going to get one of those?" Megan asked.

"I guess I'll have to make one somehow." I looked around the office to see if there was anything lying around for me to use. I found a black permanent marker which I handed to Megan.

I opened up my right hand and said to her, "please draw a big eyeball on my palm." It's not an official hamsa, but it's definitely a hand! It will do for now until I figure out how to make one that I can wear or carry around."

"Are you sure you want to use permanent marker?" she asked. "It may not come off!"

"That's okay," I answered, "I don't want it to come off."

And so my best friend drew a big, fat eyeball right in the middle of my palm. I blew on it to dry it off, and honestly, I did feel more powerful and strong. With a red string on my left arm and an eyeball in my right hand, nothing bad could possibly happen to me or anyone around me from that moment on. I kind of felt like I should have been wearing a cape and going by the name Super YaYa.

"And...what's with the washcloth?" Megan asked pointing at my back pocket. "Is that another good luck charm?"

"Nah, that's there just because I need to spit three times on my fingers, so I'm carrying the washcloth around to wipe it off."

"Aha! That's what you did when I walked in. But really? Why? It's so gross!" Megan said.

"Yeah, it's gross, but that's what I read."

Megan rolled the chair over and sat down in front of the computer. "I want to read this for myself. That seems like an outrageous thing to have to do all the time!"

She scrolled around, reading this and that, and finally pointed to an article that said: *While some people spit three times to ward off the evil eye, others tend to make the sound of spitting, saying 'ptu, ptu, ptu' three times quickly."*

"Why don't you try doing that?" Megan suggested. "I think that might be a better way to go."

"I like that. What else does it say?"

"It says that some people say the word *kenahora* which comes from three Yiddish words, *kein* which means 'no,' *ayin* which means 'eye,' and *hora* which means 'bad.' Saying it means there should be no evil eye."

"Oh!" I exclaimed, "My grandma uses that word all the time. I had no idea what it meant! And she seems to be doing pretty well. Maybe I'll give that a shot too."

"Okay, then," Megan said, "I think my mom's going to be back to get me soon. Do you need me to do anything else to keep away the evil spirits, like shave part of your head or stick some string cheese up your nose?"

"Yuck!" I exclaimed. "Now you're just being ridiculous!"

"Nah, just joking around," Megan replied. "I don't always get you, Ellie Silver, but you know I've always got your back. Or your palm," she said looking at my hand.

We heard a car horn outside.

"Okay, time to go, she's here," Megan said.

I waved my hand at her and said, "Here's looking at you, kid!"

"You're such a weirdo! But a lovable weirdo. Bye bye, BFF!" she said, making her way to the entryway.

I walked her to the door, opened it, and waved my eyeballed-palm at her.

"*See* ya!" Joel would have been so proud of me for that pun.

And then, the moment that I closed the door, the light fixture fell down from the ceiling and landed right on top of me.

Just kidding...ptu, ptu, ptu. Kenahora.

18

I've Got to Hand It to You

My finger was sore from all the scrolling I did while searching for information about hamsas. Normally, our parents limit our screen time, and we're not supposed to be on the computer or watching TV for too long, but I didn't think they'd mind because this was educational and I was learning something new and worthwhile. Plus, it was just shy of being an emergency. I mean, if I didn't stop the ayin hara, who knows what might happen to us?

I saw images of all sorts of hamsas online. Some came in the form of jewelry that you could wear on a necklace or a bracelet, even earrings. Some were pretty wall hangings. There didn't seem to be too many rules about how to make one, so I sat in my room and looked around at all the stuff on the floor, on the shelves, hanging out of drawers, and under my bed and tried to figure out what I could use to make my own. Maybe I'd even make two: one to hang in my room and one to wear. The more ways to chase away the bad luck, the better.

After thinking about it for a long time, I finally came up with a solution. I walked carefully down the hallway to the stairs, reciting "Ptu, ptu, ptu, kenahora" along the way. I passed Joel who was half-lying down, half-sitting up on his neatly made bed in his room, reading a book.

"Hey, YaYa, whatcha doing? And who are you talking to?"

"Just working on a little project," I answered. Then in almost a whisper, more to myself than to him I added into my fingers, "Ptu, ptu, ptu."

"What the heck?" he said, and sat all the way up, looking at me like I was walking by with a giraffe on my head. "What are you doing with your fingers?"

"Nothing, nothing. I've got to go," I answered, and quickened my pace away from his room and down the hall to the staircase.

"You're getting mighty strange in your old age," he called to me from his bed. I didn't respond. I just kept on going until I arrived at the front hall closet in the entryway.

I shifted several jackets across the closet bar until I found my winter coat. I reached into the pockets and pulled out my gray wool gloves.

Already in the shape of a hand! I thought triumphantly.

I took the gloves upstairs to Mom's studio so I could work on them up there. I used her scissors to snip a hole through the front and back of the cuffs on each one. Then I picked up the red yarn that I had left lying there on the floor earlier and cut off a piece, which I slipped through the two holes that I had just made in the first glove. I figured that if I was supposed to use red string on my wrist, I should probably use it around my neck as well. Next, I tied the two ends of the string together and, voila! I had a hand on a string that I could wear around my neck. I did the same thing to the second glove.

I looked at the gloves and at once felt a sense of great accomplishment. But after a few moments I realized that they really just looked like gloves on a string. They didn't look anything like the hamsas that I had seen online.

What can I do to turn these from plain old ordinary gloves into real hamsas? I wondered.

Then I remembered the eyes. I looked down at my palm and saw a big eye staring back up at me. Kind of creepy!

I looked around the room, trying to come up with a creative solution to the eye problem. I searched in every bin, bucket, and drawer, trying to see if Mom had something that would work. I found markers of every color, buttons, ribbons, and beads. I found different types of paper, colored pencils, and glue sticks.

And then I hit the jackpot! It was like I was at my own Mount Pine Casino and Resort!

I found a whole entire box of wiggly, jiggly, googly eyes!

"Yes!" I shouted out loud. "Kenahora!" I took out two googly eyes and some fabric glue and attached one eye onto each glove.

I slipped my head through one of the red string necklaces and looked down to see my excellent hamsa-glove hanging there, keeping me safe. The googly eye moved around like my own personal bodyguard, making me feel like it was watching out for any bad stuff that might come along. With the eyeball in my palm, the red string on my left arm, and the hamsa-glove hanging from my neck, I felt like I was wearing a life-vest, a seat-belt, and a harness all at once. Nothing was going to get through this top-notch security system!

With no worries to weigh me down, I floated back to my room. I even said a few less kenahoras and ptu, ptu, ptus. I hung the second glove on the outside doorknob, went in, and closed the door.

I had to hand it to myself, I really saved the day!

19

The Case of the Missing Bride

I looked at the cross-off marks on my calendar. "Only eight days left until the wedding!" I sang out in my bedroom the following Shabbat morning.

As I was getting ready for synagogue, I thought back to the conversation we had a few weeks earlier at dinner when I was already out-of-my-mind excited about the big day.

"I can't believe the wedding is only four weeks away!" I had said.

Dad corrected me. "I have good news for you, honey. You really only need to wait three weeks because the wedding festivities actually begin one week earlier with the *aufruf*. When he said that word, it sounded like he was saying "oof roof."

I looked at him and then at LuLu. "Are you speaking in LuLu language?"

"What are you talking about, YaYa?" Dad asked, amused.

"You sound like you're barking. Ruf ruf!" I answered.

Dad chuckled. "Sometimes I wish I could speak in Dog! It would make understanding LuLu a lot easier!"

"Sometimes I wish I could speak in Fifth-Grade-Girl," Jeremy snarked. "That would make understanding my sister a lot easier."

"Ha ha," I said to Jeremy and wrinkled my nose at

him.

Dad explained, "What I said was that we're going to the aufruf. That's when the couple getting married goes up on the bimah in the synagogue during the Torah service before their wedding. They recite the blessing over the Torah and then get a blessing from the rabbi, wishing them a good life together."

"Oh, I know what you're talking about! I just never knew what it was called! That's the thing when everyone in the synagogue gets to throw candy at them!" I exclaimed.

"Or the bar mitzvah kid," Jeremy said.

"Or the bat mitzvah kid," Joel added.

"Right," Mom joined in. "But it's only called an aufruf for a wedding couple. It's like they're getting rained down upon with sweetness and blessings."

That's the really fun part! It's not very often that we're encouraged to throw things at people, let alone in the synagogue. It's seriously the best ritual ever invented! After all the candy has landed (and sometimes even while it's still flying in the air!), all the kids under the age of thirteen get to run up to the bimah and collect it. After we collect the candy we're even allowed to eat it right in shul!

For some reason, according to Jewish tradition, thirteen is the age when a kid becomes an adult, and that's why they have a bar or bat mitzvah ceremony then. I looked across the table at my older brother and found him trying to get his spoon to balance on his nose. I don't know why they chose thirteen as the magic number. Jeremy's only a couple of months away from being thirteen, and let me tell you, he is miles away from being anything like an adult.

Whenever I go to Shabbat services, I hope that

there'll be a bar or bat mitzvah or an aufruf that week. Lucky for us, not only was there going to be an aufruf, this time it was our family's aufruf!

So there I was in my room, getting ready for the aufruf and the start of the wedding week. As I was about to get dressed, I looked down at my hamsa, which I had worn over my pajamas. I slept with it on all night and I didn't have any bad dreams. Coincidence? Maybe, maybe not!

I knew for sure that I wanted to wear my hamsa to services because I didn't want anything bad to happen at the aufruf. I could just imagine Uncle David getting pelted in the face and ending up with a black eye, or Aunt Rachel slipping on a piece of candy and breaking her arm. It was bad enough that one of us already had her arm in a cast!

I decided to wear my dark gray dress because it had short sleeves and was easy to slip on over the cast. I debated whether to wear the hamsa hidden underneath the dress or to wear it out. I decided to let it hang on the outside to be sure that it would work at full effect. Also, it would have been really lumpy and bumpy if I kept it tucked inside.

The gray glove did kind of blend in with the gray dress, but the red string and the googly eye made it stand out. People would definitely see it and I was sure that I would be fielding questions all morning. Oh well. Up until now, if anyone asked me why I was wearing a glove around my neck, all I had to do was tell them that it was my new style. No one questioned me further. I guess being a bit quirky has its perks!

I giggled as I bounced down the stairs because I could feel the googly eyeball bouncing right along with me. *Thanks for the protection!* I thought and patted the eye gently. Once I got down to the foyer, I slipped my jacket on and zipped it up quickly so Mom wouldn't tell me that I shouldn't wear it over my nice dress.

The five of us all walked to shul together. We live pretty close to our synagogue, which is nice, especially when the weather gets cold because our family doesn't drive on Shabbat, which is the Jewish Sabbath. I like that because it really makes the day feel different and important. We got there early since it was a special day for our family, also so we wouldn't possibly miss the aufruf. Even I, the notoriously latest, slowest-to-get-out-the-door person in the world, was the first one ready. I couldn't wait to see Aunt Rachel and Uncle David smiling together up on the bimah. And, of course, I couldn't wait to bombard them with candy, either.

We usually get to services around the time of the Torah service and that's almost an hour after shul starts. But we're never the last people to arrive. Some people come so late that they get there just in time for *musaf*, the very last part of the service. Well, I guess arriving late is better than not getting there at all, right?

We were so early that most of the seats in the sanctuary were empty. It felt kind of weird. We often sit somewhere in the middle, but we sat right up front so that we'd have a perfect view of the happy couple. (Also to be sure we'd hit our targets when we flung the candy at them!) Grandma Ruth and Grandpa Jack were already seated so we slid into the row with them. I looked around. Aunt Rachel and Uncle David weren't there yet. I couldn't believe we got there before they did.

Grandma and Grandpa stood up and kissed each of

us as we joined them.

"Where's Rachel?" Dad whispered to Grandma.

Grandma looked at her watch and shrugged. "I always used to joke that she'd be late to her own wedding," she whispered back with a quiet chuckle and clucking her tongue. "I didn't count on her being late to the aufruf too!"

"That sister of mine," Dad said shaking his head with a little smile on his face, "she's nothing but trouble!"

"She'll get here. Relax," Grandpa, the eternal optimist, said.

I noticed Grandma eyeing my hanging glove, but she didn't say anything. She kind of made a confused face but went back to worrying about Aunt Rachel not being there.

I looked up at the bimah and saw Rabbi Green sitting in his big chair looking down into his *siddur*, the prayer book. When he looked up, I waved to him and he gave me a huge smile, a wink, and he waved back. I realized I was waving with my hand that still had the eye on it, even if it was pretty faded since it was a few days old and had been washed many times. So I closed and opened my fingers to make it look like the eye was winking back at him. It made me giggle. Joel also waved to him. Rabbi Green is the coolest rabbi ever. He's our teacher for Shul School and I think he's just the greatest. He's funny and silly but he also teaches us a lot. I feel really lucky that we get to have such an awesome teacher.

I opened my siddur and followed along with the prayers. The service went on for a while and then it was almost time for the Torah service. I looked behind me and all around the sanctuary and noticed that it had started filling up with people, none of whom were Aunt Rachel or Uncle David. They still had not arrived, and Grandma was starting to search worriedly around the room from her seat. Even Grandpa, who had been so calm and sure earlier, kept going back and forth between looking at his watch and at the door in the back of the sanctuary. Rabbi Green had a concerned look on his face too. He stepped down from the bimah, came over to our row, and bent over slightly to talk to Grandma.

"Where are Rachel and David?" he asked quietly.

"I don't know," she responded. I could tell by the strange sound of her voice that she was upset. I patted my hamsa, hoping it would come to the rescue.

Aunt Rachel is notorious for her practical jokes, just like Joel, and she is always late for everything, just like me. So it wasn't unusual for her to be running late, but you'd think she'd be on time for one of the most important days of her life.

"I hope they're okay," Grandma said anxiously.

"Oh, you know Rachel," Grandpa reassured her, patting her arm. "She runs on her own clock."

"Well, thanks to her own clock, she's going to miss her own aufruf!" Grandma said out loud, not even trying to whisper anymore. "You see all these gray hairs?" She pointed at her head. "I should name each one of them Rachel!"

Grandpa chuckled and gave Grandma a squeeze.

"Maybe they're just hanging out in the lobby," I suggested. "I'll run out and check. Maybe they don't realize that it's almost time for the aufruf to get started."

"Thank you, sweetheart," Grandma said and she kissed me on the cheek. Once I got far enough down the aisle and out of her line of vision, I wiped the side of my face, knowing full well that Grandma left me one of her red lipstick souvenirs. One of the old men sitting in an aisle seat winked at me when he saw me do that. I smiled politely at him, slightly embarrassed that he caught me in the act.

When I got to the back of the sanctuary, I pushed open one of the large doors and bolted to the lobby. I saw lots of familiar faces and some friendly congregants wishing me a "mazel tov," but no Aunt Rachel and no Uncle David. I ran to the hallway with the bathrooms and went into the ladies' room. I looked under each stall. Nope, not in there. I even called for Uncle David through the closed door of the men's room.

"No, dear. It's me, Morris Selnick," came a deep voice from the bathroom.

"Oh, hi, Mr. Selnick," I replied awkwardly to the men's room door. "Sorry to bother you." I felt my face get hot and assumed that my ears were turning red as they do.

"No trouble at all, dear," he answered.

I hustled back to the sanctuary and speed-walked down the aisle to where my family was sitting. Grandma looked up at me expectantly and I shook my head to let her know they were nowhere in sight. She clucked her tongue again, this time with more intensity and frustration. She seemed simultaneously worried and annoyed, bordering on angry. She tapped her long, red-polished fingernails nervously on the page of her open prayer book.

Rabbi Green was back up on the bimah and had started giving his *d'var Torah*. That's the part when he talks about the Torah portion we're reading that week and what we can learn from it. When there's a bar or bat mitzvah, the kid usually shares his or her d'var Torah, but this time it was just Rabbi Green. I'm pretty sure he usually does that once the Torah service has already begun, after the Torah is paraded around, but I guess he was trying to buy a little more time.

I was getting nervous, just like Grandma. I was so busy scanning the room the whole time Rabbi Green was speaking that his entire talk was a blur. When he finished, it was time for the Torah service to actually begin. Everyone in the room stood up as Mrs. Idelson, a lady I see at synagogue all the time, opened the curtain to the ark where the Torah scrolls are kept. She wore a fancy, shimmery gold-colored suit, a big hat, and lots of jewelry. When I was much younger I used to think that she was a queen. She always dresses like she's going to an important meeting or to a fancy party so I always assumed that she was famous and hobnobbed with celebrities.

Mrs. Idelson's chunky gold bracelet with a bazillion charms rattled around and made noise as she pulled the string to open the curtain in front of the ark. Mr. Pinsky, a man who always helps out on the bimah and with services in general, took the Torah out of the ark and handed it to Mrs. Idelson. Grandma mumbled something under her breath while Dad was still smirking and shaking his head. The Torah procession or "Torah parade" as I used to call it when I was little, was beginning...and still no sign of Aunt Rachel or Uncle David.

As Cantor Grossman sang the prayers and Mrs. Idelson carried the Torah around the sanctuary, everyone turned to watch the Torah travel around the room. As the Torah passed by each person, most touched it with their prayer book or a corner of their tallit and then kissed it. It's the way we show respect to the Torah and kiss it without actually putting our mouths on it. Rabbi Green once told us that it's almost like a reverse kiss, like we're taking in what the Torah has to offer and bringing it to our lips.

Rabbi Green walked behind Mrs. Idelson, who followed Cantor Grossman down the aisle. Rabbi Green shook hands and greeted all the congregants while making his way around the room. They went down the aisle on the right-hand side of the synagogue, then walked across the back of the room by the big entrance doors.

Just as they turned the corner to come up the center aisle and head back toward the bimah, the giant wooden doors in the back of the room were flung open wildly, and there, panting, red-faced, and out of breath were Aunt Rachel and Uncle David.

20

Candy Showers

T hey made it!" I exclaimed. I lifted the glove that hung around my neck and gave my hamsa a little secret thank-you kiss without anyone noticing and whispered a quiet little "kenahora."

"She's going to put me in an early grave, I tell you," Grandma muttered, sighing, laughing, and crying all at the same time.

Dad quietly chuckled to himself. Aunt Rachel's antics always seem to amuse him.

"See, dear, I told you that you didn't need to worry," Grandpa said, once again patting Grandma affectionately on the arm.

As if they were part of the procession, Aunt Rachel and Uncle David walked down the center aisle, right behind Rabbi Green. People extended their hands to shake and wish them a mazel tov and the two of them greeted everyone just like Rabbi Green did. In fact, even after Mrs. Idelson, the rabbi, and the cantor made it back up to the bimah, the two of them were still going strong, schmoozing, smiling, kissing, and greeting the congregants. As they came down the aisle I imagined them as if they were movie stars walking down the red carpet at a big, glitzy premiere with all the reporters taking pictures of them, calling out their names, and yelling questions at them:

"Rachel, who are you wearing?"

*"David, do you think this performance will earn you
an Oscar?"*

I laughed to myself as I imagined the scene.

Aunt Rachel's face was pink and practically glowing, probably because she had just run into shul, but
also, I assumed, due to all the attention and hubbub.
She and Uncle David finally made it up to the front
row, both of them smiling and beaming, looking happier than I'd ever seen them. It felt like all the troubles
leading up to their wedding were washed away and
gone forever.

Grandma scowled and shook her head at Aunt Rachel and said sarcastically, "Glad you could make it."
But then to show that she wasn't too mad, she reached
over and kissed Aunt Rachel on her cheek. Then she
did the same to Uncle David.

"We're here in plenty of time!" Aunt Rachel said,
defending herself, still smiling and glowing. "Look,
they haven't even started reading Torah yet!"

Grandma clucked and shook her head yet again as
Aunt Rachel climbed over her and sat down next to
me. I very discreetly wiped Grandma's lipstick off Aunt
Rachel's cheek with my thumb.

"Thanks," she whispered and winked at me. I
smiled back and snuggled in next to her.

"What's with the glove?" she whispered.

"Tell you later," I answered. That seemed to be
good enough, as she nodded and dropped the topic.

Uncle David quietly said a blessing as he draped his
tallit over his shoulders and sat down on Aunt Rachel's
other side. At our synagogue all the men and lots of
the women wear a tallit and a kippah. My mom and
grandma don't, but Aunt Rachel does. Mom likes to
wear hats to cover her head and Grandma wears a

white lace doily thing that she folds in half and clips to the back of her hair. Aunt Rachel was wearing a blue and white tallit, the kind that the shul has available in the lobby. She probably forgot hers when she ran out of the house. She's often as forgetful and scattered as I am.

Aunt Rachel reached over and wiped the lipstick off of Uncle David's cheek the same way that I did to hers, then winked at me again. I tried to wink back, but I'm not very good at it, so I did more of a blink with both eyes. Then I winked at her with the eyeball in my hand. She chuckled with a puzzled yet amused look on her face.

The service continued as different people went up to read from the Torah and recite the blessings. Finally it was time for Aunt Rachel and Uncle David to go up for their *aliyah*, the part when they say the blessing over the Torah. The *gabbai* (kind of rhymes with "bah-bye"), the person who stands up next to the Torah during the service and calls people up, chanted their names in Hebrew and they went up together.

Aunt Rachel and Uncle David stood next to each other to the right of the Torah reader. Uncle David reached over and touched the open Torah scroll with a corner of his tallit and kissed it. Aunt Rachel did the same thing. Together they chanted the blessing that's read before each section and then the reader bent over the podium and started chanting from the big Torah scroll on the table.

Uncle David wrapped his arm around Aunt Rachel's back and the two of them followed along in the scroll while the Torah reader read aloud. I was probably supposed to be following along in the book I had on my lap, but I was too busy watching them up on the bimah. I looked over at Grandma. She was dabbing tears from her eyes.

Meanwhile, Mr. Pinsky came over to our row and quietly asked me and my brothers if we would be willing to pass the candy around so that people could throw it when it was time. We happily agreed. He handed each of us a small white basket filled with the soft jelly candies that were each wrapped in plastic.

"Let's pull some out first so we don't miss out on throwing them," Joel suggested.

We each took a handful of candies and left them in a pile on the floor by our seats. Then we split up and each walked through a different section of the sanctuary, passing the basket around, and letting people take candy. It didn't take too long before our baskets were empty, so we returned to our seats to listen to the Torah reading.

When the Torah reader was done, Aunt Rachel once again reached over with her tallit and touched the scroll and just like before, she kissed the tallit; then Uncle David did the same. They recited the blessing that follows the Torah reading, after which everyone in the congregation said "Amen."

Rabbi Green said something quietly so that only they could hear it and the three of them laughed. I wish I knew what he said to them! He then stepped back and read a blessing in Hebrew for the couple. I recognized some of the words such as *HaHatan*, which means "the groom," and *HaKallah*, which means "the bride." Yup, that was them!

"May you be blessed with a life full of joy and happiness, warmth, and love, and maybe even, God willing, a new generation with whom you can share your love and to whom you can pass on your family's traditions and values."

Grandma and Grandpa both shouted out together "Amen!" and the whole congregation laughed.

Rabbi Green laughed too and said, "And now, may we *all* say 'Amen'."

The congregation said one big "Amen" altogether. Then Rabbi Green placed a cover over the Torah and Cantor Grossman started clapping and singing, "*Siman tov u'mazel tov*," a happy, celebration song which sort of means 'congratulations'. Everyone joined in and then, finally it was the moment I had been waiting for!

Candy started flying through the air, all heading straight for Aunt Rachel and Uncle David. Uncle David held his tallit up over both of their heads to protect them from the candy missiles. I threw my first one and hit Aunt Rachel on the shoulder. When Uncle David popped his head out from under the tallit to see if it was all clear, Jeremy stood up and clocked him right in the forehead. Uncle David laughed and wagged his finger at Jeremy. Then he bent down, picked up the very same piece of candy, chucked it right back at Jeremy from the bimah, and hit him on the nose! Jeremy laughed and pelted him again. The two of them went back and forth lobbing the candy at one another while the tossing and singing continued. Sometimes Uncle David behaves like he's one of us kids. That's one of the many things we love about him!

Out of nowhere little kids appeared as if they had popped out of the walls, scrambled up the steps of the bimah and began collecting all the candy. Kids were putting them in their pants pockets, and those who had pockets in their shirts filled those up too. Some of the little girls made makeshift sacks with their skirts to hold as much as they could scoop up. I was so busy throwing candy that I almost missed out on picking it up! By the time I got to the bimah, there wasn't much left. Those kids were fast! I found three pieces of candy that I was able to fit in my one good hand. It was really hard to pick them up and hold them with only one hand. *Ugh! Why did I have to break my arm right before the wedding?* It was so unfair!

Unlike me, Joel arrived at the bimah right away and looked ridiculous with candy stuffed in every single one of his pockets. I wouldn't be surprised if he shoved some into his socks, too. Jeremy didn't join in. Technically he could have since he was still under the age of bar mitzvah, but he was way too cool to do little kid stuff like that. But I had no doubt that he'd ask me for a piece of candy when I got back to my seat. He wasn't too cool for that!

The singing finally came to an end and things started to calm down in the sanctuary. I was about to walk down the steps with my tiny haul when I noticed a little boy who must have been about three years old crying on the bimah. He stood there with his bottom lip stuck out and quivering, and big, fat tears rolling down his cute little face.

I went over to him and got down on my knees so I could look him in the eye. "What's wrong?" I asked him. "Do you need help finding your mommy or your daddy?"

"I...I...I...," he tried to speak through his sobs, "didn't...get...any...candy," he managed to say.

Oh, man! I had so been looking forward to eating my candy in shul. But I couldn't stand to see this little guy crying. I opened my hand to offer him a piece of candy. I really thought he'd just take one, but before I knew it, he had scooped all three pieces into his two little pudgy hands. I guess he thought I was offering him all three. He looked at me with gratitude and awe like I was the Tooth Fairy. His tears turned so abruptly to joyful giggles it was as if they were controlled by an on-and-off switch.

"Momma! Momma! I got candy!" He cried out so loudly that the whole congregation probably heard him. He ran down the steps, victorious, his tiny fists clutching the candy. He ran into the arms of his mother, who was squatting down low, waiting for him in the center aisle.

I felt so good about making the little boy happy that I didn't even care that he didn't say thank you. I didn't care that I was left without a single piece of candy. I didn't care that I was the last one standing right smack in the middle of the bimah.

Well, actually, that's not true. When I noticed that everyone was back in their seats I got super embarrassed. Aunt Rachel and Uncle David had moved over to the other side of the podium and Cantor Grossman and Rabbi Green were back at their seats on the bimah as well. I felt my face, and especially my ears, do their red hot deal, so I quickly got up off my knees and stepped down from the bimah, not looking up at anyone on my way.

"Thank you so much," the little boy's mother said quietly to me as I was about to enter my family's row. I smiled at her and at the kid gobbling up his first piece of candy, feeling the red of embarrassment slowly flow out of my face.

"No problem," I said.

I climbed back over all of my relatives to my spot and sat down empty handed, but only a little bit disappointed. I could still hear the little boy letting out squeals of delight from the back of the room and his mother shushing him.

"That was very sweet of you," Mom whispered to me and pecked the top of my head with a little kiss.

"Nice work, kiddo," said Dad as he offered me a fist bump.

Joel reached over and dropped a handful of candies in my lap. He didn't say anything. He just gave me a warm smile.

"Thanks," I mouthed to him with a grateful smile in return.

Jeremy reached over across Joel with his hand open to me, palm facing up. I was pleasantly surprised by his gesture. I gently tapped his hand to slap him five with my eye-balled palm.

He held his hand open. "Can I have a piece of candy, YaYa?" and then he stretched his arm across Joel and helped himself to three from my lap.

Yep. That seemed about right.

I unwrapped one candy and popped it into my mouth. Then I took the rest of them and dropped them into the empty glove hanging around my neck. It was a perfect candy holder. See? The good luck had started already.

21

Cookies and Kugel
and Wine, Oh My!

After the service, everyone shuffled out of the sanctuary and gathered in the social hall for the kiddush lunch. There's food after practically all Jewish events. No matter how happy or sad the occasion, there are always, at the very least, cookies and some sort of cake. Bagels too.

On a round table in the center of the room was a big lump with a cloth covering it. I knew it was a big, braided loaf of challah bread. Next to the big challah was a basket full of bite-sized, already-cut-up pieces of challah. On that same table were tiny plastic cups, each filled with either purple grape juice or white wine. Beyond the challah station stood a long table loaded with platters of food for lunch. And way in the back corner was the dessert table, complete with all the cookies and cakes I've come to expect at these events.

Rabbi Green stood up on a chair in front of the table with the wine and bread. Standing up on a chair or even a desk has become one of Rabbi Green's signature moves during Shul School when he wants to make a big announcement or to start off class with some sort of surprise. He's really tall, so when he stands up on a chair you can't help but see him. He shushed everyone to get the room to quiet down. I figured he was going to lead us all in the blessing over the wine and the grape juice. Before he said the blessings, though, Rabbi Green announced, "I'd like to do a l'chayim in honor of the *hatan* and *kallah*, Rachel Silver and David Resnick! Rachel and David, where are you two?"

"Here we are!" they called back. Holding hands, they squirmed their way together through the crowd to the middle of the room, like fish swimming upriver. As they squeezed their way toward Rabbi Green, the little cups of wine and juice were passed in the opposite direction to all the people clustered around the table.

Everyone was gathered in concentric circles around Rabbi Green, Aunt Rachel and Uncle David. I was in the inner ring right behind Aunt Rachel. I giggled to myself because it reminded me of when we were little and we used to play The Farmer in the Dell in preschool and all the kids would be in a circle around the farmer, his wife, the cat, the rat and so on. I wondered which one of them would be the cheese standing alone.

Rabbi Green stepped down from his chair and faced the couple. He held up his cup of wine and broadcasted in his big, bellowing voice, "We wish you a lifetime of health, happiness, and much mazel!"

"And babies!" Grandma yelled out from somewhere in the huddle. "Don't forget my future grandbabies!"

Everyone laughed. *Oh, Grandma!* Aunt Rachel looked down at her feet, shaking her head. I wasn't sure if she was embarrassed or thought it was funny. Either way, she was a good sport about it. Grandma is always razzing her about giving her grandchildren, so why should this day be any different?

"And babies?" Rabbi Green asked with a shrug looking at Aunt Rachel with an almost apologetic look.

Aunt Rachel gave him a matching shrug followed by a big smile and a thumbs up, so he echoed Grandma's words louder the second time, "AND BABIES!" Uncle David rolled his eyes and the two of them laughed. "To Rachel and David! L'chayim! To life!" Then everyone else held up their cups and yelled "L'chayim!"

Before we all drank from the cups, Rabbi Green recited the blessing over the wine and grape juice. "*Baruch atah Adonai, Eloheinu melech ha'olam, borei p'ri hagafen.* Blessed are you, Adonai, our God, Ruler of the universe, creator of the fruit from the vine."

At the end of the blessing, everyone once again said, "Amen" in unison and people randomly shouted, "L'chayim! L'chayim!" And all the cups went from being raised up in the air to being tipped back into people's mouths as they gulped down the purple or golden-white liquid.

Rabbi Green stood up on the chair again, shushed everyone one more time, then stepped down to stand in front of the water pitcher and bowl. As soon as the crowd quieted down he washed his hands and recited the blessing. "*Baruch atah Adonai, Eloheinu melech ha'olam, asher kid'shanu b'mitzvotav, v'tzivanu al n'tilat yadayim.* Blessed are you, Adonai, our God, Ruler of the universe, who makes us holy through your mitzvot and has commanded us to wash our hands."

And once again, everyone shouted, "Amen!"

Next, he uncovered the challah and recited, "*Baruch atah Adonai, Eloheinu melech ha'olam, hamotzi lechem min ha'aretz.* Blessed are you, Adonai, our God, Ruler of the universe, who brings forth bread from the earth." The little baskets of cut-up bread were passed around throughout the cluster of congregants. After each person took a piece and ate it, the crowd broke up as people headed toward the various tables. Most went straight to the food table. Some of the kids skipped the lunch food and made a beeline right for the sweets. Some grown-ups went to get hot drinks like coffee or tea. I walked over to get some lunch.

The line was moving very slowly. People were gabbing and taking their time picking out what they wanted to add to their plates. While I stood there holding my empty plate, waiting semi-patiently, I looked around the room and saw a girl that I recognized. I remembered her from Aunt Rachel and Uncle David's engagement party last year. She was Uncle David's niece Samantha, the other huppah holder. I figured it would be nice to get to know her and to be friendly. I left the line and walked over to re-introduce myself.

"Hi," I said.

"Hi," she replied in almost a whisper, barely looking up from the little plastic kiddush cup that she was still holding.

"I'm Ellie. I'm Rachel's brother Mark's daughter." Jeez, that was a mouthful.

"I'm Samantha," she said quietly again. She looked up into the air as if trying to get her title straight. I decided to help her out.

"You're David's sister Pam's daughter, right?" I giggled at how silly that all sounded.

"Yeah," she said seriously.

"I remember meeting you last year at the engagement party. We're going to be huppah holders together!"

"Uh-huh." She nodded in agreement.

Awkward silence.

"Do you want to get in line for some food together?" I asked. I realized how hungry I was as my stomach growled. I'd been too excited to eat much for breakfast.

"Sure," she said, still not making much eye contact with me.

We walked a few steps and got in line for the buffet, each of us on opposite sides of the table. The line was still moving slowly, but after a short wait we made it to the hot tray of noodle kugel. I couldn't hold my plate and serve myself food since I only had one good arm, so I had to put my plate down on the table and take the food with my good hand. What a pain!

"What grade are you in?" I asked across the kugel tray as I cut a massive piece for myself. I love the kugel they make at our shul. It's sweet and crunchy on top and filled with soft noodles on the inside.

"Sixth," she replied.

I waited for a couple of seconds, thinking she'd say something to me like, *"How about you?"* but when she didn't I just volunteered, "I'm in fifth." She nodded silently to let me know that she heard me.

"What's your favorite subject in school?" I asked trying to make a conversation and hoping that maybe I'd ask a question that would bring about some excitement or at least an answer with more than one syllable.

"Science," she said flatly.

Again, I waited to see if she'd ask me what I liked. She did not.

"I like science too," I said, starting to get annoyed by this one-sided conversation. "But I also like to read a lot, so English is another one of my favorite classes," I said while plopping a spoonful of sour cream on top of the kugel.

We continued down the line. I'm not a big fan of raw vegetables so I skipped the salad, but I did take a few grilled asparagus spears and red pepper slices. Those I love!

We kept moving along on our own sides of the buffet filling our plates with food. When we got to the end of the table, we each took silverware and napkins and without even having to say anything, we both headed straight to the dessert table. Of course!

I put a chocolate chip cookie and a spoonful of cut-up fruit on my plate alongside the kugel. I was very careful not to let the asparagus touch the cookie. I like both of those things but the thought of them together? Yuck! Samantha chose a slice of chocolate cake.

From the dessert table, we walked over to get a glass of ice water.

"Do you want to sit with me?" I asked. I carefully placed the cup on my plate and balanced it there as I started walking, holding the plate with my one good hand, but resting it on my cast.

"Okay," Samantha answered with a little shrug.

I couldn't tell if she was unfriendly or just shy. She was so quiet that getting her to give more than a one-word or two-word answer was quite a challenge. I was beginning to regret inviting her to sit with me.

Oh well, I figured, *it's just one little lunch. No big deal.*

But as it turned out, it was a big deal. A very big deal.

22

Aunt Trouble

Samantha and I sat together at a round table, neither one of us knowing what to say next. After an uncomfortably silent few seconds, I finally said, "Aren't you so excited about the wedding?"

"Mmhm," she said while taking a sip of water. She sounded about as excited as I would be if someone asked me if I was looking forward to next week's math test.

"I can't believe we get to be the huppah holders! That's like the best job in the whole wedding!" I added.

She nodded, taking a bite out of her bagel.

I was trying not to take this personally. I wasn't sure what her deal was, but her conversation skills were making me very uncomfortable.

I'm not sure why, but I felt like I needed to keep trying to be friendly and get to know her. We were going to be almost cousins. We'd probably see each other at a lot of family events.

"What are you wearing to the wedding?" I decided to ask. Unlike the bridesmaids, we're not wearing matching outfits. Aunt Rachel just asked that we all wear black. So my brothers will be wearing black suits and Samantha and I will each wear a black dress.

"A black dress—"

"Of course it's black," I jumped in. "We have to wear black!" Immediately after I realized that I cut her off, I wanted to kick myself. For the first time in the past fifteen minutes she actually uttered more than a one-word answer and I had to go and interrupt her. I guess I was excited to finally have someone besides my brothers and my parents to talk to about the wedding.

"Sorry," I said, "I didn't mean to interrupt you like that. Go ahead, tell me about it."

"Um, it's black with long sleeves—"

"I wish mine had long sleeves, but I have to wear short sleeves because of this dumb old cast," I said holding my arm up to show her. Ugh! I did it again! Why did I feel the need to keep barging in? It was like my mouth was running ahead of my brain and I couldn't keep up to get it to stop. I guess when my friends and I talk we probably jump in and interrupt each other a lot, not in a mean way, but because we have so much to say!

"Sorry, sorry," I said, "keep going."

And then it happened. The corners of her mouth actually went up a little on each side and I saw the slightest hint of a smile. I felt like I had just cracked a secret code. I made her smile! How did I do it? Was this a good thing? Or was she laughing at me? Was she mocking me because I broke my arm? Or did she think I was funny? I didn't know her at all, so I had no idea.

So I asked, "What did I do? Did I say something funny?"

At that very moment, someone came up behind me, put their hands over my eyes and said in a phony, deep, low voice, "Guess who?"

"I don't know, Joel?"

"Nope," the deep voice said.

"Jay?"

"Nuh-uh," the voice said again. I didn't really think

my older brother would actually come over and play a game like that with me.

"I give up," I said and I took the two hands in mine, uncovered my eyes and turned around to find my favorite aunt standing there.

"Aunt Rachel!" I exclaimed. But the weird thing was that it wasn't only my voice that said that. At the very same time, Samantha lit up like the sun with a humongous smile. She jumped out of her seat and wrapped her arms around Aunt Rachel's waist and gave her a huge hug.

I felt this awful, weird sensation in my gut. Why was this girl hugging my aunt? And why was she calling her Aunt Rachel? *She's MY aunt!* I thought angrily to myself. *Get your grubby paws off her!*

"I'm so glad that you guys found each other!" Aunt Rachel exclaimed. "I was planning to introduce the two of you, but I see you took care of that yourselves. Awesome!"

We both nodded. I tried to smile politely.

"Aunt Rachel, you look beautiful!" Samantha gushed, hugging my aunt's waist like a belt. I felt queasy watching the two of them. I quickly pulled my hair forward to make sure it was covering my ears, which were no doubt turning red hot. They always give me away.

"Aw, thanks, Sammi!" Aunt Rachel said giving her a peck on the head, kind of like what she did to me earlier in services. My insides felt like they were going to fall out.

I sat there smiling at the two of them, trying to mask just how terrible I felt watching this girl steal my aunt away from me.

"Okay, ladies," Aunt Rachel said, "I have to get

something to eat. I've been so busy schmoozing, I haven't had a chance to get any lunch yet. I'll hang out with you two later, okay? Love you guys!" She blew kisses to each of us.

Samantha sat back down in her seat and continued eating her bagel. I couldn't eat. My stomach was doing flips. I suddenly felt like Samantha was my enemy and I couldn't be with her for another second. I definitely didn't want to talk about the dresses with her anymore. I didn't feel like I could talk about anything. I felt like I might be sick, actually.

"Will you excuse me for a minute?" I asked Samantha. Even though I was so upset, I managed to still use my manners. My parents would have been proud of me.

"Sure," she said, with another one of her weary shrugs, and resuming the one-word responses. She took another bite of her bagel.

I started running out of the room, kind of at a slow trot. As I got nearer and nearer to the doors, I picked up some speed. I didn't want to look at anyone, so I kept my eyes down on the carpeted floor and focused on moving my feet as fast as they could go. I almost made it to the exit when I bumped into someone.

"Oof!" I looked up. It was Uncle David, who was shaking out his arm, which was now full of water that spilled all over him, thanks to our collision. "Where are you running off to, YaYa?"

"I just need to go to the bathroom," I told him, trying so hard not to cry.

"Looks like an emergency!" he said with a smile.

"It kind of is," I answered. Then, completely out of my control, I felt my eyes well up and before I knew it, salty tears streamed down my cheeks.

"Oh no! What's wrong?" Uncle David asked, getting down on one knee so that he could look me in the eye.

"Nothing, nothing, it's nothing," I said waving my hand in front of my eyes as if that might dry them.

"It's not nothing. It's obviously something!" He said reaching over to a nearby table to grab a pile of white cocktail napkins for the two of us. He handed me one so that I could dry my eyes and he used a bunch to dab the water off his sleeve. "Come with me. Let's go out into the hall and talk."

He put his arm on my shoulder and led me out into the hallway. Thankfully there was no one out there that I knew. We sat down on a bench and he looked me right in the eye and said, "What's up, kiddo?"

"She called her 'aunt!'" I blurted out.

"Who called who what?" Uncle David asked confused.

"Samantha...she called Aunt Rachel 'Aunt Rachel!'"

Uncle David sat and looked at me quietly, his brow furrowed. He didn't seem to be following what I was talking about so I explained.

"She called her 'Aunt Rachel.' But she's not her aunt, she's my aunt!"

He hesitated for a moment and then asked, "Who am I?" His question seemed kind of random and out of place.

"What?" I didn't get what he meant.

"Who am I?" He repeated. "Who are you talking to?"

"I'm talking to you."

"And my name is...."

"Uncle David," I answered with a sniffle.

"Uncle David?" he asked, as if he didn't actually know.

"Of course!" I answered.

"Why are you calling me Uncle David?"

Do I really have to spell it out for him? "Because your name is David and you're my uncle." He just sat there looking at me as if waiting for me to continue, so I added, "Well, you won't officially be my uncle until next week, after the wedding, but it's like you're my uncle already."

"Mhmm," he nodded. "Do you know who else I'm an uncle to?"

"Joel and Jeremy."

"And...?" he added.

Now I understood where he was going with this. "Samantha," I said quietly.

"And don't forget Anna." I nodded. "You've been calling me Uncle David ever since Aunt Rachel and I got engaged, even though it's not official yet."

"Yeah," I said with my head down.

"Well, Aunt Rachel is Samantha's and Anna's aunt in the same way."

I started crying again. I couldn't help it. I didn't even know why.

"YaYa, listen, nothing's going to change between you and Aunt Rachel. She'll always be your aunt and she'll always love you. And now you get to have a new friend in the family."

"But I don't want to share her!" *Did I really say that out loud?* It's totally what I was thinking, but I couldn't believe I admitted that to him. Hearing the words outside of my head made me feel like I was acting like a baby but it was honestly how I felt.

"I understand that you and your aunt have a very special bond, but I promise you, nothing's going to change. I mean, my nieces have been calling her Aunt

Rachel for as long as you've been calling me Uncle David. It's just that this is the first time you're hearing it. Besides, you've been sharing Aunt Rachel with your brothers for years. Why should this make such a difference?"

"Because I'm her only niece!"

"Ah," he said nodding with understanding.

"Plus," I had to add, "no offense, Uncle David. I know Samantha's your niece and all, but she isn't very nice. I've been trying to have a conversation with her all through lunch and she won't say anything." I felt guilty saying that to him, but I also felt a little bit relieved to let it out. So I continued, "She's barely willing to talk to me! She's unfriendly and it's unfair that I have to share my aunt with someone un-nice like that!"

"Un-nice?" he chuckled with a warm smile and a wink. "I don't think that's actually a word."

I shrugged, looking down at my hands. "Whatever." I knew he was doing that thing grown-ups do when they try to change the subject or make you laugh about something when you're upset. But I was glad he came back to the subject at hand right away.

"Actually, YaYa, Samantha is a really good kid, she's just extremely shy. And to tell you the truth, she's come a long way. When she was a little girl she wouldn't talk to anyone other than her parents. Her teachers used to get so frustrated. And how do you think I felt? My own niece wouldn't talk to me! Even worse, she would run away and hide when I came over to their house. Luckily, she started breaking out of her terrible shyness a few years ago. She's made huge progress. The fact that she was sitting with you is a giant step for her. And I promise, the more she gets to know you, the more comfortable she'll be and the more open she'll become. I guarantee it. You'll see."

I nodded silently as I let all that sink in. It did make sense. I suppose I should have given her the benefit of the doubt. Rabbi Green always tells us to "judge people favorably." I guess this was one of those times.

Uncle David said, "I happen to have the best nieces in the world. Just look at the one sitting right here with me." I smiled.

He got serious again. "At first we were worried about Samantha being in the wedding. We didn't know if she would be willing to be a huppah holder or not because it meant standing up in front of everyone. It's kind of scary for her."

"Well, do you think she'll go through with it? Being a huppah holder, I mean?" I asked.

"Yeah, I do. I think she's trying very hard and is excited to be a part of the wedding. And believe it or not, I think she's looking forward to being up there with you." He handed me another napkin. I wiped my runny nose with it.

"Really?" I asked, looking up at him.

"Really," he said. "Come here," he spread his arms wide open. I snuggled in for a big Uncle David hug. I suppose he was right. He is one hundred percent my uncle and has been for a while now. In all that time, he hasn't stopped loving Samantha. And if all this time Aunt Rachel has had a new niece or two, I certainly didn't feel a difference in how she treated me.

I scooched back from his hug and dried my eyes one more time. "Thank you, Uncle David."

"Love you, kiddo," he said to me, rubbing my back gently.

"Love you too. I'm going to go finish my lunch now."

I dried my eyes, took a deep breath, and walked back into the social hall to eat my kugel and get to know my new sort-of cousin-to-be.

23

Friends and Glovers

Another day crossed off the calendar and—bam!—it was Sunday morning. Only one week left before the wedding and it was time for Aunt Rachel's bridal shower. Her best friends, who were also her brides-maids, planned a very nice brunch party for her at her friend Jodi's apartment. It was a "women's only" event and I felt really special because I was included as one of the "women." Of course Samantha was there too, but Anna wasn't. I guess five-year-olds don't make the cut as "women."

After my little breakdown at shul and the chat that followed with Uncle David, I decided that I would make an effort to get to know Samantha. I was relieved to learn that she was just shy and not unfriendly. I hoped that if I could help her feel comfortable, maybe she'd open up a little bit just as Uncle David had promised. I only had one week to accomplish this, so I figured I'd better start right away.

I walked up to her with my plate of brunch food.

"Hi again," I said with a friendly smile.

"Hi," she said back. Short and to the point. Pretty much what I expected.

"Can I sit with you?"

"Sure," she replied.

Here we go again with the one-word answers.

But then to my shock and surprise, she asked me a

question! And it was more than just one word! It was two!

"What happened?" She asked, pointing at my cast.

I looked down at the green thing on my arm, covered in scribbles and doodles. "I tripped on something in the dark when I was walking my dog and I broke my arm. I should be okay to hold up the huppah, though," I added quickly. I didn't want her to think that I was unfit for the job.

"Oh," she said, and got quiet again. And there I was thinking we had made progress.

We sat quietly next to one another eating our food. I had a piece of broccoli quiche and some breakfast potatoes. It was all delicious. At the exact moment that I put a big forkful of quiche in my mouth, Samantha surprised me again. "Does it hurt?"

I swallowed and said, "Oh my gosh! So much when it happened! But it's okay now. It only hurts when I bang it into something, which, obviously I try not to do. To be honest I'm constantly living in fear that I might trip over something somewhere and fall on it again. I'm especially nervous about walking and tripping down the aisle at the wedding. That would be a disaster!"

She giggled. "You sound like me!"

"What do you mean?" I asked, realizing that we were actually embarking on a real honest-to-goodness conversation.

"I'm so nervous!"

"About being a huppah holder?" I asked.

"Yeah. I don't like being in front of people." I nodded and gave her a sympathetic smile, trying very hard not to take over the conversation the way I did the day before. I hoped that by keeping my mouth shut, I would encourage her to be more talkative. It worked.

"I'm scared, " she continued, "but I really want to do it for Uncle David and Aunt Rachel...."

My skin prickled when I heard her say "Aunt Rachel." I took a deep breath and reminded myself that we're going to share our aunt and uncle for the rest of our lives, and that's just the way it is. Also, if they ever have kids, we're going to share cousins too. I was comforted at least by the fact that Samantha wasn't unfriendly like I had thought at first. I was starting to think I could even get to like her.

"I'm sure you'll be fine. Maybe you can hold one of the poles in the back, behind the rabbi and the bride and groom. That way, you won't be able to see the audience and they won't be able to see you because you'll be blocked by everyone else," I suggested.

"Good idea!" she said with a huge smile. I felt like I had really accomplished something.

We continued eating quietly for a while, but I noticed that she was staring at the hamsa-glove around my neck, and it made me realize that I had a solution for her. "Actually, we don't have to worry about walking down the aisle or holding the huppah because I know for a fact that everything is going to be okay." I held it up for her to see. "This is a hamsa. Do you know what that is?"

"A glove?" she answered more as a question.

"Yeah, but this one is a hamsa. It's kind of like a good luck charm."

"It's a glove. With a googly eye," she remarked doubtfully.

"You're right, it is, but it's my own homemade hamsa. I guess it's more of a bad-luck keeper-away-er than a good luck charm, but either way, as long as I wear it to the wedding, it will guarantee we won't have any problems. That's why I'm wearing it all the time. I've been having a lot of bad luck lately." I held up my arm in the cast to make my point. "Now that I'm wearing my hamsa, things seem to be better. And, of course, I don't want to have any trouble at the wedding!"

"You think it'll work?" she asked, still doubtful, but seeming to leave some room open to the possibility that I might be speaking the truth.

"I really do! I even made one for Aunt Rachel so she wouldn't have anything to worry about, either." I went into detail about it all: the red string, the ayin hara, everything.

Samantha seemed to be thinking this over when Aunt Rachel's friend, Leslie, called everyone to the living room. It was time to open the presents. How fun! It was kind of like a birthday party, but for grown-ups!

As we were gathering around for the opening of the presents, I noticed something that didn't seem right.

"Uh oh. Awkward!" I said kind of to Samantha and kind of just in general.

I went over to the bride and whispered in her ear, "Aunt Rachel, I don't know if you realized this or not, but there's a man in your women's-only party."

Aunt Rachel smiled and waved her hand nonchalantly. "Oh, that's just Steve. It's actually a women's-only-plus-Steve event," she said.

I must have looked as confused as I felt because she continued. "Steve is one of my closest friends. I decided that it didn't seem fair that just because he's not a woman he couldn't be in my bridal party. So Steve is my 'bridesman!'"

"A bridesman? Is that a thing? I've never heard of

that before!"

"I don't know if it's 'a thing' or not," she answered, "but it is now!"

"Okay," I said. "I'm glad to know that you didn't have a party crasher."

I went back to report what I'd learned to Samantha. Just then, Karen, another one of Aunt Rachel's friends asked me and Samantha to do a special job. After Aunt Rachel opened each gift, we were supposed to keep the ribbons and bows and make a silly-looking hat out of them all. She asked us to try to keep it a secret so we could surprise Aunt Rachel with it at the end.

"This'll be fun!" I said to Samantha. She nodded, but she seemed to be climbing back into her shell. I could understand that. We were going to be hanging out with all of these adults that we didn't know. I definitely could see why she felt uncomfortable. I decided to try and keep her attention focused on the silly ribbon hat so she'd be distracted from the things that make her uneasy.

Aunt Rachel sat down on the couch and her friends brought her a bunch of beautifully wrapped gift boxes, one at a time. With each gift she opened, the guests discreetly passed the ribbons and bows to me and I passed them to Samantha, who taped each one onto a paper plate. It would have been easier to staple them, but the stapler would have made too much noise and revealed our secret hat-making.

The gifts were kind of boring, like dishes, pots and pans, and a coffee maker. But then she started to get some interesting ones.

"Open this one next," Leslie suggested, handing Aunt Rachel another box with a fancy ribbon on top. She delicately tore the wrapping paper and opened the box to find a big, beautiful, white tablecloth.

"Oh, this is great!" Aunt Rachel exclaimed. "We need one of these!"

"Now you can host many wonderful Shabbat and holiday dinners in your new home together," Mom said. "And maybe now I won't have to host quite as many!" she added with a wink.

"And may I be invited over every now and then!" Grandma chimed in. Everyone laughed. She was joking around, but I think there was also some truth to her comment. Grandma loves to host our big family dinners, but it's nice to be the guest sometimes, too.

"Okay, Mom," Aunt Rachel said, "but make sure you get there on time!" They both laughed, and Grandma wagged her finger at her always-late-for-everything daughter. Aunt Rachel went over and gave Grandma a big hug. Then she hugged Mom, too, for the gift. She approached me to give me a thank-you hug as well, but I held her off.

"Nope, that one isn't from me." I told her. "Those two are!" I pointed at a box wrapped in silver paper with a bright blue bow on it and a silver gift bag tied with blue curly ribbon. "Open the box first."

"You got us a gift yourself?" she asked, surprised.

"It's from all three of us," I answered proudly. To be honest, my brothers didn't even think of getting them a gift, maybe because they weren't included in the shower, but once I suggested the idea to them they got on board with it.

Aunt Rachel untied the blue bow, opened the shiny paper, and pulled out all of the soft white tissue paper that was inside the box covering the gift. She reached in and dug out the beautiful candlesticks that my brothers and I bought for them with our own money.

We had gone online and bought them totally without our parents' help, well, except for the use of their credit card. We paid them back with our allowance money.

"Wow! These are gorgeous!" Aunt Rachel raved, turning the shiny silver candlesticks around to see every side and to show the guests. "We'll use them each and every Shabbat!"

She came over to me and gave me a big hug.

"Wait," I said, "we're not done yet. You still need to open the other gift."

"Two gifts? How'd I get so lucky?"

"Funny that you should ask that," I said pointing to the silver gift bag.

24

Hats and Gloves

This one's not from my brothers. It's just from me," I told Aunt Rachel proudly as she held the gift bag. Out of the corner of my eye I noticed Samantha squirming uncomfortably in the corner. I started to think that maybe she hadn't brought a gift of her own for Aunt Rachel and Uncle David. "I mean, it's from us—me and Samantha," I corrected. Samantha, who had been slumping in her spot, suddenly sat up straight and tall and looked at me with a questioning expression. I smiled to let her know it was cool.

She shot a secret look at me as if to say, "Thanks!"

"Wow! I'm not sure how you pulled that one off since you really only met yesterday, but I'm so impressed! I will love it no matter what it is because it came from the two of you! Thanks, girls." She blew us an air kiss.

She removed the tissue paper and peered into the bag for a few long seconds. She looked confused. Finally she lifted the glove by the red string, pulled it out of the bag, and held it up for everyone to see. It felt like the googly eye was looking right back at all the people staring at the glove.

"So sweet!" she said, but I could tell she was really just being polite. "Check it out, guys. Ellie and Samantha gave me a pair of gloves. Look how cute! They even have a red string so I won't lose them!" She dug around inside the bag clearly searching for something else. "Uh-oh. I think you may have lost one of the gloves," she said. "I only see one."

"No, it's only supposed to be one," I stood and held up the hamsa that hung from my neck. "It's the match to this one. But it's not just an ordinary glove."

"It's not?" she asked turning it over in her hand, trying to figure out what I was talking about and what made it special.

"Nope, in fact, it's not a glove at all anymore. It's a hamsa."

Aunt Rachel smiled at me. "Oh, so that's why you've been wearing that glove!" I could see from the expression on her face that it was all beginning to make sense to her now. She slipped her head through the loop of red string and wore her hamsa just like I did.

"Ellie?" Mom said, "Are those your winter gloves?"

"Oh yeah, I forgot to tell you. I'm going to need a new pair of gloves this winter." Mom covered her eyes with her hand and shook her head quietly.

I explained the whole thing to everyone in the room. I didn't go into all the details about every single thing that had gone wrong in the past couple of weeks, and for sure I didn't mention Aunt Rachel and Uncle David fighting or what had happened to the ketubah, but I did explain about the red string and the eyes. By the end, everyone understood why I, and now Aunt Rachel, wore googly-eyed gloves around our necks.

"Thank you so much, girls!" Aunt Rachel came over and gave me a big hug and then gave an equally big one to Samantha. I was glad that I included her in the gift. I could tell how happy she was about it.

Aunt Rachel returned to the business of opening

the rest of her gifts and I went to sit down by Samantha on the floor again.

"Thanks for including me," she said.

"See, I told you the hamsa made things better!"

The gift opening continued for a little while longer. Aside from some more everyday gifts like a blender and towels, they got some really nice Jewish things like a Hanukkah menorah, a seder plate and a tzedakah box.

Right after Aunt Rachel opened her last gift and she thought she was all done, Leslie announced, "Rachel, before you go anywhere, we have one last present for you. Your huppah holders made something special for you to wear. You may want to even wear it on your big day!" And then Karen nodded at us as a sign to bring out the special surprise.

"My huppah holders?" Aunt Rachel exclaimed. "They've already given me so much!" she said while looking down at her hamsa glove admiringly.

Samantha whispered, "You do it."

I stood up with the silly hat behind my back and told Aunt Rachel to close her eyes. She followed my instructions, and sat there with a hesitant grin.

"Should I be worried?" she asked, letting out a nervous chuckle.

"Not too worried," I replied as I tied the two long blue ribbons hanging down from each side under her chin. I straightened the ridiculous looking bow-hat on her head.

"Okay, open your eyes now!" I said, and as soon as she did, all of her friends started snapping pictures of her wearing the hat.

Steve brought over a mirror and held it up for Aunt Rachel to see herself.

"Lovely, you guys. Just lovely!" she said playfully, laughing at her reflection in the mirror. "I don't know about the wedding, but I'm certainly ready to go to the Kentucky Derby."

"You should wear it on your honeymoon!" One friend called out.

"I think you should wear it to the wedding!" I said with a giggle.

"Yeah, sure," she said, "but I simply can't decide, should wear it over or under my veil?" And she gave me one of her famous winks. I, in turn, gave her one of my famous two-eyed I-can't-actually-wink-with-one-eye blinks.

Karen announced it was time for dessert. As all the grown-ups moved toward the kitchen to get cake and coffee, Samantha tapped me on my shoulder as I was getting up from the couch. "Thanks again for including me in the gift. My mom bought a gift from our whole family, so I didn't even think of getting one myself. I really appreciate what you did."

I stood there and thought to myself how far she'd come in the past twenty-four hours. Not too long ago she wasn't speaking to me in full sentences!

"No problem!" I said. "I'm sure you would have done the same for me if the tables were turned. Right?"

She nodded.

Then, to my astonished delight, Samantha, my new cousin-to-be-potentially-new-friend quoted my latest favorite Corey McDonald song, *Crushin' on You Like a Garbage Truck.*

"*If the tables were turned, you know you'd never get burned....*" She looked at me with an expectant, curious expression, waiting to see if we spoke the same language.

I stared at her as if someone had just plopped a huge pot of gold down in the middle of the room. *OMG! She likes Corey?* The smile on my face must have answered her question because she now had a smile that matched mine. This was a major breakthrough! We had unlocked the door to our inevitable friendship!

I continued the song where she left off: "'Cause when you're down on your luck, I'd always pick you out from the muck....'"

Then together we both sang, "CRUSHIN' ON YOU LIKE A GARBAGE TRUCK!"

OMG!

"You like Corey?!" she asked me excitedly.

"Like him? Um, he's just like my whole reason for living! Duh!" I replied.

Then we both jumped up and down right there in the middle of the living room, screamed, hugged, and at the speed of light, began to rattle off every single one of our favorite things about Mr. Perfect himself.

As we headed into the kitchen to get our slices of cake together, I looked down at, and then patted my hamsa-glove. I couldn't believe this new turn of events.

Take a hike, evil eye! I thought. But then I whispered a quiet, little kenahora, and a ptu, ptu, ptu. Because, you know, just in case.

25

Something About a Bad Chicken

"Tell me again why we're going over to Uncle David's," Joel asked.

"Yeah, I still have some homework left to do," Jeremy added from his seat.

It was five o'clock in the afternoon, the same Sunday as the bridal shower, and Jeremy, Joel, Mom, Dad, and I had all piled into the car to drive over to Uncle David's apartment for dinner.

"We're going over for dinner and a movie," Mom answered. "Don't worry, we won't stay too late. I'm sure Uncle David and Aunt Rachel have a lot of things to do before the wedding."

I was kind of surprised that the two of them wanted to cook for us and have us over to watch a movie one week before the big day, but I certainly wasn't complaining. I've always loved going to Uncle David's place! Plus, that sounded much better to me than doing my social studies homework.

We arrived at the place we called Uncle David's "Fun House" because the apartment was full of fun stuff and was a kids' paradise. As soon as we walked through the front door, we were in the living room facing the two big windows that were spaced about three feet apart on the opposite side of the room. On every inch of wall space where there wasn't a window, Uncle David had these huge, floor-to-ceiling bookcases filled with all sorts of books, movies, video games, music CDs and even old-time records. But mostly books. His shelves were filled with almost every single category from real science to science fiction, to biographies, spy novels and history books, and even a few cookbooks.

In fact, it was his love of books that Aunt Rachel says drew her to him and vice versa. I've heard the story so many times that I know it by heart. They met in an English class in college. They completely disagreed about the plot of a certain book. They began to argue in class and took the debate into the hallway when class was over. They continued walking through the quad, discussing and arguing and before they knew it they were sitting at a coffee shop together. They started meeting every day after class to talk about their favorite and least favorite authors, which movies based on books were better than the original, and so on. I think later on, when Aunt Rachel mentioned that her older brother was buying a bookstore, that pretty much sealed the deal for Uncle David.

Right in front of his big walls of books, he had the most comfortable places to sit and read them! I waved to Uncle David and Aunt Rachel and then, as I always did when I went to his place, I made a running leap onto the big, gray, cushy couch in the living room. It was like plopping into a vat of cotton candy! I loved flying onto it and landing in the softness. Our couches at home are nowhere near as cushy and I don't think Mom would be very happy with us if we jumped onto them like that. There's a reason we called that place the "Fun House!"

Joel and Jeremy each took their spots in the two gray, equally soft, cushy chairs on either side of the couch. Within seconds of our arrival, Jeremy had already taken his shoes off, grabbed a book from one of the shelves and tuned everyone else out, lost in his reading. He planted his big, giant feet, complete with a sock with a hole in the heel, on top of the coffee table and made himself comfortable.

The only thing that Uncle David had hanging up was an enormous flat screen TV that took up almost the whole wall facing the couch. That's all he had for decoration in the whole living room—a huge TV screen and walls of books. No framed pictures, no knickknacks, nothing. Just places to sit, a place to put your drinks, and a gigantic screen. At least the books added lots of color to the room. What made his place perfect was that he always had ice cream in the freezer, and an awesome video game system hooked up to the TV.

"Hey, Aunt Rachel," I called over to her while she was in the kitchen, "did you or Uncle David bring this huge TV here by bicycle?"

"Ha! Good one, YaYa!" she replied. "Actually, it was a unicycle! And I was juggling watermelons, too!"

My brothers each gave me a strange look.

"Huh?" Joel asked.

"Inside joke," I answered with a grin, pleased that Aunt Rachel had saved that for me, without sharing the joke with the boys when she invited them to be in the wedding.

A few minutes later, the doorbell rang. I was surprised when Uncle David opened the door and a parade of people streamed into the apartment. I thought we were the only ones coming over. I didn't realize it was a whole party!

Grandma and Grandpa came in first, followed by all of Uncle David's family including Samantha and her parents. It quickly got crowded in the cozy, not-so-gigantic space. Since "the other side of the family" was there, we knew we had to be polite, so Joel and I all got up to say hi to everyone. Jeremy grudgingly put his book down on the coffee table and got up too. Had it only been Grandma and Grandpa, we probably would have merely yelled hello from the couch.

At some point we'd met all of Uncle David's relatives before except for "Nana," his ninety-something-year-old grandma. She was a teeny, tiny, frail lady with short white hair. When she shuffled into the apartment with her cane, her whole face lit up when she saw her grandson and soon-to-be granddaughter. The loose skin on her arms waggled around as she let go of the cane and hugged the two of them with all of her might. I couldn't believe it, but when I stood up and walked over to meet her, I was even taller than her! I never feel tall around grown-ups.

Even though we had just seen everyone at synagogue for the aufruf the day before, Uncle David reintroduced us since it had been so long since we'd all really hung out together. Samantha and I simply grinned and waved at each other. We didn't need an introduction, that's for sure!

"Look what I made!" she said, proudly showing me her own hamsa that she created with a purple glove. "I didn't have any red string, so I used pink. It was as close as I could get. And I didn't have those eye things like you had, so I made one big eye out of a t-shirt that I cut up, colored in and sewed on. Now none of us will have bad luck!"

We looked across the room and sure enough, Aunt Rachel was wearing her hamsa-glove too. I felt very proud! *Maybe it will become a new trend,* I thought.

Maybe in the future when people go online and search for images of a hamsa they'll find pictures of celebrities wearing hamsa-gloves!

Uncle David was in the kitchen, which was right behind the living room wall with the TV. He pulled a few homemade pizzas out of the oven, and Aunt Rachel brought a huge salad to the table in the dining room, which was right off the kitchen. Everyone took their food and then we all sat around the tiny apartment, wherever we could find a place. Some of the grown-ups sat in the dining room, some hung out in the kitchen. I grabbed a spot next to Samantha on the floor in the living room. We sat with our legs out and our backs against the coffee table. Joel came over and sat next to me. I realized that I'd been spending tons of time with Samantha over the past twenty-four hours, but Joel and Jay hadn't been reintroduced to her yet.

"Samantha, this is my *younger* brother Joel," I said, hoping she wouldn't clam up and be too shy. Joel rolled his eyes at me.

"Hi," Joel said.

"Hi," she said back.

"And that guy over there is our older brother Jeremy. He prefers to go by Jay." I pointed across the room. "Jay! Wave!" I called over to him.

Instead of waving his hand like anyone else would, he waved his slice of pizza at us, apparently thinking that he was being funny. But a mushroom fell off and onto the floor and Dad happened to walk by at that exact moment and stepped in it without noticing. It squished onto the sole of his shoe, so as he walked we could see a mushroom clinging to the bottom of his foot.

For some reason, Samantha thought that was hysterical. It was nice to see her laughing and being at ease. Joel thought it was pretty funny, too, and watching Samantha laugh so hard made him laugh. Watching the two of them crack up made me crack up. Before long, the three of us were in hysterics together.

Joel caught his breath long enough to roll over onto his back and pretend that he was the mushroom, "HELP!" he called out in a high squeaky voice, his arms and legs flailing, "I'm trapped!"

Samantha lost it. She was bent over, laughing so hard, holding her stomach. Joel, who loves a good audience, continued in his mushroom voice.

"Hello, dog hair, hello, cookie crumbs, hop on! Come join me for the ride!"

Samantha had tears streaming down her face. I didn't actually find the whole mushroom thing to be all that funny, but their laughter was contagious and we all caught it from one another. I think it's fair to say that Joel made a good first impression on Samantha. She warmed up to him right away after that and never spoke to him with one-word answers.

Eventually, the laughter died down and Samantha said to me, "I didn't realize that you had a younger brother. I thought Uncle David said that you guys were twins."

"We are," I said, predicting the puzzled look I got from her. I waited a couple of seconds to let her think about that one and give it time to sink in. Then I explained, "I'm thirteen minutes older. I came into the world five minutes *before* midnight on October eighth and he waited to make his appearance eight minutes *after* twelve on the 9th, so that makes me a whole day older!"

"Hmm!" she said, considering this.

"Yep, I'm the big sister," I said with a smug smile. "And he's my—." I caught myself. I almost said Little Bro but I had already promised I would stop calling him that because he hates it, so I quickly corrected myself, "younger brother."

"Cool!" she said.

Aunt Rachel and Uncle David stood arm in arm right in front of the huge TV screen and asked for everyone's attention.

"Thanks for coming over, you guys," Aunt Rachel started. "We wanted to have everyone here with us as we head into the final week of our engagement."

"Plus, since Rachel and I are going to stop seeing each other after tonight—" Uncle David started to say.

"What?!" I yelled out, cutting him off. "What do you mean you're going to stop seeing each other? That is NOT okay!" I felt a rush inside me and had a terrible flashback to that awful afternoon in our kitchen when I thought I heard Aunt Rachel say that they were breaking up and not going to get married.

Both of them giggled. "Does it look like we're breaking up?" Aunt Rachel asked with a big smile and her arm still draped around Uncle David's middle.

"Um, no," I said meekly (and full of relief).

Uncle David explained. "There's a custom that we're choosing to follow, which is that the couple getting married doesn't see one another for a whole week prior to the wedding. The first time that we'll see each other will be at the *bedeken*...."

I turned and whispered to Joel, "At the what?"

Joel shrugged and whispered back, "Something about a bad chicken?"

Samantha overheard this and cracked up. Joel was on a roll. He had quite an audience in Samantha. I was thinking that if he kept this up maybe she'd start a Joel Silver fan club!

Samantha's dad was the one who spoke up next. "Can you please translate that for those of us who don't know what you're talking about?"

"Absolutely," Aunt Rachel said with a grin.

"We thought you'd never ask!" Uncle David added. "In keeping with tradition, Rachel and I will be doing a ceremony called a bedeken before the actual wedding under the huppah begins. We're going to start out in separate rooms, but then the people who were with me in the groom's room are going to lead me, with singing and dancing, to where Rachel will be sitting on a big chair, almost like a queen on her throne. Once I get there, I'll place her veil over her face."

"Tell them why you're doing it," Grandma egged him on. Then to the rest of us, "Such a nice tradition. I don't know why more people don't do it. I guess they don't know about it. Jack and I didn't do it at our wedding because neither one of us had ever seen it before. I wish we had." Then she turned back to Uncle David with an encouraging wave of her hand, "Go on, tell them, tell them."

"Okay!" he said with a big smile, amused by Grandma's antics. "One idea goes back to the story of Jacob in the Torah. Remember how he was tricked by Laban into marrying Leah instead of her sister Rachel, the woman he truly loved? Jacob married a woman with a veil covering her face, and ended up marrying the wrong sister. By placing the veil over my bride's face, I'll know for sure that she's the right woman!"

Aunt Rachel added her two cents to the conversation. "Another take on it, from a different Torah story, is that when Rebecca saw Isaac coming toward her, she covered her face out of modesty."

"I've heard another explanation, that the covering of the bride's face is to show that her inner beauty is just as important as her outer beauty," Uncle David said, turning to look directly at his bride-to-be. "Covering Rachel's beautiful face with her veil shows that I am marrying her beautiful soul, too."

Everyone in the room let out a big "Awww...." Joel and I, on the other hand, made faces at each other while rolling our eyes. Jay pantomimed like he was throwing up. Way too mushy for our taste, that's for sure!

Aunt Rachel kissed Uncle David on the cheek, blushing a little.

"So, anyway, since this is our last time together before we become a married couple, we wanted to watch a movie with you," Uncle David said, picking up the remote control for the TV. "Everyone get comfortable and find a spot where you can see the screen." We all laughed because it was impossible not to see the screen that took up almost the whole wall.

"Is it *National Treasure*? I love that movie!" Joel called out.

"Nope," Uncle David replied.

I gave it a go. "How about *Night at the Museum*? That's a good one."

"Nuh-uh," Aunt Rachel said, shaking her head.

Everyone started calling out names of their favorite movies:

"*Hello, Dolly!*"

"*Fiddler on the Roof!*"

"*E.T.!*"

"*Raiders of the Lost Ark!*"

"*Finding Nemo!*"

"The Empire Strikes Back!"

"Okay, okay, you can all stop guessing. Only my brother and sister-in-law know, because they brought the movie. You did bring it, didn't you, Mark?" Aunt Rachel asked, joking around with Dad.

He pretended to fumble around like he was looking for it, and then said, "Oh, did you want me to bring that *today*?" Then he laughed and handed her a square DVD case.

Aunt Rachel slid the disk into the player while Uncle David passed around bowls of yummy-smelling popcorn and we all settled in to watch the surprise movie.

"I wonder what it is," Samantha whispered to me.

"Me, too," I said tossing a piece of popcorn in my mouth.

We both got comfortable with our backs against the coffee table as we eagerly awaited the big movie premiere.

26

Watching Movies
at the Fun House

Jeremy, who was now sitting on the sofa behind us, threw a piece of popcorn at Joel's head. Joel turned around and glared at Jeremy but didn't say anything. Then he turned back.

Jeremy did it again. And again. And again.

"Cut it out, Jay!" Joel finally snapped.

Jeremy looked up at the ceiling as if there was something completely and utterly fascinating going on up there. Once again Joel turned back around, and once again, a few seconds later, Jeremy threw another piece.

"Mom!" Joel complained, "Jeremy's bugging me! Tell him to stop!"

"Shhh!" Aunt Rachel loudly shushed the boys, "Pay attention! You're going to love this!"

Jeremy lobbed another piece at Joel's head.

"Boys!" Mom reprimanded, "Stop it now!"

"What do you mean, 'boys'? I'm an innocent victim here! I'm sitting here minding my own business and he's throwing popcorn at me!" Joel protested.

Uncle David paused the movie before it even started.

"Come on, guys," he said in a friendly but serious voice. We all love Uncle David so much, none of us would ever want to disappoint him, not even Jeremy.

"Don't look at me!" Jeremy said, "I'm just sitting here waiting for the movie to start. Joel's the one making a racket."

Mom didn't buy that for a second—that boy has a reputation, after all. She gave Jeremy one of her angry mom stares and he shrank down into his seat. He mumbled something inaudible into his popcorn bowl and started digging into it as if it was a box of Cracker Jacks and he was looking for the prize.

Uncle David hit "play" again.

The movie opened with a heart being drawn on a piece of paper like a Valentine's Day card.

"Ugh!" Jeremy grunted, not even trying to hide his disgust with the movie choice. "Do I really have to sit through this?" he asked Mom.

"Yes," Mom answered calmly.

"Gross!" Joel called out.

"Trust me, it's not what you think. You'll like it," Mom responded calmly once again.

"I know what it is. It's a cheesy romantic comedy!" my older brother whined.

"It's not a romantic comedy," Mom assured him.

Dad looked at Mom from across the room and gave her a knowing smile. "It's a bit of a comedy," he said. "It does have a few giggles...."

"Oh, come on!" Joel added to the protest.

I had to side with my brothers on this one. I was not in the mood for a sappy love story. *They could have taken a vote or something before popping the movie in! They could have asked what we'd like to see. I thought we lived in a democracy!*

Meanwhile, the heart on the screen turned red and the hand that drew the heart originally, wrote in fancy calligraphy, "Mark and Debbie."

Suddenly I was a little more interested.

"Mark and Debbie?" I said to my Mom who was sitting on the couch behind me.

"Keep watching," Dad said.

When the hand finished writing the names, a banner appeared across the top of the screen that said, "The Wedding of...."

"Hold on! Is this your wedding video?" Joel asked with the same sort of panic in his voice as if he just realized that he was in line for Space Mountain.

Mom and Dad were both grinning like they had pulled off the world's greatest college prank. For years they'd been trying to get us to watch their wedding video with them, and, conveniently, every year around their anniversary when they would get ready to watch it, my brothers and I would somehow get "busy" with one thing or another. We'd leave them sitting there, all cuddled up and cozy together on the couch, sharing a blanket and a bowl of popcorn. (Of course, I'd usually steal a handful of popcorn before making a quick escape from the room!)

"Oh, man!" Jeremy grumbled from his seat, admitting defeat.

Uncle David pushed the remote with his thumb to pause the movie and yelled, "Surprise!"

"What's going on?" I asked him. "Are we really watching their wedding video?"

It was Aunt Rachel who responded to my question while speaking to the whole crowd. "We are. Since David and I are planning to include a lot of Jewish customs that many of you are not familiar with, we wanted to show you this fabulous video of these two young lovebirds getting married so that we can stop and explain things to you. That way, it will all be familiar to you next week and you'll feel comfortable participating in all the parts of our wedding ceremony and celebration and hopefully you'll even get other people to join in."

Uncle David seemed to feel the need to explain to us. "Even though I grew up in a Jewish home, we didn't really do a lot of 'religious' stuff. You know, we lit Hanukkah candles and got together on Passover for a seder, but that was about it. Over the past few years, though, Rachel and I have been to several friends' weddings that included a variety of traditions. We've been learning about all the different ways there are to create a Jewish wedding, and we found a lot of meaningful rituals that we decided to include in ours."

I felt the need to explain too.

"In our house, we keep a lot of traditions, like lighting candles and eating challah every Friday night. But even still, my brothers and I have never been to any weddings at all, so the only ones we know about are the ones we've read about in books or seen in movies or on TV. I'd never even heard of a huppah before! I mean, I knew that there was a canopy, but I didn't know what it was called." I smiled at Aunt Rachel, remembering our phone call. She smiled back and it was like we were reading each other's minds.

Uncle David jumped in.

"Well, since none of us has three hours to spare, we're going to fast-forward to specific parts and highlights. Right now we're going to watch the *bedeken* and the *tisch*."

"Bedeken and tisch?" Samantha's mom asked from the other corner of the room. "That sounds like a TV cop show from the eighties!"

Joel laughed out loud. He saw this as an opportunity to make his own little joke.

"Maybe the 'bad chicken' has allergies and needs a 'tissue,'" he said with a sly smirk and looked over at Samantha to see if she approved. I thought his joke wasn't funny but Samantha laughed quietly and let out a little snort. Seriously. It was almost at the point where all Joel had to do was look at her and she'd crack up. This was a far cry from the girl who was too shy to talk to her uncle!

"Dork," Jeremy muttered, rolling his eyes at Joel.

Uncle David un-paused the movie. There was a much younger, skinnier version of our Dad on the screen, standing behind a table, trying to give a speech. Every time he said a word or two, people would yell and scream or even break out into songs, totally interrupting him. Some people held up glasses and yelled "L'chayim!" just like they did at the kiddush at shul.

Of course I'd seen many pictures from my parents' wedding, but it was so different to see it in action with everyone moving around and talking. It was especially strange to hear Dad's voice sounding so much younger than it does now.

"Why are they being so rude to you?" I asked, staring at the screen. "Why aren't they letting you speak?"

But I could see on the video that young-groom Dad was laughing. He wasn't offended by everyone jumping in. In fact, as I watched Dad watching himself on the video there in Uncle David's living room, I could see that he had a huge smile on his face.

"That's part of the tisch," Dad explained to us. "It's all part of the celebration. My job was to try to share some words of wisdom on this most important day, and everyone else tried to distract me and lighten the mood. I knew it was coming. It was funny, not insulting at all. I was amazed that I was able to get out as much as I did!"

"Why is it called a tisch?" Samantha's mom asked.

"Tisch is Yiddish for table," Aunt Rachel answered. "It's just the groom's table."

"Is there a bride's tisch?" I asked.

Aunt Rachel said, "There can be. I have some friends who got married and each one had their own tisch. I'm not doing that, but yes, some people definitely have two tisches going on at the same time."

Mom added, "Some people might even choose to do one tisch all together. I like the way we did it. You'll see why in a few seconds."

Uncle David hit "play" again and zipped forward to the next scene that he wanted to show us.

He stopped in time for us to see a crowd of people dancing and singing all around Dad. Although, honestly, some of them were singing so loudly that it sounded more like shouting. They had left the tisch room and were now dancing their way through a long hallway, singing (more like bellowing!) a song in Hebrew that I'd never heard before. It was a happy, fun (and loud!) song. Some people were behind Dad and some were in front of him, walking and dancing backwards. Some were even jumping up and down. Then they made it to a big room and the camera turned toward the bride.

Young Mom was sitting on a big white chair, looking beautiful in her pretty white dress. She looked like a princess. Seated on either side of her were both of my grandmothers in dark blue dresses. They looked so different back then!

Joel must have been thinking the same thing that I was. "Grandma! Your hair was so much longer than it is now!"

"And much, much darker." Grandma said, running her fingers through her now chin-length silvery-white hair.

"Look at Bubby Miller!" Jeremy called out, showing some excitement for the first time since we started watching the video. Bubby and Zayde are our mother's parents. They live in Florida. The names Bubby and Zayde mean Grandma and Grandpa in Yiddish. In the video Bubby was sitting on Mom's other side. "She kinda looks like one of the teachers at my school."

"She doesn't look so grandmother-y," I said.

Mom laughed. "Maybe that's because she wasn't a grandmother yet!"

Uncle David paused the video again.

"Okay, everyone. Here comes the bedeken that we promised you." Then he turned to Joel, "Let me know if you find a chicken in here!" And he winked at him as he hit "play."

As the video started again, the camera shifted to a man playing a very bouncy, happy tune on the trumpet as the mass of people surrounding Dad all moved together like a big ball as they entered the room and moved in blob formation toward Mom.

"You kind of look like the nucleus of an atom, Dad, and they're all a bunch of electrons orbiting around you!" said Joel, my science-loving brother.

"Hmm, I never thought of it like that, but yeah, I can see it!" Dad said, clearly enjoying this trip down memory lane.

As the group neared the big fancy chair, the people in the front stepped back and cleared a path so Dad and Mom could see each other. It made me feel like Dad was Moses walking through the Red Sea as it split into two sides.

"This was the first time we'd seen each other in a week!" Mom gushed. "It was an incredible moment. You see, this is why we wanted to be in separate rooms to start."

"And this is why we're also not going to see each other for a week," Aunt Rachel jumped in. "All for this moment!

Young Mom was beaming, sitting on that big white chair with a huge smile on her face, her eyes locked on Dad's. Both grandmothers were wiping their eyes delicately with little white handkerchiefs. Our two grandfathers were on either side of Dad and then along came a rabbi I didn't recognize.

"Hey, that's not Rabbi Green!" I pointed out.

"No, he was probably still in school and wasn't even a rabbi yet. Plus, we didn't know him then," Mom explained. "We had our wedding at the synagogue where I grew up, not Ohav Zedek. That's Rabbi Shapiro."

The music kept playing while Young Dad walked up to Young Mom and whispered something in her ear and they both laughed. He kissed her on the cheek, put the veil over her face, then stepped backwards, never taking his eyes off her. It was kind of a mushy romance, but much to my surprise, I loved watching it! It was so much fun to see a young version of my parents looking and acting so differently than they do at home. Sure, they smile and laugh a lot, and every now and then I even catch them holding hands, but I'd never seen them as happy as they looked in that video. And in Mom's case, I'd never seen her quite so bouncy! She was bouncing along with the music, right there in her seat.

Next the rabbi put his hands over Mom's head and

she stopped moving and sat still with her head slightly bowed. He recited a blessing or something. When he was done, he stepped away, and Mom looked at Dad and started bouncing in her seat to the music again. Then she stood up, took Dad's hands and the two of them started dancing right there in front of the chair and in front of all of the other people. Before long, all of their friends made a big circle and they danced and sang around the two of them. Then another circle formed and then another until finally the rabbi called out, "Hold on! They're not married yet! Let's go make a wedding—then we'll dance!" At that point the crowd scattered, Mom and Dad let go of each other's hands and the atom blob closed in around Dad and danced him back out of the room.

"By the way," Uncle David said to us as he paused the video, "I've never seen a bride get up from her chair like that and join in the festivities. Just so you know, that's not the way it usually works!"

Mom piped up, "Why should I be left out of the fun? It was the happiest day of my life. I couldn't just sit there!"

"Ahem," Joel cleared his throat.

"Yeah, yeah, having you guys was pretty great too!" Mom responded. "But at that point, that was the happiest day of my life."

Uncle David said, "So, that's the tisch and the bedeken. Any questions?"

"No, keep going!" I shouted out. I didn't want them to stop! This was so amazing. Why did I fight it for so long? I couldn't believe I'd never seen this video before. I decided that when we were home I was going to watch the whole thing from start to finish without skipping any parts, even if it did take three hours.

"Oh, don't worry," Uncle David said with an impish grin, "we'll keep going. The best part is yet to come."

How cool that I could "attend" my parents' wedding and my aunt and uncle's wedding all in the same week! I couldn't wait to see the best part that Uncle David was talking about!

I tossed a piece of popcorn into my mouth. I considered throwing one at Jeremy, but thought better of it, knowing that the consequences of starting up with him could be dangerous. Instead, I casually flung it at Joel and hit him in the face.

Just as he was about to get super-angry, I smiled at him.

"Just kidding, Little Bro!"

He lightly tossed a piece at me. "That's in retaliation for the one you threw." Then he threw a second one at me, "And that's for calling me Little Bro!"

I shrugged, picked up one piece of popcorn from my lap and then pulled the other one out of my hair and ate them both, smiling at my twin brother and waiting to see what was coming next in this awesome wedding video.

27

A Trip Down Memory Lane

Uncle David zipped ahead to the actual ceremony. The person taking the video panned the camera all around the room, so for a while we played the "Who Do You Recognize?" game. It was so much fun trying to see if we could recognize anyone. Some people, like our Mom's Uncle Jerry, looked exactly the same, but some looked so different that we couldn't even tell that it was them.

"Hey, there's Cousin Tzipi from Israel!" Joel called out.

"I see Grandma and Grandpa's friends, Mr. and Mrs. Solomon!" I yelled.

Finally the music started and the camera focused on the middle aisle. First, a little girl who was about three or four years old walked down in a fancy white dress, dropping red rose petals along the way.

"Who's that?" I asked.

"That's cousin Allison."

"No way! That's Allison? Allison who's in college now?"

"It is!" Mom said with her eyes glued to the TV screen.

When Allison made it to the end of the aisle she took the handle of the white basket that had been hanging on her arm and held it upside down over her head, dumping the remaining flower petals out of the basket, making them rain down all over her and the floor. First she jumped up and down in the pile of flowers like she was splashing in a puddle. Then she sat down right in the middle of the pile and started playing with the petals as if she was in a sandbox. On the video, we could hear everyone in the synagogue laughing. And of course, we all started laughing in Uncle David's living room. I guess the movie was kind of like a comedy!

"That," Dad said with a chuckle, "is *not* a traditional Jewish wedding custom!"

A woman in a pink dress, who I'm assuming was cousin Nina, Allison's mother, swooped in and picked Allison up from her play area. Allison started to wail. There was an audible "Awww," on the video. A few people in the living room let out a similar, "Awww!"

"You can plan and plan, but you never know what to expect at a wedding!" Mom said.

The next person to walk down the aisle was Mom's sister, Aunt Julie. She looked really young, too!

"How old was Aunt Julie there?" Joel asked.

"She was around twenty-eight, I guess," Mom answered. It was so weird to see her as a young adult. Then Aunt Rachel walked down the aisle.

"Whoa!" Jeremy called out.

"Is that you?" Samantha asked loudly. It took me a couple of seconds to process what had just happened. I looked over at her, surprised and shocked. I couldn't believe it! Shy, quiet Samantha was so caught up in the video that I guess she forgot for a minute about being so shy and actually spoke up in front of everyone!

"Yep," Aunt Rachel said smiling, "that's me! I was nineteen!"

"Whoa!" Jeremy called out again. "You were only

like six years older than I am now. That's so weird!"

Next, people started walking down two at a time. We knew almost everyone, except there were a couple of Mom and Dad's friends who I guess they don't really keep in touch with anymore because we didn't recognize them.

As people walked down the aisle, I noticed that no one came down holding the huppah and I remembered that Mom said that the one they had was free standing.

The bridesmaids came down the aisle, each paired up with one of Dad's buddies, who served as his ushers. Then Grandma Ruth and Grandpa Jack came down the aisle, each with one of their arms wrapped through Dad's arms. They walked together with smiles on their faces, but Grandma kept using her free hand to wipe her eyes with a little handkerchief. That thing must have gotten a lot of use that day! I looked over at present-day Grandma sitting on the couch, dabbing her eyes gently with a tissue in the exact same way that she was in the video. Some things never change!

"I can't believe we get to do this again next week!" Grandma said.

Finally, Young Mom came down the aisle with Bubby and Zayde.

"So what's the deal with Bubby and Zayde anyway?" Jeremy asked. Uncle David hit "pause." "Are they going to make it to the wedding?"

I knew what he was talking about, but Mom turned to the "other side of the family" to explain.

"My mother hasn't been feeling well, and unfortunately, the doctor told her that she probably shouldn't travel right now, so they aren't going to make it to the wedding. She's resting and getting better, and they absolutely plan to be here for Jay's bar mitzvah in February."

How sad! "I sure hope they're here for the bar mitz-vah!" I said.

"Me, too," said Jeremy.

"Okay, okay," Mom said, trying to lighten the mood. "No need to be such a downer at this happy occasion. Let's get back to the wedding."

Uncle David hit "play" again.

Young Mom was a beautiful, happy bride. She held her large bouquet of flowers in front of her, and Bubby and Zayde looped their arms through Mom's on either side. The people in the aisles all looked on with smiles as the three of them walked together toward the front of the room.

When they got to the front row of seats, Bubby and Zayde lifted Mom's veil enough to each plant a kiss on the cheek nearest to them, and then walked up to the bimah to take their places under the huppah with Grandma and Grandpa and the rest of the bridal party.

Dad walked down the steps from the bimah toward Mom. He had a big goofy smile on his face. In fact, he was so busy staring at Mom and looking ahead at her that he didn't notice the little white basket still sitting on the floor that Allison had left behind. Dad's foot must have gotten stuck in the handle of the basket or something because all of a sudden he went from standing and walking to being on his hands and knees on the floor right in front of Mom. There was a sudden loud gasp as if the congregation was all one voice. Even the music stopped. It was like a scene in a movie. For a moment, the room was totally silent, except for the sound of Allison singing *Mary Had a Little Lamb* somewhere in the background.

We sat there stunned, open-mouthed, waiting to

see what would happen next. I felt so bad for Dad. He must have been so embarrassed. I would have been mortified!

"That, too," Dad said while the video continued on, "is *not* a traditional Jewish wedding custom!" Well, if he'd been embarrassed then, he certainly didn't seem embarrassed anymore.

What a funny scene that was, Young Dad, on all fours on the floor looking like a dog about to bark, and Young Mom, holding her flowers in one hand and covering her mouth with the other. She bent down and reached her flower-free hand out to Dad, who took it and jumped up to his feet. He threw his arms up in the air like a gymnast who had just stuck the landing from the balance beam, faced the people in their seats, and sang out, "Ta-da!" At that moment, he bent over from his waist, practically folding himself in half and took a long, deep bow for the guests. Everyone in the video (and the living room) cheered.

Mom, meanwhile, had gone from shock to an all-out laugh attack. She was bent over in the other direction, facing the bimah, while Dad faced the congregation. Mom was laughing so hard that the flowers in her hand were shaking and petals were falling and joining the pile on the floor that Allison had left behind.

"Wait for it...," Aunt Rachel said.

"Wait for what?" I asked.

Aunt Rachel pointed at the screen. "Watch this."

While Mom stood in the aisle cracking up and Dad was dusting off his pants, Grandma Ruth came running down the stairs from the bimah waving her little white hankie in her hand. When she reached Mom, she stuck her hand under Mom's veil and started dabbing away.

We all looked over at Grandma Ruth in the living

room as she watched the video.

"What?" She said looking at each one of us. "I didn't want her mascara to run!"

We all laughed. Samantha's eyes were teary from all of her giggling.

"Oh my goodness! How did we not know about this comedic goldmine?" Joel asked, almost sounding insulted.

"We've been inviting you to our little viewing parties every year," Mom said. "And every year you've chosen not to watch!"

"You should have told us that it wasn't boring!" Jeremy hooted, "This is classic!"

"Yeah, well, you should trust your parents now and then!" Dad replied with a wry smile.

"See, I told you. You never know what to expect at a wedding," Mom said.

I put my hand on my hamsa, closed my eyes, and secretly wished that if the unexpected was going to happen next week, please let it be something good. And if it's not good, please let it not be my fault!

28

Life in the Fast Lane

We went back to watching the video. The musicians started playing again and Grandma hurried back up the steps, returning to the bimah to stand under the huppah next to Grandpa. I noticed once again that the huppah stood on its own, without anyone holding the poles. That was a nice way to do it because it wasn't crowded up there. But even still I was so happy that my aunt and uncle chose to give us that job.

Back in the aisle, Mom took a deep breath and Dad took her hand. The two of them looked at one another and laughed one more time before walking up the stairs together.

"Good thing you guys have a sense of humor!" I said.

"I guess that's where I get it from," Joel added.

Once they got to the bimah, the music did not stop. Instead it continued as Mom made seven circles around Dad.

"Please tell me you didn't trip over your dress!" I cried out.

"Nope," Mom said with a smile looking over at Dad. "Even though I was the one wearing the giant dress and the high heels, I was *not* the one who tripped that night!"

We watched Mom go around Dad with our two grandmothers holding up the end of the long train of her dress. Each time she passed Dad, the two of them smiled at each other. They seemed to be having a good time up there. I always thought a wedding would be very serious and dignified, but theirs was so much fun! I kind of wished I could have been there.

"We chose to go the old-fashioned, traditional route," Mom said. "It's traditional for the bride to make seven circles around the groom, but some people choose to only do three."

Dad added, "There are many ways to do it—or not!"

I looked over to see Aunt Rachel and Uncle David give each other an almost-secret smile. I remembered that circling was one of the details they had been arguing about. I guess they figured it out and came up with a solution, but they didn't share it with us.

Aunt Rachel looked down at her wristwatch and said to Uncle David, "Let's skip ahead. It's getting late and I need to go home and get to bed early tonight. I have a super-busy day tomorrow. They'll catch on to the rest when they see it next week."

Uncle David nodded and fast-forwarded to the final scene. "This is when the rabbi announces that they are now a married couple." Uncle David said. "You've probably all seen someone stomping on a glass at a wedding before, but it's a highlight, so let's watch it."

Rabbi Shapiro took a glass, wrapped it up in a napkin and put it down on the floor by Dad's foot. I assumed that the napkin was just there so that they didn't get glass all over the place. In the video, Dad lifted his leg way up high, bent at the knee and then he stomped on the glass.

"Mazel tov!" shouted everyone in the video, as well as Grandma Ruth in the living room.

Young Mom and Young Dad kissed under the huppah, gave each other a big hug, then went around hugging and kissing everyone else under the huppah, including the rabbi. And then they joyfully made their way back down the aisle, smiling, waving, and even high-fiving a few people in the aisles.

Aunt Rachel then explained, "The next thing that happens is the wedding couple gets a little time alone before joining the guests. It's called *yichud*, and during this time we'll get a chance to sit for a couple of minutes and have a few private moments before celebrating with everyone."

"And don't forget to eat!" Grandma added. "Remember what happened with you two?" she asked Mom and Dad.

"Of course," Mom said. "We didn't realize we'd be so busy during the wedding greeting people at the tables and dancing and celebrating that we'd hardly have any time to sit down and eat our meals—"

Grandma cut her off. "We made sure there was plenty of food waiting for them in the yichud room, but these two were so busy laughing and talking that they never ate any of the food in the room and then they never ate any of the food during the reception either."

"You missed a scrumptious Chicken Wellington," Grandpa Jack said. "I can still taste it now. Best I've ever had."

"See! There was a chicken!" Joel joked.

"But not a bad chicken!" Uncle David said. "Sounds like it was pretty good!"

"Truly outstanding!" Grandpa said with his eyes closed, looking like he had just finished the most delicious meal.

"It's true," Dad said. "We missed the food. And

worst of all is that I had been fasting that day. One custom that some people choose to take on is that they
fast on the day of the wedding."

Mom added, "Some people view the wedding day as
a personal Yom Kippur. It's a day for starting over fresh
and new, so they fast as a way to focus on the big life-
changing event that's about to take place."

"Did you fast too, Mom?" Joel asked.

"No, I get too sick from fasting. I didn't want to ruin our special day by being sick, so I opted to eat. Your
dad, on the other hand...."

"We were both hungry by the end of the wedding,
but I was SO hungry...." He put his hand by his mouth
as if he was telling us a juicy secret and added, "that on
our way to the hotel after the wedding, we stopped and
picked up a pizza to eat in our room."

Grandma crossed her arms and shook her head.
"All that money we spent on food at the wedding and
you ate pizza!" She was clearly still stinging from this,
even more than fifteen years later!

"Okay, okay, let's move on," Mom suggested, just
like before. Then to Aunt Rachel and Uncle David she
said, "Let this be a lesson to you two! Eat when you
can! Now, on to the fun stuff—the party!"

The band leader announced that Mom and Dad
were entering the room and the band started playing
some happy Jewish music. Everyone in the room stood
up, gathered around the entryway, and showered Mom
and Dad with confetti. It was so cool! They all made
their way to the dance floor and started dancing in circles around them.

"Do you know what this kind of dancing is called?"
Grandma asked the crowd, but then answered without
waiting for a response. "It's called a hora." I think we

all knew that.

We watched everyone dancing the hora for a while, but then Aunt Rachel asked Uncle David to hit "pause."

"I know this is so much fun to watch, but we're going to skip ahead to one particular part of the dancing that we want to show you. Then we're going to stop because David and I have a lot of things to do before I go home and we stop seeing each other for a whole week. It's not that we don't love having you here, but we're going to have to kick you out so we can get our stuff done."

"No!" Samantha and I cried out together. Once again I looked at her in disbelief, astonished by how bold she was being. But I understood where she was coming from. The video was so much fun to watch! Just like Samantha, I wanted to see every single minute of it.

Mom said, "Girls, if you want, maybe Samantha can come over sometime this week and you two can watch the whole video together. But let's be fair to the wedding couple. They have a huge week ahead of them. We don't want to overstay our welcome."

Samantha and I looked at each other and smiled.

"Yeah, let's do that!" I said. She nodded excitedly. Had you asked me just twenty-four hours earlier if I thought I'd ever be inviting Samantha over to hang out with me, the answer would have been "No way!" It truly seemed like the beginning of a cool friendship.

"Okay, here's the final thing we want to show you," Uncle David said. "You've all seen people being lifted in chairs before, right? Maybe you've even been lifted up yourselves."

Everyone nodded. Jeremy added, "I want to be lifted in a chair at my bar mitzvah party!"

"Noted," Uncle David said, winking at Jeremy. "Well, here's something that happens at some weddings that you may not have seen before. It's a custom to entertain the bride and groom as if they were the king and queen of the day. People may dance in front of them, put on silly hats, and so forth. Here, take a look."

In the video we could see Mom and Dad sitting in chairs in the middle of the circle, clapping to the music, surrounded by people who were doing all sorts of crazy things in front of them. Someone draped Hawaiian leis over their necks. Someone else came by and put a king's crown on Dad's head and a queen's crown on Mom's. Then someone else came along and switched them making Dad the Queen and Mom the King! I could see people laughing, pointing, and having a great time.

People danced around them in a big circle. Many people wore silly hats. We saw one woman wearing a firefighter hat, someone else with a big cowboy hat, and one person even joined the circle wearing a full gorilla suit!

"This looks like so much fun!" I called out. "I wish I could have been there!"

"Yeah, I can't believe you didn't invite us!" Joel joked.

We continued watching and saw different people going into the middle of the circle to entertain the wedding couple. Grandma and her two sisters did a kick line in front of them. Two women turned cartwheels, which was kind of funny since they were wearing dresses and fancy high-heeled shoes. Two guys got in the middle and pretended that they were in a bullfight. The first guy waved a napkin around like he was a matador and the other guy, the "bull," put his fingers up next to the sides of his head like they were horns and danced over to the waving napkin. When he got there, the matador guy whisked the napkin away and they started all over again. Many people in the circle didn't go into the middle, but stood on the side and waved streamers or blew bubbles. I'd never seen anything like that, not even at a kid's party, let alone at a grown-ups' wedding!

"So much fun!" I exclaimed again.

Then one guy wearing a black cape and a top hat got into the middle, waved a magic wand around and produced a paper bouquet of flowers that he presented to Mom. It made her laugh.

"We can do magic tricks?!" Joel asked excitedly.

"You bet!" Uncle David said, "Anything you want."

"Oh, I'm SO going to do a magic trick for you!"

"Can't wait!" Uncle David said, smiling.

And with that, he hit "stop" and ejected the disk from the video player.

"So there you have it," Aunt Rachel said. "Do you think you guys are ready for the big day next week?"

Ready? We were more than just ready. We were pumped! The week could not possibly go fast enough!

29

A Nightmare of a Wedding

I looked in the mirror of the synagogue bathroom and couldn't believe that I was really wearing the black dress and that the big day had actually arrived. I also couldn't believe that Mom allowed me to wear lip gloss! I never wear any sort of makeup, but Mom said that this was a very special day (as if I didn't already know that!) and so she took me to the store and let me pick out a light pink lip gloss. I thought I looked pretty good except for the dumb old cast on my arm.

The hair lady put my hair up in a fancy bun that morning. I fixed a stray strand that was sticking out and when I felt like I looked ready enough, I headed out to the lobby to find everyone.

Jeremy was standing outside of the sanctuary wearing his black suit and his blue, white and black bow tie that matched Joel's. He was holding a box of tissues and sneezing. "I don't know if it's allergies or a cold, but I can't stop," he said, punctuated by a loud "achoo!"

"I hope you're not sick," I said. "Mom was afraid of someone getting sick before the wedding."

Upon hearing her name, and as if coming out of thin air, Mom appeared and asked, "What's going on?" *How DOES she do that?*

"Nothing," we said in unison. "Nothing to worry about."

"Jeremy, why are you holding that?" she asked

pointing at the tissue box.

"I was feeling very emotional because of the big day," he said, hamming it up.

"Yeah, right!" she said.

Then he sneezed.

"Oh no!" Mom called out. "Are you getting sick? I was worried this might happen. I told you kids to take care of yourselves and to try to stay healthy!"

"I'm fine, Mom, I'm fine. What time are we taking the pictures?"

"Pictures will be in the sanctuary in about twenty minutes, assuming that the photographer actually gets here. I can't believe she's so late! We're trying to keep Aunt Rachel distracted so she won't worry. In the meantime, she wants the four of you to go in and practice walking down the aisle, but maybe you," she said to Jeremy, "should go lie down for a little while instead." Mom reached over to feel his forehead. "You feel a bit warm."

"Nah, I'm okay," he said, followed by a loud sneeze. "I'll rest later."

"If you think you're up for it I'll help you guys with the rehearsal," Mom said. "YaYa, please go find the other kids and I'll meet you in the sanctuary in five minutes. After we're done you can go lie down for a little while, Jay. We'll do all the pictures that you're not in first. Then we'll come and get you."

Grandma called Mom over, and when she walked away Jeremy said to me, "I don't know if I'll be able to hold up the huppah like this. I can't stop sneezing!" He blew his nose.

"Not only that, but you're starting to look like Rudolph the Red Nosed Reindeer," I said pointing at his face. Jeremy was not looking so great. Along with his red, runny nose, his eyes were kind of puffy and watery, and his voice was taking on that stuffed-up sound.

"I do want to go lie down," he said. "But first let's do this practice thing and get it over with."

I went into the social hall where most of the people were hanging out at the not-yet-made up tables around the room, sitting, talking, and waiting for the photographer. I found Joel and Samantha and asked them to join us.

The huppah was resting against the back wall of the sanctuary like a cowboy leaning casually against a saloon saying, "What took you so long, partner?"

"Hold on!" I called out nervously, "I thought we weren't going to walk with the huppah. I thought it was going to be waiting for us up on the bimah!"

"Change of plans, I guess," Mom said nonchalantly. "You'll be fine, don't worry."

But I was worried. What if Samantha's shyness took over and she freaked out, dropped the pole and ran out of the room? My mind wandered to all sorts of disastrous scenarios. This was not good. I thought we had it all worked out. What changed?

The four of us each took a pole. We lined ourselves up so that Jeremy and Samantha would walk down first because that way Samantha would end up hidden behind everyone else on the bimah. Joel and I walked behind them.

"Let's try to step together at the same time," Joel suggested. "Let's all start on the right foot."

"Good idea," Mom agreed. "Jeremy, you should lead since you're going first."

Jeremy nodded, pleased with this responsibility.

"Walk slowly," Mom instructed. "This isn't a race."

We all started walking as Joel whispered, "Right, left, right, left," like a very quiet army sergeant. I think he was saying it more for himself than for us, but I found it helpful.

The synagogue aisle never felt so long to me before. It felt like the bimah was miles away and it was taking an hour to get up there.

Samantha was so nervous that her pole was shaking. I was mostly looking down at my feet, making sure I was in sync with everyone else. Right, left, right, left.

Then it all went downhill.

Jeremy sneezed such a huge sneeze that he dropped his pole, which Samantha tripped over, which made her fall onto her knees. Joel and I were so focused on watching our feet, that we didn't see her fall. Joel then tumbled right over Samantha. I let go of my pole out of sheer instinct but Joel hung on to his and rolled right over Samantha taking his end of the huppah with him. The huppah covered the two of them and they ended up wound inside the cloth like a sushi roll.

Mom came running down the aisle to rescue and untangle them. If it hadn't been such a disaster it might have been the funniest thing I ever saw in my life.

"Are you guys okay?" I asked Joel and Samantha as their heads emerged from the huppah-roll.

"Yeah," Joel answered. Samantha just nodded.

"Is the huppah okay?" Mom asked in a concerned voice.

Joel and Samantha climbed out of the huppah and we all checked it. There was a rip on the seam between two of the squares that were quilted together.

"Oh no!" Mom cried out while examining the tear. "Well, at least it's right on the seam. I think I can fix this, not that I have much time, but I think I can handle this. I have a little sewing kit in my purse. YoYo, can you please go get my purse for me?"

Joel ran out of the room while Jeremy sneezed again. And again.

I felt both terrible that the beautiful huppah had ripped but also a little relieved that I wasn't the one responsible for the accident this time.

Joel came trotting back into the room with Mom's purse.

"All right kids," Mom said, "I think you get the idea of how to carry it down the aisle. Jeremy, go to the lounge for a few minutes and get some rest while I fix this."

Jeremy obediently followed Mom's orders and left the room to the sound of his nose blowing like a horn.

This rehearsal did not boost my confidence one bit. I did not feel ready at all for this job. All I could do was hope that we wouldn't make a mess out of everything.

Little did I know what was yet to come....

30

Nightmare on Chelm Street

We walked out of the sanctuary, and sitting right outside the doors was a little round table covered with a white tablecloth. On it was a small white basket filled with wedding programs that said, "Wedding of Rachel Silver and David Resnick." I took a program out of the basket and opened it up. It was so exciting to see my name printed right in there.

Huppah Holders: Samantha Adler, Ellie Silver, Jeremy Silver, and Joel Silver.

I felt like a movie star, like my name was in the credits scrolling across the screen at the end of a movie. I never felt so proud in my life!

Aunt Rachel appeared in her gorgeous white dress. Everything about her was stunning. Maybe I felt like a movie star because my name was in the program, but she actually looked like one. I ran over and hugged her.

"You look so beautiful, Aunt Rachel!" I gushed.

"Thanks, YaYa! So do you," she replied with a huge smile. She looked so happy. I was glad to see her looking that way. I guess all the fighting that she and Uncle David had done was long in the past, just like Mom said it would be.

She looked around the lobby, her mind seeming to be somewhere else. When her friend Leslie walked by, Aunt Rachel asked, "Is the photographer here yet? We're supposed to be taking pictures already."

Leslie shook her head no and said, "I'll go see if I can find out what's going on," and she turned to go to the social hall.

I tried to distract the worried bride. "Look!" I said holding up the booklet. "My name is in the program!"

Aunt Rachel laughed. "I know that, silly! I put it there."

We giggled together for a minute but then she let out a shriek even louder than when I broke my arm.

"OH MY GOD! NO!"

I didn't know what she was screaming about. A typo in the program? The photographer not showing up? Neither situation seemed worthy of such a huge reaction.

And then I saw it. I saw it and then I screamed along with my aunt. "NO!" We both kept on screaming like we were in the middle of a terrible, scary horror movie.

There were four bright red dots on the train of her dress, right where I was standing. It looked like fresh blood. Where on earth did that come from? Oh my goodness, her beautiful movie star wedding dress was ruined!

Then her nightmare turned into my own nightmare when I looked down and saw the matching red color on the program that I was holding. And worse, it was on my finger. As it became clear to me what had happened, I felt like I was going to throw up. I had gotten a paper cut from the program and I was bleeding. I didn't even feel it happening, but apparently my finger was dripping bright red blood.

Aunt Rachel's eyes filled with tears, which made her mascara run, which made her look like she had raccoon eyes with dark blackish brown rings around them. I stood there feeling useless. I remembered seeing a tissue box on the counter in the bathroom, so I ran back there and grabbed the box and darted back to the scene of the crime. I handed a tissue to Aunt Rachel and pulled one out for myself to clean up my hand and try to stop the bleeding.

Aunt Rachel nodded as if to say thank you, then reached over to the box to pull out another six or seven tissues. She simultaneously blotted the makeup under her right eye with one tissue in one hand, while blowing her nose with the other.

"MOM!" she called out, "DEB! HELP!"

"What happened?" my mother called out from across the room as she ran toward us with the sewing kit still in her hand. All the bridesmaids came wobble-running in their high heels, hiking up their long gowns so that they wouldn't trip on them. Steve the Bridesman didn't have to worry about that. He sprinted over to Aunt Rachel.

Grandma scurried right behind them. "What's with all the screaming?" she asked, panting.

"Look! My dress!" Aunt Rachel pointed at the red spots, unable to get any other words out. She started sobbing and breathing heavily.

I wanted to crawl under the carpet. I RUINED MY AUNT'S WEDDING DRESS! I'd never felt so awful in my whole entire life. I thought it was bad when I almost ruined the ketubah, but this felt even worse. Aunt Rachel had been dreaming of this day her entire life. Heck, *I'd* been dreaming of this day for *my* entire life. And in that dream, everything was perfect from the dress to the flowers to the Chicken Wellington (which, to be honest, I'd never heard of until Grandpa mentioned it the other night, but still...).

Mom gasped when she saw the blood. "Oh no! What happened?" But before anyone could say anything, I followed her gaze as she looked over to my hand, which was now wrapped in a blood-soaked tissue.

"YaYa! Are you okay? What happened here?" Mom squeaked.

"Paper cut," I croaked, holding up the blood-stained program to show her.

"That's an awful lot of blood from a paper cut!" Mom exclaimed.

And then, as Aunt Rachel stood there like a statue, all of her friends started twittering like a pack of parakeets and buzzing all around her. It sounded like they were screeching orders at one another, but somehow in all that chatter and chaos they must have made a plan because suddenly they scattered and went into action like the little forest animals in Snow White's cottage. They came back almost in formation, with paper towels from the kitchen, club soda from the bar, and flowers from a vase in the social hall. They huddled around the back of Aunt Rachel's dress, and all I could see was a mound of blue dresses and one black tuxedo surrounding Aunt Rachel from her knees down. Mom and Grandma stood in front of her trying to calm her down, and Grandma, just as she did for Mom at her wedding, patted under Aunt Rachel's eyes and tried to clean the makeup that was all over her face.

"You didn't use waterproof mascara?" Grandma asked sounding both upset and annoyed. "It's smearing."

This only made Aunt Rachel cry even more. What a mess!

I took a step back and watched the scene in horror,

knowing that this was all my fault. I didn't want to stick around. I didn't know what I could do to help and worried that if I stayed I might make things worse. The woodland-creature bridesmaids and bridesman seemed to have everything under control and I wanted to believe that they would fix Aunt Rachel's dress the same way that the birds and mice put Cinderella's dress together. I've heard people talk about "fairytale weddings," but I was sure that this was not what they meant.

Should I stay? Was I going to ruin the whole wedding? I didn't know what to do but I knew that I couldn't handle watching the disaster I had created. After all the months of planning and preparation was I going to be the one who brought the whole event crashing down? I decided to run back to the bathroom to hide.

During my escape, I saw Uncle David, looking very handsome in his black tuxedo, standing and talking with Rabbi Green in the hallway. Uncle David was showing him the wedding rings that he and Aunt Rachel would be giving each other under the huppah. It was clear that the two men had no idea about the chaos going on in the other room.

I didn't stop to talk or even say hello, which I know was rude, but I had to get myself into that bathroom and out of the way.

Well, that was the plan, anyway.

Uncle David saw me coming and turned around with his arms wide open. "Hey, gorgeous!" he said. "How's my super huppah holder doing today?"

Under normal circumstances I would have run straight into his arms for one of my favorite Uncle David bear hugs. I especially love it when he hugs me so big that he lifts me off the ground and sometimes even spins me around. But these were not normal circumstances and I didn't feel like hugging anyone, so instead I raced past him.

As I ran by, I accidentally bumped into his outstretched hand. Somehow I managed to inflate the nightmare even more because when I bumped into him, I knocked the box out of his hand and the wedding rings went flying.

Of course I should have stayed to help look for the rings, which were lost in the patterned carpeting. Of course I should have stayed to say I was sorry. But I did neither of those things. Instead, I continued running and crying all the way to the bathroom. I pushed the door open with my good hand, which made it slam into the wall, making a loud THWACK. I leaned over the sink, trying to catch my breath. Trying to stop the sobbing.

I'll just stay in here for the rest of the night. That way I won't cause any more trouble, I thought. *And why isn't my hamsa working? I even wore it over my fancy black dress. It was supposed to make everything better.*

When I finally looked up into the mirror I noticed something terrible! My hamsa! It was gone! No wonder everything was falling apart. The evil eye was back and it was doing everything in its power to ruin this wedding. Well, there was no way I was going to let that happen. I had to go back out there and find it.

So even though I had planned to hide out in the bathroom for the rest of my life, I decided to take matters into my own hand, as it were, and find the hamsa and put it to work again.

I yanked the door open and ran back out into the hallway, where Uncle David and Rabbi Green were on their hands and knees, crawling around on the carpet still looking and feeling around for the rings. The bridesmaids were still huddled around the bottom of Aunt Rachel's dress and Aunt Rachel was still shaking and crying as Grandma dabbed her eyes and Mom tried to comfort her. What a mess I made! I had to find that glove!

I looked frantically all around the synagogue. I traced my steps to every single place I had walked through or stood in. I scoured the floor looking for my hamsa. When I couldn't find it, I went outside in my short-sleeved dress. I didn't have a jacket and it was really cold out. I looked all around from the top step of the entrance and thought I spotted something red against the gray concrete of the parking lot. Could it be the string on my hamsa-glove? I rushed toward it. I quickened my pace from a slow jog to a trot to an all-out sprint. It *was* my glove! I raced toward it. Then, when I was only a matter of inches away from it, I tripped on something. I don't know what it was, but I felt myself falling.

Oh no! Not again! This can't be happening again! IT CANNOT BE HAPPENING AGAIN!

And when I landed on my arm, I screamed louder than ever before.

31

It's All Starting
to Make Sense Now

I screamed so loudly that it made me sit straight up. My hair was soaking wet and I was out of breath, as if I'd just stepped out of a swimming pool after doing a hundred laps. My damp pajamas were sticking to my body. I opened my eyes and looked around.

I was in my bed.

In my bedroom.

In my house.

Wait, what?

I touched my hand to my sheets and they, too, were damp. I felt a surge of panic. I bent over and took a whiff. Thank goodness it didn't smell. It was just sweat.

I looked down at my chest and the eye of my hamsa-glove was looking up at me. If it could have winked, I bet it would have.

It was a dream? Was that really all just a terrible dream?

I lifted the t-shirt that was draped over the alarm clock on my nightstand. Sure enough, it was only seven o'clock in the morning and the wedding was still hours away. Suddenly it all started to compute.

I still had my hamsa!

Joel and Samantha didn't get tangled up in the huppah!

The huppah didn't rip!
I didn't stain Aunt Rachel's dress!
I didn't knock the rings out of Uncle David's hand!
My arm wasn't throbbing!
I DIDN'T RUIN THE WEDDING!
(At least not yet, anyway....)

I couldn't believe it! I was so excited that I jumped out of bed and ran over to my calendar to make sure. Yes! Each of the other days had a big X in the box, but this one had a big red heart around the box. It was wedding day! Finally! And all the awful things that had felt so real only moments ago were just in my head!

I leaped over all the obstacles on the floor as I ran over to my closet to look at my beautiful black dress. It was hanging there, unworn, unspoiled, just waiting to be put on. I opened my door quietly so as not to wake the others, and tiptoed quickly through the hallway to the stairs. I flew down the steps to the entryway where I saw the ketubah leaning against the front door, wrapped in plastic, all ready for the wedding.

I skipped into the kitchen, where I found Mom and Dad sitting at the table, reading. Each had a cup of coffee. Dad was reading a newspaper. He's probably one of the only people left on the planet who still gets a newspaper delivered, but he says he still likes the feel of the paper, the crinkle of the pages when he turns them, and even the smell of the ink. He feels the same way about books, which I guess makes sense since he owns a bookstore. Mom was reading something on her phone.

"Hi, guys!" I sang cheerily. "I didn't realize you were up already."

"Hey, sweetie!" Dad said, "You're up early, too."

"A little excited?" Mom said with a huge smile.

"I can't believe the wedding is today! It's really, really today! And I have a feeling it's going to be an awesome day!" I said patting my hamsa.

Mom's smile faded a little.

"YaYa, you're not actually planning to wear that glove to the wedding, are you?"

Dad whispered out of the side of his mouth to Mom, "Why is she wearing a glove around her neck?"

Mom replied, "She's been wearing it all week. You haven't noticed?"

Dad shrugged.

She waved him away as if to say, "I'll tell you later." Dad shrugged again and hid behind his newspaper.

"Are you kidding me? I *have* to wear my hamsa! It's my obligation, my duty! If I don't, the whole wedding could fall apart. I could get blood on Aunt Rachel's dress! Jeremy might have a sneezing attack! Uncle David could lose the rings! Aunt Rachel might get raccoon eyes! Joel and Samantha could become a sushi roll! You bet I'm going to wear it!"

Mom stared at me. Dad lowered the newspaper and looked at me like I had just announced that I was only going to wear cereal boxes for clothes from now on.

"What?" they both said at the same time.

"I need to wear it to keep the bad luck away," I explained simply.

"Well, Little Miss Raincloud. I guess we can't say that you don't have a vivid imagination," Mom said.

"Sure, okay," I said, wanting to end the conversation already without having an argument with my mom. I simply knew that I had to wear it. End of story.

"Are you sure Aunt Rachel won't mind?" Mom asked.

"Mind?" I exclaimed. "She'll thank me! I'm saving

her doomed wedding with this thing! Kenahora!"

Mom and Dad looked at one another and I could see that they were both trying to hold back from laughing.

"Kenahora? Who are you? Grandma?" Mom asked with a chuckle.

"All right, honey," Dad said. "You should do whatever you think is best." And up went the newspaper.

They thought I was being silly. I knew that. But it didn't matter because I knew what I was doing, even if they didn't believe me. Even if they didn't understand.

I opened the refrigerator door, leaned in, and with my head up against the milk carton said a quiet, "ptu, ptu, ptu" before removing the orange juice container. I poured myself a glass, drank it and announced that I was going to go upstairs to get ready.

"Ready for what?" Dad asked.

"The wedding!" I answered.

"But we don't need to be there for almost six hours!" Mom said.

"That's okay," I replied as I walked out of the kitchen. "I need to take a shower."

"Your hair is so damp, I thought you just came out of the shower," Mom responded.

"Nope, just a busy night," I answered over my shoulder as I left the kitchen. I could totally picture my parents looking at each other, shrugging their shoulders and returning to their reading and coffee sipping.

I went back into my room to start getting ready. I was planning to lay out all of my clothes so everything would be waiting for me when I got out of the shower. I pulled my dress out of the closet and laid it out on my bed. Then I looked for the tights that Mom had bought for me to wear with the dress. But I couldn't find them!

I dove into Laundry Mountain since that's where most of my clothes seemed to be. In my search, I completely mixed up the clean and dirty clothes that were already hanging out together on the floor. No tights.

No big deal, I thought, *they've got to be here somewhere.*

Next, I calmly opened my sock and underwear drawer, which is where they probably should have been. *Maybe Mom put them away. Or maybe I did it and don't remember.* Nope, not in there.

I opened my t-shirt drawer. Uh oh, not in there either. With each drawer I went through, panic began to grow within me. I yanked out more and more clothes until I got to the last drawer. It was official. I was freaking out. I was tossing my clothes in the air in panic causing a blizzard of pajamas, shorts, and sweaters to fill the room.

I turned around to see Joel standing in my doorway with a pair of Levi's on his head, the pants legs hanging down over his shoulders like long, flowing, denim hair.

"What's going on, YaYa?" he asked pretty calmly for someone who just had a pair of jeans land on his head.

"I can't find my new tights! I need them for the wedding! They're not anywhere!" I shouted, my voice shaky.

"Can't you just buy another pair before the wedding? We have a few hours." Joel asked.

"I guess so," I answered, calming down a little, "but it took Mom a while to find them online. They were fancy and matched my dress and were super special for the wedding. I have to find them."

"You want some help?" Joel offered.

I wondered if he was setting me up for yet another one of his practical jokes, or if he was actually, honestly and truly being nice. Come to think of it, he hadn't played any tricks on me in the past couple of weeks. He had promised to stop, *but sometimes habits are hard to break,* I considered as I gazed around my room, which looked like the aftermath of a clothing-volcano eruption. I remained hopeful that he really was being sincere and wanted to help.

"Really?"

"Sure," he answered.

"That would be great! Let me just put on some searching music," I said as I blasted my new favorite Corey song, *Cute Monkey Wrench.* I turned around in time to see Joel rolling his eyes as he stepped further into my room. He has no patience for Corey or his music.

Anyway, since he was so busy rolling his eyes, he wasn't looking down, and he tripped over an ice skate that was propped up against a soccer ball that happened to be in the middle of the floor. He landed in a tangle among the myriad of treasures covering my carpet. His arm was wrapped under his body.

"Oh no!" I cried out. "Are you okay?" I didn't wait for a response. "Is your arm okay? Is it broken?" That would be a most unfortunate coincidence.

In typical Joel fashion, he looked up at me from the floor and said, "My arm is fine, but yours needs about twenty bucks."

"Huh?"

"Your arm needs twenty bucks. Because it's broke!" Okay, I actually did laugh at that one.

32

Buh-Bye, Evil Eye

It was a little spooky, like déjà vu. There I was, in the synagogue bathroom, looking into the mirror just like in my dream. I pinched my cheek to see if I could feel it, to see if this was real or another dream. *Oh yeah, I could feel that!* It was definitely real. And now I had a little red mark on my face to prove it.

I was wearing my black dress with the short sleeves and my fancy tights (which LuLu had somehow swiped from my room and I found hidden under a towel in her crate!). The light pink lip gloss made me look almost grown up. (Mom really did take me to the store and let me get some—that part was real.) And just like in my dream, I thought I looked pretty good except for the grungy green cast on my arm. The red string that Megan had tied on for me was still there over the cast, but it too, was looking a bit darker and well-worn. And unlike in my dream, I had my chasing-away-the-Ayin-Hara hamsa hanging down over my dress. I wondered if Aunt Rachel was going to wear hers. Probably not, but maybe Samantha would wear hers and so we'd have double protection for the day.

It was kind of cool, actually. It was like getting a real-life do-over. I mean, my dream felt so real, but everything had gone wrong. I was living out the exact same scenario, but now I had the chance to do it right.

I skipped out of the bathroom and headed to the

lobby where the photographer was snapping away, picture after picture in different combinations: Aunt Rachel on her own, Aunt Rachel with Grandma and Grandpa, Aunt Rachel with her bridesmaids and bridesman. At first I worried because Uncle David was nowhere to be seen and I thought back to the whole scene when they were late for their aufruf. Then I remembered that Aunt Rachel had told us they were going to sneak away and do their pictures together after the wedding ceremony because they weren't going to see one another until the bedeken. In fact, they hadn't seen each other since the movie night at Uncle David's apartment and that was a whole week ago!

At the photo shoot, there was a lady wearing a dark suit who, Mom explained to me, was called the Wedding Coordinator. Her name was Marilyn and she was there to make sure that things ran smoothly. After each picture, she fussed with Aunt Rachel's dress, fixed her hair, and made sure everyone was where they needed to be. While the pictures were being taken she called out orders to all the men and women who were working at the wedding.

"Joey, do you have enough ice in the bar?"

"Sue, start putting the tablecloths on the tables!"

I was fascinated by all the action. As I stood and watched, Samantha snuck up next to me from behind. She tapped me on the shoulder and waved to say hi when I turned around.

"You wore it!" I shouted out, excitedly pointing at her purple hamsa-glove. "You're the best, kenahora!"

"Yeah, I did," my almost-cousin replied. "But who's Kenny Hora?"

I giggled and said, "Never mind that. I'm so glad you wore yours too."

I turned my face and secretly did a ptu, ptu, ptu on behalf of both of us.

Samantha and I stood off to the side watching the photographer give directions to the beautiful bride as she posed for the camera, sometimes alone and sometimes with other people.

"I'd like to take a picture with my huppah holders," Aunt Rachel said to the photographer.

"Sure. Are they all here?" she asked letting her camera dangle by the strap that hung from her neck.

"I'll go get the boys," Mom offered, and left to find them.

Aunt Rachel came over and gave each of us a big hug.

"You look amazing!" Samantha said, gazing at her as if she were one of the Seven Wonders of the World. Aunt Rachel naturally glows and looks healthy without ever needing any help. On this special occasion she wore a little bit of wedding-day makeup and her light brown hair was put up in a fancy bun, covered by a white see-through veil. She was as perfect as one of Mom's masterpieces.

"You do!" I agreed. "You look amazing! You're such a beautiful bride!"

"Aw, thanks, you guys! You're making me blush! And aren't you the stunning huppah holders! Hey, come here for a minute." We followed her to a little round table that was right outside of the sanctuary. Just like in my dream, there was a white basket sitting on the table, filled with programs. I didn't go near them! It felt way too familiar. In fact I even took one small step backwards.

She reached into the basket, and from underneath the pile of programs, she pulled out two small wrapped boxes that she must have hidden in there earlier. She handed one to each of us.

"Wait, why are you giving *us* presents?" I asked, confused. "I thought this was your wedding! *You're* the one who's supposed to be getting the gifts!"

"I wanted to thank you two for playing such an important part in our wedding. It's just a little something to show you my appreciation."

"Being a huppah holder is the best present ever!" I said excitedly. "You didn't have to get us anything else." But honestly, as I held the little box in my hand I couldn't wait to see what was inside. I love presents. I mean, come on, who doesn't?

"I know, but I wanted to," she said sweetly. "I think you'll like them."

"Should we open them now?" Samantha asked.

"Yes, please do!" Aunt Rachel said, smiling. "And don't worry, I have something for the boys, too."

Being that I was all dolled up in a fancy dress, with my fancy tights and a fancy hairdo, I figured that I should try to act dignified and mature. I attempted to open the box slowly and delicately by gently running my fingernail under the tape. But the tape was so strong that the only thing I was successful at doing was chipping the shiny pink polish on my freshly manicured nail. In the end, I tore into it like a tiger tearing into its lunch.

Samantha and I opened our gifts at the same time. Inside the wrapping paper was the kind of tiny box that holds earrings or a necklace or a fancy, sparkling ring. I lifted the top and removed the foam that was under the cover."

"Oh! It's beautiful!" I cried.

"This is gorgeous!" Samantha exclaimed.

"I thought you might like to wear them today." Aunt Rachel said.

I gently lifted the delicate silver chain from the box and looked at the beautiful, dainty, silver hamsa charm dangling at the bottom of the necklace. It was a shiny, silver hand. In the palm of the hand was an eye with a turquoise-colored stone right in the middle. Samantha got a matching one, just like mine.

Samantha and I looked at each other and shouted, "Yes!"

"Can you help us get them on?" I asked.

Aunt Rachel took the necklace from me and clasped it around my neck. Then she did the same for Samantha. I carefully slipped out of my red-stringed glove, making sure not to mess up the fancy hairdo that the hair lady gave me earlier, and Samantha slipped out of her pink-stringed one. I have to admit, the silver hamsa necklaces were a pretty good replacement for the homemade ones.

"Thank you so much, Aunt Rachel!" we said at the same time, and we both went in for a big, group hug.

"You're welcome, girls!"

We each stood on our tiptoes and kissed her on the cheek that was closest to us.

"Can we go look at ourselves in the mirror to see what they look like?" Samantha asked.

"Sure," Aunt Rachel answered, "but hurry back because we're going to take our huppah holder pictures as soon as the boys get here."

The two of us dashed off to the restroom, flung the door open and stood side by side facing the mirror.

"How cool is this?" Samantha asked.

"I know! These hamsas are so much lighter than the gloves! And they're so pretty, too!" I replied.

"Not only that," Samantha said. "I mean, they are beautiful, but how cool is it that we have matching ones? It's kind of like a friendship bracelet. I guess that means we're officially like real friends now!"

I stopped and thought for a moment about how only one week ago she would barely talk to me, but thanks to this adventure called "The Wedding," I was not only gaining an almost-cousin, but a real-life friend, too.

"Yeah, it's really cool," I said, looking at the two of us in our black dresses and matching hamsa necklaces in the mirror.

It seemed that the evil eye had bought a one-way ticket and jumped on the bus out of town.

Buh-bye, evil eye!

33

The Real Deal

After what felt like an eternity, we finally finished taking all of the family pictures. Well, the first batch, anyway. My cheek muscles already hurt from smiling so much. I thought back to the picture of Mom and Dad that was hanging in their bedroom, with their big, happy smiles, and wondered if their cheeks were as sore back then as mine were now.

It was almost time for the wedding to start! After all the weeks of preparation, after all the drama with the ketubah, the dresses, the arguing, the discussions, even my terrible nightmare, at last the big event was about to begin. Slowly but surely, cars started pulling into the parking lot and people filled the lobby of the shul.

Marilyn the Wedding Coordinator nodded to Grandma as if they had planned a secret code or something. Grandma nodded back and started shooing us out of the room.

"Come on, come on," Grandma urged us. "We need to be out of this room before the guests see us. We need to greet them in the other room."

"Where are we supposed to be?" Joel asked.

"You can either go into the library for the groom's tisch or you can come into the social hall for the bride's *kabbalat panim*, where we will be greeting guests, and people will be seeing our lovely bride for the first time," Mom explained. "At some weddings, men and women go to separate rooms, but at this wedding, everybody gets to choose."

"Well, except for the bride and groom," Joel added. Mom smiled.

"I'm going to the tisch," Jeremy announced.

"I'll go to the bride's thing," Joel said.

So Joel, Samantha, and I followed Grandma, Mom, Uncle David's mom, the bridesmaids, and Steve the bridesman into the social hall (which the Marilyn the Wedding Coordinator, who tried to make everything seem so fancy, now referred to as the "ballroom"). Even Uncle David's Nana hobbled along with her cane.

Aunt Rachel was already in the "ballroom" waiting for us. Her dress sparkled as she stood there in the middle of the big room. There were some shiny beads on the top half of her dress that caught the light from the chandeliers overhead and almost made it look like she had fireflies lighting up on her every time she moved.

She had the whole group of us huddle up like a football team and then she handed each of us a program. I momentarily flinched when I saw them, remembering the bloody disaster in my nightmare. I took one cautiously, careful to avoid getting a paper cut.

"These will explain everything that you're going to see tonight. I'm giving them to you in case you have any questions. In the meantime, for now, please stay right here and greet the guests as they enter."

Cool! I thought, *I'm going to be a huppah holder AND a greeter! A bonus job!*

Aunt Rachel continued.

"Now, I'm going to go behind that wall divider with my mom and David's mom. In a little while, the musicians will play a song and the three of us will come in and sit on those chairs over there for the kabbalat panim." She pointed to a big, white wicker chair on a platform that was right in front of the wall divider. On it were three smaller chairs on either side of the big white chair. She turned to Uncle David's grandmother. "Nana, do you want to sit here and wait or do you want to make a grand entrance with us? It's up to you."

"I'll come with you, darling!" Nana said to her soon-to-be granddaughter. She hooked her shaky hand into the crook of Aunt Rachel's arm and they walked together. We watched the four of them escape behind a wall divider just as the guests began to file into the room.

As the onslaught of grown-ups exploded into the room, a violinist and harpist started playing background music but I could hardly hear the music because people were greeting and hugging one another and making such a racket! I overheard things like: "Don't you look lovely?" "It's been so long!" "How are the kids?" I did my best to do my job and greet people, but honestly, they didn't need me. They were doing fine on their own, so instead I hung out with Joel and Samantha.

Men and women in tuxedos passed around yummy appetizer things. One lady came by with a tray full of something wrapped in pastry dough.

"Yum! I love pigs-in-a-blanket!" Samantha exclaimed.

"Pigs? What are you talking about? They don't serve pig in the synagogue!"

"No, no," she explained, "they're just called 'pigs-in-a-blanket.' They're cute, little, tiny hot dogs. They're delicious! You have to try one."

"Hot dogs? At a fancy wedding? How could I say no to that? I love hot dogs!" We each took one, dipped them into the little mustard cup that the lady had on her tray and popped them into our mouths.

"Oh my goodness!" I shouted out over the background music and the chatter. "These are awesome!"

"See, I told you," Samantha said, dabbing her mouth with a white mini-napkin.

"So good!" Joel said through a mouthful of hot dog. "We need more!"

But the lady with the pigs-in-the-blankets had walked away, and before we could catch her, a man came by with a tray of mini-eggrolls.

"Yes, please!" Joel said before the guy even offered them to us. I hadn't noticed how hungry I was but come to think of it, I hadn't eaten since breakfast. How did that happen?

We each reached over and took one.

"Yum!" we all crowed in unison.

Before long, the knish lady came by.

"I could get used to this!" I said, biting into one of the two delicious mini potato knishes I had taken.

"I'm going to track down the hot dog lady again," Joel announced.

"Me, too," Samantha said, following him.

I was going to join them, but a woman came up to me and introduced herself as a distant cousin, and before I knew it, more and more people that I didn't know began coming over to talk to me. They kept on asking me the same questions over and over again. I lost track of how many times I had to say things like:

"I'm Mark and Debbie's daughter."

"Joel is my twin brother, Jeremy's the older one."

"I tripped over something on the sidewalk and

broke it."

"It doesn't hurt too much."

"I'm in fifth grade."

"Yes, I'm very excited to have a new uncle."

"No, I haven't really given much thought to which college I want to go to." (Someone actually asked me that! Sheesh! I'm only eleven years old!)

Answering those questions was so boring, but I knew I had to be polite and answer them all—over and over and over again—no matter how annoying it was.

Then I was saved by the trumpet! One of the musician guys came out from behind the room divider, blowing his trumpet, followed by a clarinet player. Everyone turned and looked to see Aunt Rachel make her grand entrance followed by her entourage of mothers in fancy, sparkly dresses. Aunt Rachel helped Nana settle into her chair, then made her way to her royal white throne. I loved that even though this was her special day and she was the queen of the evening, she still took the time and the effort to take care of Uncle David's grandma. I sure do love that Aunt Rachel of mine!

The mothers of the couple sat down and the bridesmaids and bridesman took their places behind the chairs. People lined up and waited their turn to give each of the seated ladies a kiss or a hug and to say hello. Aunt Rachel was all smiles as she received each visitor. She really was like a queen holding court.

I was glad that all the grown-ups were now in line waiting to greet the bride so I could stop answering all those questions!

Joel and Samantha returned with a plate full of little dough-wrapped hot dogs. "Here, these are for all of us," Joel said offering me the plate and a napkin.

"Score!" I sang out happily.

The three of us contentedly stood in our own private little circle enjoying the pigs-in-a-blanket.

"Hey, what do you call a frozen frankfurter?" Joel asked out of the blue.

"I don't know. What?" Samantha said.

"A chili dog!"

Samantha let out a much-too-big laugh for such a corny joke. Uh oh. I remembered our time together at Uncle David's apartment on movie night and I knew where this was going. Of course, Joel took Samantha's positive reaction as an invitation to keep going.

"What do you call a poodle with a fever?"

Immediately I said, "Hot dog. It's a hot dog." It was such an obvious joke. I was not impressed.

"Yes!" Joel said, unfazed by my lack of enthusiasm.

Samantha laughed again, even louder and stronger than before. "Bah ha ha! A hot dog!" She almost spat out her own hot dog. I was starting to think that Samantha had a very warped sense of humor.

"Keep going," Samantha managed to say. "You're ON A ROLL!" The two of them pointed at each other and cracked up together. I stood there and enjoyed my pig-in-the-blanket, watching the two of them laugh until they had tears streaming down their faces. I just didn't get it.

"Okay," Joel continued, "what do you give a poodle with a fever?"

Samantha looked at him with great anticipation. I merely shrugged and popped another hot dog in my mouth. I didn't have very high expectations for this one either.

"Mustard—it's the best thing for a hot dog," he managed to say through his laughter.

Major groan.

Samantha was now doubled over laughing. I really liked her, but this was one side of her that I truly didn't understand. After enduring a few more of Joel's horrendous jokes I turned to the two of them and said, "I guess we don't need to say hello to the bride and her court since we've all been together all day long."

"That's true," Joel agreed. Samantha nodded. "Maybe we should go check out the tisch," Joel said. "Or should I say, 'the tissue.'" Of course Samantha giggled.

So the three of us wiped our mouths with our napkins to make sure we didn't have any mustard on our faces, and made our way out the door. On the way, we each swiped one last eggroll for the long trip to the library.

34

The Rowdy Tissue

The kabbalat panim was a nice, sophisticated gathering with people smiling, talking and greeting one another. The tisch in the library, on the other hand, was a completely different scene. We could hear the singing all the way down the hall, and as we got closer and closer to the library doors, the singing got louder and louder.

"That's one rowdy 'tissue'," Joel joked.

In the library we found Uncle David at the head of a long table. About twenty men and women sat around the table and even more stood behind them. Everyone in the room was singing and clapping, and those who were sitting were banging on the table. There wasn't any room at the table for us, so we joined the group of people standing behind the chairs.

People were yelling "l'chayim" like they did at shul, and drinking from small cups. There was a stack of larger, empty cups on the table, so Joel reached over and poured a ginger ale for each of the three of us. Every time the people yelled "l'chayim!" we each took a swig.

In between the singing, banging, and shouting, people randomly stood up to tell funny stories about Uncle David. He sat in his spot giggling, maybe even blushing a little, but mostly looking happier than I'd ever seen him. I've heard that sometimes people are nervous when they're getting married, but my aunt and uncle seemed nothing but thrilled. They were soaking it all in and enjoying every minute.

Jeremy stood up.

"I'm Jeremy."

"Hi, Jeremy!" everyone in the room said at once, as if it was rehearsed.

"David is my uncle. Well, almost. Rachel is my aunt. She's my dad's sister. I want to tell you the story about the time Uncle David lost me and my siblings on a bus...."

"Hey, wait a minute," Uncle David protested with a huge smile. "That was not only on me. Your Aunt Rachel was just as guilty as I was!"

"Yeah, but she's not here now, so I'm just going to embarrass you!" Jeremy replied, with an equally big smile on his face."

"L'chayim!" someone shouted, and everyone laughed and took another sip.

"Oh, great," Uncle David said, covering his eyes and shaking his head. "Here it comes!"

Joel and I giggled together, because we obviously knew this story!

"So, Uncle David and Aunt Rachel were supposed to take me and my brother and sister—" he pointed at us across the table. Joel and I waved. "—to the mall to see a movie one Sunday afternoon. We went on a bus."

"We had to transfer and take two buses," Joel interrupted.

"Right," Jeremy continued.

"Anyway, the two of them were so busy flirting and making eyes at each other that when it was time to get off the bus, they left and forgot about the three of us. We weren't paying attention, so we didn't notice at first that they weren't there, but then all of a sudden, right when the bus was pulling away from the curb we saw—"

"I saw!" Joel interrupted again.

"Hey, let me tell the story!" Jay protested. "Fine. Joel saw the two of them walking down the sidewalk, holding hands. The three of us banged on the windows, and when Uncle David looked up and saw us, he began yelling and chasing after the bus. We also yelled and shouted for the bus driver to stop. The driver pulled up to the next stop two blocks down and told us to wait at the front of the bus until Uncle David caught up with us. He was there in a matter of seconds, panting, and out of breath."

"He was all sweaty!" I added.

"Here's to Uncle David," Jeremy concluded. "I hope you'll do a better job with your own kids if you have them someday!" Everyone in the room laughed and raised their glasses.

"But may you always be so in love with your bride that you can't take your eyes off her," Grandpa added.

"L'chayim! L'chayim!" everyone cheered, and drank whatever they had in front of them. Joel, Samantha and I clinked our ginger ale cups together and took a sip.

After a few more embarrassing stories about Uncle David, he stood up, and just like Dad did in the wedding video we watched, attempted to share a d'var Torah. And just like in the video, every time he said something, people called out and interrupted him. Mostly people jumped in singing Hebrew songs related to words he was saying. My favorite was when he said something about, "So, you can see...," and someone began to sing the "Star Spangled Banner." "Oh say can you see?" And before long, everyone in the room was standing up, holding their hands over their chests, and belting out the national anthem like they were at a baseball game. It was awesome!

The moment the singing stopped, Rabbi Green looked down at his watch and said, "It's time to go see your bride!"

As everyone stood and got ready to go, Rabbi Green climbed up on a chair in his own unique style and bellowed for all in the room to hear, "As it is written in the book of Jeremiah, *'Od yishama b'arei yehudah uv'chutzot Yerushalayim. Kol sason v'kol simcha, kol hatan v'kol kallah.* Once again it will be heard in the cities of Judah and in the streets of Jerusalem. The voice of joy and the voice of gladness, the voice of the groom and the voice of the bride.' Let's go, everyone! To the bedeken!"

Joel leaned over to me and Samantha and said, "Woohoo! Time for the 'bad chicken!'" Once again, Samantha giggled.

Then, just as in Mom and Dad's wedding video, a circle of people formed around Uncle David with their arms around each other, and they started singing the song *"Od Yishama"* that Rabbi Green had just quoted. Uncle David was escorted out of the library and into the hallway. A saxophone player walked alongside the group and played the song we were singing. As we neared the social hall, the clarinet and the trumpet guys, who were already in the room, came over and joined in. Right as we were about to enter the "ballroom," some of Uncle David's friends actually lifted him up and put him on two of the men's shoulders. He was already so tall, and now he was super tall! He had to duck way down to get through the doorway!

People in the circle around him jumped and

bounced as they sang and shouted. Of course, Jeremy, Samantha, Joel, and I jumped and danced and sang along. They kept singing the same song over and over, so even though I didn't know it at first, I caught on.

It was the happiest, most joyful thing I had ever seen but then came the bedeken.

35

Secrets and Blessings

Just as our dancing circle around Uncle David arrived at the chairs on the platform where Aunt Rachel and the mothers were seated, the guys who had Uncle David up on their shoulders put him down, and everyone formed two lines facing one another. A couple of people put their arms up and held hands like they were making a roof, so the rest of us did the same, creating a tunnel for Uncle David to walk through. Jeremy and Joel held hands and Samantha and I held hands. When Uncle David reached our part of the tunnel he had to bend down low because we're so much shorter than he is.

As soon as he passed under our arms, the four of us kids ran up to the front so we could see everything. What a scene! Uncle David was clapping and smiling the biggest smile ever. Aunt Rachel also clapped, but stopped occasionally to wipe away a tear. Grandma passed her a tissue but Aunt Rachel didn't even notice. She kept her eyes fixed on her husband-to-be.

Uncle David went over to Aunt Rachel, put his hands on her shoulders, bent down and whispered something in her ear for a long while. She was looking down at her lap as he spoke to her and just kept nodding and smiling and nodding and smiling. Finally, he stopped his whispering and she said something quietly to him. They hugged and then Uncle David knelt down in front of Aunt Rachel who stood up and switched the kippah he was wearing for a fancy, white knit one. She fastened it onto his hair with a kippah clip and handed him the original one, which he tucked away in his pants pocket.

"What was that all about?" I whispered to Mom.

"That's what they agreed to do instead of Uncle David wearing a kittel," she answered. "They read about it in a book and thought it was a good compromise to end their disagreement. Wearing something white and pure was what mattered to him. He's also going to wear a white tallit during the ceremony."

I smiled a huge smile and felt warm all over. "I'm so glad they were able to come up with a solution that they're both happy with!"

"Me, too," Mom said with a nod.

"Shalom bayit!" I said happily. Then we went back to watching the action.

Uncle David stood up, reached behind Aunt Rachel, and brought the veil over her face. He then backed away from her and went over to Grandma and gave her a kiss, then went to his mom and his grandmother and gave each of them a kiss. In the meantime, Grandpa went up to Aunt Rachel, whispered something to her, kissed her forehead and backed away, too. Not to be left out, Grandma went over and whispered something to Aunt Rachel, and she giggled in response.

Finally, Rabbi Green took his turn and I guess blessed her or something. We couldn't hear what was going on because everyone was still singing and the band was still playing. When all of the secrets and blessings were done, the crowd closed in around Uncle David and started to sweep him away. It reminded me of a movie where a blob covers up everyone and everything in its way. But Uncle David popped up from the middle of this blob, once again sitting on someone's shoulders. Joel, Samantha, and I clapped and sang along, but we stayed with Aunt Rachel as the blob danced the groom all the way out of the room.

"What happens now?" Samantha asked.

I shrugged but remembered that Aunt Rachel had given us the programs so we would know what's going on. I opened mine up.

"Well, we're done with the kabbalat panim, the tisch, and the bedeken, so I guess the next thing up is the ketubah signing," I answered while looking at the program.

I was right. As Marilyn the Wedding Coordinator ushered the rest of the guests into the sanctuary to find seats, Aunt Rachel, the bridesmaids, Steve the bridesman, the groomsmen, and the rest of the immediate family stayed behind. On our way back to the library the most wonderful thought occurred to me. I turned to Samantha and Joel and whispered quietly, "Hey guys, did you notice that we haven't had a single mishap at this wedding yet?"

"Why are we whispering?" Joel whispered back.

"To be sure that the ayin hara doesn't hear us!" I answered indignantly, shocked that he didn't understand.

"You don't actually believe all that stuff, do you?" he asked, a little louder this time.

"Shhh! What's wrong with you?" I answered angrily. "What if I do? And more important, what if I'm right?"

"I just don't believe there's an evil spirit floating around that's out to get us, that's all. It seems kind of ridiculous to me," Joel said.

"But what if there is?" I persisted. "Shouldn't we

play it safe?" Then, when no one else was looking, I turned my back to everyone and spat onto my fingers three times while saying a quiet "Kenahora." Since I didn't have my handy-dandy washcloth with me, I discreetly wiped my wet fingers on my fancy black dress.

Joel must have seen me because I caught him rolling his eyes at me as he often does. At least he didn't say anything else on the subject.

Before we got to the library, I stopped to get a glass of water. I guess all those little hot dogs made me pretty thirsty.

In the library, Aunt Rachel and Uncle David were pointing to the ketubah and explaining all the secrets to Rabbi Green.

"And look!" I jumped in, "there's LuLu! Even she made it into the ketubah!"

Rabbi Green knew LuLu very well because we were with him when we found her during our class at the synagogue. He took good care of her and she absolutely loved him right away.

"This is phenomenal!" Rabbi Green raved. "Look at all that detail! I especially like all the little black dots in the flowers on the sides. It adds an interesting dimension to the colors." I almost spat out the water I had just sipped. I looked across the room at Mom who had a very pleased-with-herself look on her face. I started coughing as I choked on my water.

"Hey, hey, no food or drinks in here, please," Rabbi Green said. "We need to take the ketubah out of the frame so the witnesses can sign it. We don't want anything to spill on this beautiful piece of work."

That made me cough even harder. Little did he know there'd already been a disastrous spill on the artwork. Aunt Rachel, Uncle David, Mom, Dad, and my brothers all looked at me. I felt my ears get hot as embarrassment warmed up my whole body. Uncle David cleared his throat. Aunt Rachel let out a little chuckle and so did everyone else who knew about the terrible mishap.

"What?" Grandma asked. "What's going on here? What's so funny?"

"Nothing, Ma, nothing," Aunt Rachel assured her.

I stepped out of the room to set my glass of water down as Rabbi Green had requested. When I came back inside, Rabbi Green was carefully removing the ketubah from the temporary plastic frame, like a surgeon removing an appendix. Mom had explained that the temporary frame protects a ketubah until it is framed nicely after the ceremony.

Just as Mom had promised, the two blank spaces she had left on the bottom got filled up with the signatures of two of Aunt Rachel and Uncle David's friends—the two witnesses who were sitting at the table. I was standing behind Aunt Rachel and smiled across the table at Mom, who shot a knowing smile back at me. I could tell she knew that I was thinking about those blank spaces I had been so worried about.

Rabbi Green carefully replaced the ketubah inside the frame. "Okay," he said to the small crowd in the room, "signed and sealed. Now let's go deliver it. Time to get married!"

We filed out of the library one by one. As I headed toward the sanctuary, I touched my beautiful new hamsa and whispered a quiet, "Thank you." Because, you know, just in case....

So far, so good. Now all we had to do was get through the ceremony.

36

Knock, Knock

We lined up outside the sanctuary doors in the order that we were going to walk down the aisle. I looked over at Samantha, who was standing next to Jeremy and in front of Joel. She was shaking a little bit. I tapped her on the shoulder and said, "Don't be nervous. Think about doing this for Aunt Rachel and Uncle David."

Samantha nodded, but I wasn't sure she was convinced. She turned to face forward again. I tapped her on the shoulder one more time. "Just remember," I said, "you're wearing your hamsa. Nothing's going to go wrong."

As before, she nodded and once again turned to face the front.

I looked over at Joel and gave him a face as if to say, "You try something!" He totally understood me. Joel tapped Samantha on the shoulder. She turned around looking both annoyed and curious.

"Hey, Samantha," Joel started, "knock, knock!"

She didn't seem to know what to do. I'm sure she knew that the next thing you say is "Who's there?" but she appeared to be torn between waiting for instructions to walk down the aisle, and engaging in the joke.

Joel repeated, "Come on, you know what to do. Knock, knock!"

The corners of her mouth went up a tiny bit and

she coyly and quickly whispered back, "Who's there?"

"Shirley," Joel replied.

Samantha looked over her shoulder, probably to make sure she wasn't messing anything up and finally said, "Shirley who?"

"'Shirley' you're not nervous about this!" Joel said, landing the punchline.

Fortunately, Samantha did not go into one of her all-out laugh fests. She grinned and faced the front again. It seemed that, for the moment at least, he took her mind off her fears.

Meanwhile, Marilyn the Wedding Coordinator and one of the guys who was carrying the mini eggrolls around earlier opened the doors to the sanctuary. Uncle David's grandma was the first one in line and it was her turn to walk down the aisle. Uncle David's brother Ben escorted her into the room. Marilyn and Eggroll Guy then closed the doors behind them and we all took one step forward. We knew it would be a while before the doors opened again, since it would take Nana a long time to get to the front row.

Joel tapped Samantha again. "Knock, knock," he whispered.

She shot him a look as if to say, "Not now!" But Joel didn't let up.

"Knock, knock!" he tried once more.

The doors swung open again, but Nana was still shuffling down the aisle and hadn't made it to her seat yet.

"Who's there?" Samantha finally relented.

"Les."

The big doors were shut.

"Les who?" she asked with a small playful smile, as if the two of them were behaving mischievously.

"'Les' do this wedding thing!"

Samantha let out an audible chortle and immediately covered up her mouth with both hands. Marilyn the Wedding Coordinator gave her a dirty look, but I saw Samantha's shoulders relax a little. This was good because we were up next! I was so excited I could hardly stand it. I touched my hamsa for good luck and whispered a quiet kenahora. Under the circumstances, I skipped the ptu-ptu-ptus.

Joel tapped Samantha on the shoulder one more time. Samantha shook her head. "Not now!" she hissed nervously at him.

He tried again. "Knock, knock."

I got the distinct feeling that Samantha wasn't going to participate, so instead I answered, "Who's there?"

"Luke," Joel said. Even though she wasn't participating, I could tell that Samantha was listening by the way she had her ear turned toward us.

"Luke who?"

"'Luke' out, here we come!"

As if on cue, Marilyn and Eggroll Guy pulled the doors open.

Samantha inhaled deeply. In fact, it seemed like she was holding her breath, as if she was diving in and swimming underwater. *Whatever works for her,* I thought.

I looked ahead to the bimah and, unlike in my dream, I saw the huppah standing there, waiting for us, like a mama bird waiting for her little chickies to come home to the nest. Under the huppah was an easel showcasing the ketubah and next to that was a little round table with two wine cups.

It felt like hundreds of eyes were looking at us from

the seats. People were smiling at us and some were taking pictures. I even heard a woman whisper as we passed her saying, "Aren't they darling?"

We were doing well. We were halfway down the aisle, and no one tripped, no one sneezed, and no one turned into a sushi roll. I smiled to myself.

Samantha kept her eyes forward. She seemed to be focusing on the bimah and on Rabbi Green, who was smiling broadly at us. It was smooth sailing.

Until....

37

Hoopla on Top of the Huppah

There were loud gasps in the crowd. I panicked as a million thoughts raced through my head. *Is there a hole in my dress? Can everyone see my underwear? Is one of my brothers' shoes untied and he's about to trip? Did somebody faint?*

Then people started pointing and looking upward. Before long nobody was paying any attention to the four of us walking down the aisle because all sets of eyes were wildly following the tan streak that moved across the room. My brothers, Samantha, and I all stopped walking, and watched along with everyone else. Even the musicians stopped playing as they ducked and hid from the thing that was flying overhead.

Someone shrieked. Then someone else did. Soon there were shrieks and yells coming from all around the sanctuary. People were waving their arms around trying to keep the flying thing away from them.

When it finally landed on top of the huppah the whole room went silent.

"*Chirp!*" it said.

It seemed as if everyone in the room let out a relieved sigh. It was a little tan-colored bird. People sat down, still pointing and making a commotion, but at least now we knew what it was that we saw zipping by in the air.

"How'd a bird get in here?" I heard someone say.

"It's a wedding crasher!" someone else joked.

Joel turned to face the three of us in the aisle with him and said, "If it's flying around in this room, does that make this a bird sanctuary?"

Samantha laughed out loud. Jeremy pushed Joel's shoulder and said in his bitingly, sarcastic tone, "Hardy har har. That's so funny I forgot to laugh."

The doors behind us opened up and I turned around to see Aunt Rachel and Uncle David peeking in to see what all the hoopla was about.

Rabbi Green stepped up to the microphone under the huppah and said, "We seem to have an uninvited wedding guest!" Everyone laughed. "They say that a bird flying into your house is good luck! And in the synagogue, even better luck!"

Cantor Grossman then stepped up to the mic and said, "Actually, I've heard that if a bird 'does its business' on you, that's when it's good luck."

Samantha turned around and looked at me with a scrunched-up nose and asked, "Does its business on you? What does he mean by that?"

"It means if the bird poops on you," Jeremy was all too happy to explain.

"Gross!" we all said in unison.

"Well then, let's hope we don't have *too* much good luck!" Rabbi Green replied and everyone in the room roared with laughter. The rabbi and the cantor were a regular comedy team.

We were standing in the middle of the aisle, half-way to the bimah, when Joel muttered for only the huppah holders to hear, "This wedding is for the birds!" Samantha laughed out loud again.

"That's enough out of you, bird brain!" Jeremy retorted.

And that's when the bird puns began to "fly" among us.

"I think we'll be *raven* about this wedding for years to come," Joel snickered.

I couldn't help myself, "Joel, you think you're so clever. Well, *toucan* play at this game!"

Not-so-shy-anymore Samantha joined in, "You guys *quack* me up!"

"Yo, cut it out! This is supposed to be a dignified event." Jeremy said. We thought he was being serious until he gave us an impish grin and said, "You're *cheep*ening the experience. It's getting *hawk*ward." I love it when fun-guy Jeremy comes back. We used to have so much fun with him when we were younger. It was great to have him playing with us like old times.

"I hope the bird in the room won't fluster Rabbi Green too much. Otherwise he might have to *wing* it!" Joel said.

This went on until Rabbi Green finally asked into the microphone, "Shall we continue?" Everyone applauded. But at this point, the whole mood in the room had shifted from serious to silly. It was like we switched from Yom Kippur services to the Purim spiel!

Joel threw in one more, "I bet Cantor Grossman is thinking, '*Owl* be glad when this whole thing is over!'"

"I hope we don't live to *egret* this!" Jeremy added. We all laughed as we tried to pull ourselves together and get ready to finish our trip up to the bimah.

"Don't be *blue, Jay*, I'm sure it'll all be fine," I said. It took each of them a moment or two to realize that I made a pun with Jeremy's nickname!

"Well, that was quite *emus*ing," Joel added.

"It was a *hoot*!" Samantha said between bouts of

laughter. She tried so hard to stop, but every time she would catch her breath, she'd crack up all over again.

At first I was so worried about Samantha not being able to make it down the aisle because she was nervous and shy. Now I didn't know if she'd make it because of her laughter. She was still giggling and wiping tears from her eyes as the musicians started up again. Well, at least she was enjoying the moment!

Rabbi Green motioned for us to continue walking toward the bimah. Instead of being able to concentrate on the significance of this long-awaited day, I was too busy focusing on the bird that sat on top of the huppah. It had settled right above the pole that I was about to be holding. I hoped it hadn't had a big breakfast that morning. I certainly didn't want it to leave a little "wedding present" on me.

The four of us walked slowly up the steps of the bimah and took our places next to our respective poles. As soon as I took hold of my pole, the bird flew away. I was relieved that it wasn't perched above me, but I was also distracted. I wanted to take in everything about this most important day, but at the same time I couldn't help but watch it fly around the sanctuary.

Eventually, I lost sight of it, which was good because the procession was continuing and the four of us had the best seats in the house! Well, not seats exactly, but we had a perfect view of all the action.

We watched all of the bridal party: the ushers, the bridesmaids, and Steve the Bridesman walk in. Mom and Dad came down together as did Samantha's parents. Each of them joined us on the bimah, and they formed two lines on either side of the huppah. The men stood on the side behind Joel and Samantha and the women lined up behind Jeremy and me.

Next, Uncle David's little niece Anna, the flower girl, stood in front of the back doors looking around at the crowd. Her Mom got down on her knees at the end of the aisle and tried to coax her to walk toward her. Anna stood there, frozen. Her mom waved a little teddy bear for Anna to see and got her moving. She slowly took steps down the aisle, and tossed flower petals on the floor along the way. Her mom looked relieved. Unfortunately, it was at that exact moment that the bird decided to soar right by her and down the aisle. Anna let out a scream and raced straight into her mother's arms.

"Well, that went well," Jeremy quipped.

And then the bird "did its business" right on top of the flower petals on the floor.

38

Duck, Duck, Goose

I couldn't believe that a bird was flying around in the sanctuary, and worse, that it pooped right in the middle of the aisle.

"Duck!" someone yelled out as everyone tried to take cover in their seats as the bird flew wildly around the room. Once again, the sanctuary was in an uproar, and, like before, the musicians stopped playing.

Someone on the other side of the room called out, "Here it comes! Duck!"

"Duck!" someone else yelled.

Smart aleck Joel called out "Goose!" from the bimah.

We all laughed, including Rabbi Green. Good thing he has a great sense of humor. Samantha laughed so hard that her corner of the huppah shook as she gripped her pole.

Cantor Grossman leaned into the mic and bellowed a big, loud, "Mazel tov!" He looked at Rabbi Green as he continued with a little playful shrug, "I told you, when it leaves a little gift, it's good luck!"

"I think it's just *fowl*!" Jeremy joked to us. And we were at it again.

I said, "Jeremy, it's nice that you're being so *pheasant*, I mean pleasant, today."

"The three of you guys are all birds of a feather!" Samantha said through her giggles.

Joel said, "Do you think someone ought to *chick'n* on Aunt Rachel and see how she's doing?"

Surprisingly, it was Rabbi Green who played along next, "That would be an *egg*-celent idea—" Joel looked at him with great admiration and appreciation for joining in the pun fun. "—but I think we're about to get started again. Look," he pointed at the center aisle in which Eggroll Guy was quickly covering up the petal-strewn floor with a long white cloth that perfectly covered the carpet-bombed area.

Once everyone settled down, the musicians started playing their beautiful music again. I thought back to when we watched the video of my parents' wedding and how my dad tripped and then took a big, deep bow in front of all the guests. I guess the Silvers are destined to have funny things happen at their weddings. I wondered if anything funny would happen at my own wedding someday. I just hoped this little comedy fest had come to a close.

I remembered from the way we lined up in the hallway that it was Uncle David's turn to enter the room and walk down the aisle. A woman with a beautiful voice stood at a microphone next to the musicians and started to sing a song in Hebrew. As soon as she started I got all excited because I recognized some of the words! She was singing, "*Dodi Li.*" I recognized those words from the ketubah:

Ani l'dodi v'dodi li.

The doors in the back opened and, as I expected, out walked Uncle David, accompanied by his parents. He didn't actually need to, but he ducked as he walked through the doorway. I guess since he's so tall it had become a habit. Uncle David had a white tallit draped around his shoulders and his white kippah on his head.

244 • YaYa & YoYo: Hoopla Under the Huppah

I was so glad that he and Aunt Rachel figured out a way to both be happy with the whole kittel question. I liked their creative solution!

They walked slowly down the aisle toward us and joined us on the bimah. Uncle David's parents took their places under the huppah between Joel and Samantha. Uncle David turned to face the back of the room as he waited for his bride to enter.

Then came the big moment. The music changed to a song called *Erev Shel Shoshanim*, which according to the program, is a traditional song used in Jewish weddings and it means "Evening of Roses." The doors opened and out came Aunt Rachel holding her bouquet of flowers, with Grandma and Grandpa each holding onto one of her arms. The beautiful bride had a smile so big that I half expected her teeth to fall out. She floated down the aisle and smiled back like a mirror at all the people smiling at her. Of course, Grandma kept on dabbing at her eyes with her little handkerchief, but through each dab she managed to smile at the onlookers.

I glanced over at Samantha, who was smiling as she watched our aunt proceed down the aisle. I had a feeling that she would be just fine for the rest of the ceremony.

Grandma, Grandpa, and Aunt Rachel stopped when they got to the bottom of the steps leading up to the bimah. Grandpa lifted her veil and gave her a kiss. Grandma kissed her, too. As Grandma and Grandpa began to walk up the steps to the bimah, I watched Aunt Rachel delicately rub her cheek. She was subtly wiping off Grandma's lipstick that she'd left behind but clever Aunt Rachel made it look like she was wiping away tears. She looked over and winked at me and I smiled back at her, so happy that our little inside jokes remained between us.

Grandma and Grandpa joined us on the bimah and stood right next to me under the huppah. Grandpa reached over and gave my hand a little squeeze. I smiled up at him and he winked at me. I blinky-winked back at him.

Uncle David walked down the four steps from the bimah to meet Aunt Rachel, and the two of them walked together, hand in hand, up the steps. There, Aunt Rachel began the circling. She went around Uncle David three times and each time she passed him she looked him right in the eyes and grinned. Then she stopped and stood on his right side.

Okay, so they're just doing three. I guess they decided, I thought to myself. *I like that, short and sweet.*

But then Uncle David began. He circled Aunt Rachel three times and stopped.

Oh, that's cool, I thought, *they each did three. That's really nice!*

But then, the two of them turned toward one another, held hands like they were going to dance together, and made one big circle together.

Oh, that's really great! I thought once more. *So in the end, they each did three and they did seven in total! Let's hear it for shalom bayit again!*

When they were done circling, they continued holding each other's hands and faced Rabbi Green and Cantor Grossman. Aunt Rachel and Uncle David were both glowing and looking full of expectation. I could see all of it happening right in front of me! I couldn't believe I was right up there under the huppah watching them get married.

THEY'RE REALLY, ACTUALLY, FINALLY GETTING

MARRIED! I silently shouted in my head.

As I clutched the huppah pole with my good hand, I glanced up at the patchwork-quilt huppah above our heads. I totally understood why Aunt Rachel and Uncle David wanted to make their huppah that way. Each square had different messages or pictures or even handprints from people in their lives and in a way, it sort of did feel like they were on the bimah with us.

I looked out at the crowd of people in the seats. Everyone was watching and listening. There was a sense of anticipation in the air as we were all awaiting that final moment when the glass would smash and the two of them would be married. I couldn't help but feel so proud that I was such a big part of the whole thing and had the honor of standing right up there on the bimah, under the huppah, inches away from the bride and groom.

Rabbi Green started by taking one of the cups of red wine. I saw Grandma flinch a little, then I over-heard her whispering to Grandpa, "I told her to use white! What if she spills or drips?"

Grandpa took Grandma's hand in his and patted it to let her know everything would be fine. I noticed he didn't let go. It's kinda sweet to see old people who still hold hands.

"Friends," Rabbi Green started, "we are about to partake in the first of two cups of wine and as such, the first of the two parts of the wedding. This is the part called *erusin*. It is also known as *kiddushin*, which comes from the same word in Hebrew as *kadosh*, which means holy. After that we will bless and drink a second cup of wine for the part we call *nissuin*."

Rabbi Green held the cup a little higher so everyone could see it. Cantor Grossman sang the two blessings in Hebrew and Rabbi Green recited them in English. I recognized the first one, which was the regular blessing over the wine that we always say: *"Baruch atah Adonai Eloheinu melech ha'aolm, borei p'ri hagafen.* Blessed are you, Adonai our God, Ruler of the Universe, Creator of the fruit of the vine."* I didn't recognize the second blessing. Rabbi Green then handed the cup to Uncle David who took a sip. Uncle David lifted Aunt Rachel's veil and passed her the cup and she took a sip.

Grandma took in a sharp breath and held it until Rabbi Green safely placed the cup back on the small round table by his side. Then I heard her slowly exhale.

No one spilled or dribbled! I thought triumphantly. *Ptu, ptu, ptu!*

Next came the ring ceremony. "Rachel, I'd like you to please point at your groom."

She did. In fact she started wagging her finger at Uncle David as if he was in trouble. Rabbi Green chuckled.

"Now, David, I'd like you to please say the following words to Rachel. *Harei at mekudeshet li b'taba'at zo, k'dat Moshe v'Yisrael.* With this ring you are consecrated unto me according to the laws of Moses and Israel."

Uncle David repeated the line as instructed. He took her right hand with his left. He held the ring in his right hand, which he had hovering over the tip of her index finger.

"Now please slip the ring onto Rachel's pointer finger. We use this finger because according to custom, the index finger is a direct line to the heart." Rabbi Green explained.

Uncle David took the gold ring and slid it onto her finger. But it didn't seem to go as easily as he had expected. At first he just smiled and looked Aunt Rachel in the eye as he started to slide the ring, but then his whole expression changed. His brow furrowed and he looked like he was trying to solve a hard math problem or something. He held on to her hand even tighter and pushed harder and harder on the ring. Aunt Rachel shook her head, but he didn't see. He was looking down at her finger, concentrating intently on getting the ring over her knuckle. Her eyes got teary as she winced in pain.

"David!" Aunt Rachel eventually whispered forcefully.

He finally looked up.

"Stop!" she said. Her finger was turning purple.

Aunt Rachel twisted and pulled the ring off her knuckle and back onto the top half of her finger.

"Oops, my mistake," Rabbi Green said with a chuckle. "I forgot to mention that you don't put the ring over the knuckle. It won't fit that way since it was sized for her ring finger."

Uncle David's face turned pink. "Oh, yeah, that makes sense!" Then to Aunt Rachel he said with an apologetic shrug, "Sorry, hon."

"No biggie," she replied with a shrug and a smile in typical Aunt Rachel fashion.

Next it was Aunt Rachel's turn to put a ring on Uncle David's finger. Just as she had done when it was her turn, Uncle David pointed his index finger at her as she recited her lines. Unlike him however, she did not try to shove the ring over his knuckle. In fact, to be funny, she made a big deal about stopping right before his knuckle.

"Good job!" Rabbi Green joked. "So some would say that with the exchange of the rings you are officially married, but let's be real, we can't make it that quick and easy! Let's move on to this beautiful wedding document." He reached over and lifted the ketubah from the ledge of the easel and held it up for all to see.

"This stunning piece of work, made lovingly by Rachel's sister-in-law, Debbie Silver, is your wedding contract." I glanced over at Mom, who looked so proud and pleased. All I could think of was how glad I was that I didn't totally ruin the ketubah and I kind of got goosebumps watching Mom beam with pride.

Rabbi Green continued. "I will now read some of the highlights of this document."

At that point he read the Aramaic stuff from the ketubah. In my head a lot of it sounded like, "blah, blah, blah." But then he finished and he handed the ketubah to Uncle David, instructing him to give it to his bride as a gift, which he did. Aunt Rachel stood there holding it, not quite sure what to do with it.

"Now you have to hold on to that for the rest of the ceremony," Rabbi Green said seriously.

"I do?" Aunt Rachel looked and sounded surprised.

"No, no, I'm kidding," Rabbi Green said with a mischievous wink, taking the ketubah from her hands and placing it back on the easel. "Plus, we pretty much already got all of the 'I do-s' done when you exchanged rings."

I'd never actually been to a wedding before, so I didn't have much to go on besides what I'd seen in movies, on TV, and on my parents' wedding video, but something told me that this was not a typical wedding. I always assumed that the mood would be serious and solemn, but this one never stopped being lighthearted and full of jokes. To tell you the truth, I was certain that this was exactly what Aunt Rachel and Uncle David wanted, even though it may not have been what they had planned. Just as Mom had said, you never know what to expect at a wedding!

In keeping with the lighthearted nature of the wedding, Rabbi Green took a few minutes to speak to the bride and groom, to share a funny story about the first time they came in to see him after getting engaged. Just as he was getting to the punchline of his story, the silly bird flew back on top of the huppah.

"Oh, I see our visitor wants to hear the story, too!" Rabbi Green joked. Once again, I worried about the bird above our heads, but forced myself to focus and pay attention to what was happening under the huppah and not so much about what was going on above it.

Once he finished the story, Rabbi Green said, "I now invite Rachel's and David's friends to come up to the bimah for the *sheva brachot*, the seven blessings, as we begin the second stage of the wedding ceremony, the nissuin."

The seven friends came up, each taking a turn to recite their blessing in Hebrew and in English. And thanks to all the commotion and movement, the bird flew away again with a loud chirp.

Just like during the set of blessings recited earlier, the first blessing was over a cup of wine and I knew that one. I didn't know any of the others, but they sounded nice. When they were done, the friends each tried to sneak over to give Aunt Rachel and Uncle David hugs, but there wasn't enough room for everyone to fit under the huppah, so instead, they each gave them a fist bump and then stepped down off the bimah.

Once the sheva brachot crew had cleared out, Rabbi Green took a big, deep breath, smiled a huge grin at the bride and groom and said, "Almost there!" Aunt Rachel giggled a little as she and Uncle David held hands and looked up at Rabbi Green in anticipation. I looked around at everyone under the huppah and saw that every single face was full of love. Everyone was not only smiling with their mouths, but with their eyes, too.

Uncle David removed his white tallit from one of his shoulders and wrapped it around Aunt Rachel's shoulder so that they were snuggled inside the tallit together. Rabbi Green said a few blessings in both Hebrew and in English and wished them a long life together.

"And now, finally," Rabbi Green said in a clear, loud voice meant for all to hear, "it's time for the dramatic, final moment of the ceremony. We remember the destruction of the Temple in ancient times as well as the brokenness and destruction that exist in our world even today and our need for *tikkun olam*, the healing of our world. And we know that the two of you together will work as one to repair this broken world of ours. Though the glass shatters, may your bond never be broken as you strive together, through your love and your partnership, to make this world a better place for yourselves, for others, and for future generations to come."

And with that, Rabbi Green placed a glass wrapped in a napkin on the floor by Uncle David's foot. Aunt Rachel and Uncle David held hands as they looked down at the floor. Uncle David lifted his long leg and brought it down with a thunderous BOOM on the glass. It made a crunching sound under his shoe.

"MAZEL TOV!" the entire room shouted.

The shouting scared the bird, which started doing laps around the room almost frantically. But this time, the musicians didn't stop and no one in the congregation looked up to watch it fly around. All eyes were on my aunt and uncle who were now hugging and kissing and crying and laughing all at once.

They did it! They really did it!

And I didn't even ruin the wedding!

39

Put Your Chairs in the Air

Aunt Rachel and Uncle David disappeared for a while. Mom had reminded me about how they were going into the yichud room to have some time alone before coming out to party with their guests. Marilyn the Wedding Coordinator ushered everyone into the "ballroom" to wait for them and their big entrance. The band was playing some swing music and a few people were on the dance floor dancing and having fun while waiting for the bride and groom to show up.

Jeremy, Joel, Samantha, and I, on the other hand, were huddled in the corner near the door to the kitchen where we happened to notice a tray full of appetizers that had been left out from the kabbalat panim. It was just sitting there, practically begging for someone to eat something (kind of like how Grandma does!). So Samantha and I helped ourselves to one more appetizer each. Joel dove in as if he was the one fasting all day and hadn't seen food in 24 hours.

"I hope they stay in there a long time," Joel said, his mouth once again stuffed with mini hot dogs.

"Why?" Samantha and I asked in unison.

"Don't you want to dance with the bride and groom?" I asked.

"Sure," Joel said, "but as long as we're waiting for them, we can keep eating these things," he said holding up yet another hot dog.

"You know there's a whole dinner that they're going to serve us in a little while. Maybe you should slow down on all those hot dogs!" I warned sounding an awful lot like our mother. "Plus, you might get a stomach ache!"

"Gee, thanks for the heads-up 'Mom'," Joel snarked at me.

"Do what you want," I responded with a shrug. "I'm saving room for the chicken Wellington, or whatever they're serving tonight. Hot dogs we can get anytime, but tonight we're going to get a big, fancy-shmancy dinner."

As it turned out, Joel didn't get his wish to continue eating hot dogs all night long, because a few moments later Aunt Rachel's bridesmaid, Jodi, came over to us with a big bag of shiny, colorful confetti in her hand.

"Hey, you guys, come on over to the doorway. We need you to welcome the bride and groom with us when they enter the room. We're going to shower them with confetti."

We wiped our hands on napkins. Jodi poured little pieces of paper and tinsel into our cupped hands. We carefully carried our haul as we followed her to the entryway, leaving a trail of sparkles on the floor as we went. As we made our way closer to the doors, we were also moving closer to the band and the music sounded louder with each step we took.

We lined up with the rest of the guests that were standing in two lines on either side of the doors, waiting for the wedding couple's big entrance. People were chattering and talking. There was a definite feeling of excitement and anticipation. I could hardly wait!

I yelled over the music to Joel, Samantha, and Jeremy, "Why are they taking so long?"

Jeremy and Samantha shrugged. Joel said, "It's Aunt Rachel. She's always late for everything, remember?" I nodded in agreement. Yup, just as Grandma had said, Aunt Rachel would even be late to her own wedding.

"Well, at least she was on time for the ceremony," I said.

Finally, the band guy announced, "Gather around, everyone! Please welcome David and Rachel as we celebrate with them for the first time as a married couple!"

The music changed from the swing-dance music they'd been playing to a fun, bouncy Jewish tune. The doors to the social hall swung open and Aunt Rachel and Uncle David came dancing in, holding hands. The singer from the band sang the same song that everyone sang when Uncle David was entering the room for the bedeken. "*Od yishama b'arei Yehudah, uv'chutzot Yerushalayim,*" which apparently is a very popular wedding song. Throughout the night the band played many versions of the same song with different tunes each time.

As my aunt and now-official uncle walked between the two lines of guests they were blasted with confetti from both sides. Aunt Rachel had replaced her veil with a sparkling tiara but now her hair, loaded with confetti, was sparkly too.

When they made it through Confetti Alley and onto the dance floor in the middle of the room, everyone grabbed their neighbor's hand and the crowd started dancing in a huge circle around them. There were so many people on the dance floor that someone broke off from the circle and created another one around the first. That ring of people danced in the opposite direction of the inner circle. People were singing, even shouting. along with the music as they danced around.

The four of us huppah holders, the bridal party, and some other people were in the innermost circle around my aunt and uncle. I was surprised when Aunt Rachel left Uncle David's side, and came over and grabbed my hand and Samantha's hand. She motioned for Joel and Jeremy to come over too, so the four of us joined hands with Aunt Rachel and Uncle David in the middle and created an even smaller inner circle. I felt so important dancing in the center of the room with the bride and groom!

I noticed that little Anna, the flower girl, was standing and watching us from in between our circle and the one that was going around us. Her Mom was trying to coax her to join the circle with her and dance but she just stood there watching us almost longingly. I pointed her out to Jeremy. He let go of our hands and went over to her. In a flash, he swooped her up and came back into the inner circle with Anna sitting on top of his shoulders! At first she looked scared but then all of a sudden she had a smile so big plastered across her face that I thought she might burst.

We danced around like that for a while and then the bride's and groom's parents came into the middle. Eventually, Mom and Dad and Uncle David's siblings joined us. For all I knew, there were now four or four hundred circles going around. I was so busy in the middle that I truly didn't know what was happening outside of our own orbit.

Two of Aunt Rachel and Uncle David's friends danced their way into the center, each carrying a chair over their heads. They placed them right in the center of the circles. Aunt Rachel and Uncle David sat down in them and a bunch of their friends politely pushed their way into the middle. Eight people took hold of the chair legs. Suddenly, Aunt Rachel shot up like a rocket ship and was bouncing around in the air, simultaneously waving to the crowd with one hand and hanging on for dear life with her other.

It took a little longer to get Uncle David up in the air, probably because he's so tall and weighs more than Aunt Rachel. But soon enough, he, too, was bobbing around in the air, floating over the heads of the people dancing below. Meanwhile, some of their other friends were busy passing out silly hats and Hawaiian leis throughout the dancing circles. It was so funny to see grown men and women wearing such fun things over their formal clothes. Then someone passed around giant cut-out pictures of our aunt and uncle's faces that were attached to large popsicle sticks. As I looked around the room, I saw dozens of dancing Rachels and Davids. I giggled because it was so goofy.

A lady wearing a firefighter's hat reached up and passed Aunt Rachel a white napkin, which she spun around over her head like a lasso. When her chair was moved closer to Uncle David's, she held the napkin out to him and he grabbed a corner. The two of them each held on, connected to each other by this little square of cloth.

After about five minutes or so of soaring over our heads, the bride and groom returned to the earth and then the friends lifted both of Uncle David's parents and then Grandma and Grandpa up in the air. Just like Anna on Jeremy's shoulders, they all looked thrilled and terrified at the same time. Personally, I thought it looked like fun. I looked over at Aunt Rachel, who seemed to be having a blast as she clapped and cheered for her parents in the chairs overhead.

The chairs made a safe landing back on the ground with my grandparents wobbling like they had just taken a rough flight from the other side of the world. Grandma straightened her hair with her hands and Grandpa wiped his brow with his handkerchief, then tucked it back into his pocket.

I assumed that we were done with the chairs-in-the-air portion of the dancing and would move on to the part where we entertain the bride and the groom. Joel was all prepared with a couple of magic tricks he had brought with him for the occasion, having been inspired by a guest doing magic for our parents in their wedding video.

But to my great surprise, Uncle David came at me with his arms out. He lifted me off the ground and swung me in the air as he often does when he gives me one of his big bear hugs. But instead of putting me back down where I started, he landed me in one of the chairs! At the exact same time, Aunt Rachel grabbed Joel by the hand and led him to the other chair. In a matter of seconds, I was hovering above the crowd of people that were dancing in circles, and my brother was up there right next to me. Lots of smiling faces looked up at us. Uncle David and Aunt Rachel clapped and cheered for us from below. Samantha waved excitedly from her spot on the dance floor. The photographer snapped pictures of the two of us. I could even see Eggroll Guy at far end of the room filling water glasses at the dinner tables while moving to the beat.

Joel was holding on tight to the arms of his chair. I couldn't see them, but I assumed his knuckles were getting white. The look of terror on his face said it all. He was looking down at the ground, probably calculating how many feet up and at what velocity he'd hit the floor. Not me, though. I kept one arm on the chair but I threw my other one in the air, cast and all, like I was riding a bull in a rodeo, and enjoyed the best ride of my life.

Truth be told, it really was the best day of my life. There was so much happiness and joy in one room, I could actually feel it. Everything was perfect now that all the problems were behind us. I was glad I had done my part by keeping away that awful evil eye.

Bobbing up and down in the air, I glanced at the red string still wrapped around the cast on my arm, closed my eyes and whispered, "kenahora, ptu ptu ptu." Because, you know, just in case....

Acknowledgments

Even though my name is on the front of this book, the truth is that so many people helped to make *Hoopla Under the Huppah* come to life. I would like to thank everyone who contributed in one way or another.

I would like to thank:

Gary: We got married twenty-five years ago and I can still remember every detail of our wedding like it was yesterday. It was so much fun for me to re-live that day as I wrote *Hoopla*. I am so grateful to have you in my life. In terms of this book, thank you for all of the computer and technical work you do in the background and of course thank you also for all of your encouragement and support. Gary's the best! I love you.

Ari, Ilana, and Eitan: Thank you for helping me brainstorm ideas and for being the inspiration of so many things in my books! I loved reading the manuscript of *Hoopla* aloud to you and laughing with you over the funny voices for each character. You are my whole world and I love you all so much!

The kids who read my manuscript, gave feedback, and shared ideas: Addie, Ayelet, Daphne, Dov, Eliana, Ellie, Laila, Marta, Maya, Nadav, Noam, Talia, Ty, Yaron, Yoni and the students at the Chicago Jewish Day School (a few years ago!). Thank you so much for giving me your honest feedback, for telling me what you liked and didn't like in the story, and for helping me generate some new ideas. You guys rock!

The adults who also read my manuscript and provided me with invaluable feedback, constructive criticism, and insights: Rabbi Alexander Davis, Melanie Heuiser Hill, Dana Prottas, and Lisa Simon, as well as all of my friends on Facebook who shared and brainstormed those crazy bird puns. Thank you all so much for being a part of this experience!

My editors Leslie Martin and Judy Cohen: Thank you so much, Leslie, for once again holding my hand and guiding me from my initial "final draft" to my actual Final Draft! Your input and insights are incredible and I so appreciate the perspective you bring to our work together. Plus, it's so much fun! Judy, thank you so much for taking care of the final read-through and helping with the clean-up. You are a lifesaver!

Ann Koffsky: I love the cover of this book! Once again you've managed to bring YaYa and YoYo to life with your brilliant artwork and vibrant colors. Thank you so much!

I would also like to acknowledge that while most of the information and facts about Jewish weddings came from my own life experiences having attended and participated in many weddings, I did learn quite a bit about Jewish wedding customs from Anita Diamant's book *The New Jewish Wedding* (Scribner, 1986). When I read that book for the first time in 1991 as Gary and I were planning our own wedding, many of the traditional Jewish wedding rituals were unfamiliar to me, such as the idea of wearing a kittel. I bought the updated version (Simon and Schuster, 2001) to use as a guide for this book. Thank you, Anita Diamant, for helping me out with two weddings now!

And finally, I would like to thank the readers of the *YaYa & YoYo* books for your continued support. Thank you for all of your wonderful letters and emails and for being in touch with me on social media. You are the reason I do what I do! I am now beginning to work on Book 4 about Hanukkah. Stay tuned!

Sliding Into the New Year

Thrill-loving fifth grader Ellie Silver (YaYa) has been waiting all summer to visit the brand new indoor water park in town. She is ecstatic when her best friend, Megan, invites her to go—that is until her twin brother, Joel (YoYo), points out that Megan is going on Rosh Hashanah. Sure, Rosh Hashanah is a big deal, but so is Splash World! What will Ellie do?

Praise for *Sliding into the New Year*
(YaYa & YoYo, Book 1)

"Weinstein employs YaYa's voice as the very believable and delightful narrator and carefully avoids didacticism as she introduces readers to some of the rituals and traditions of Judaism as they are practiced in a warm, loving family. ... Intended as the first in a series; more adventures of YaYa and YoYo will be most welcome."
Kirkus Book Reviews

"A contemporary style and point of view that connect present-day pluralistic Judaism to the unbroken chain of Jewish beliefs and customs are at the story's heart. ...genuine, laced with humor and warmth...this first entry into the series is a good beginning."
Association of Jewish Libraries

"In *Sliding into the New Year*, Dori Weinstein captures the attention of youngsters and their parents alike with captivating storytelling that links contemporary kids, their families, and their lives to the core of Jewish traditions and values. In this first book in the series, YaYa's and YoYo's adventures create wonderful opportunities for parents and children to engage in meaningful Jewish discussions about issues that might well have emerged from their own family experiences."
Rabbi Alvin Mars, Ph.D.
Sr. Consultant to the President of the JCC Association
of North America for Education Development

"*YaYa & YoYo: Sliding into the New Year* is just the sort of wonderful and entertaining story I wish was around when my children were young. It is an organic and engaging way to teach both Jews and non-Jews about the transforming power of the central Jewish holiday of Rosh Hashanah. Weinstein does something so rare—she captures with such honesty and groundedness a healthy family unafraid of emotion and intimacy."

Rabbi Irwin Kula
President, CLAL
(The National Jewish Center for Learning and Leadership)
Author of *Yearnings: Embracing the Sacred Messiness of Life*

"It is so refreshing to find a Jewish book for tweens and pre-teens that is current, relevant and relatable. Ellie, Joel and the whole Silver clan are likable and funny. Kids will learn about the holiday of Rosh Hashanah in a new and engaging way."

Gila Hadani Ward
Director of Lay Resources, Strengthening Congregations,
Union for Reform Judaism

"Finally, a Jewish book for young readers that is well-written, engaging, lots of fun, and has important lessons to teach. I love it. And the best of all, it is the first in a series."

Rabbi Kerry M. Olitzky
Executive Director, Jewish Outreach Institute
Author of *The Complete How To Handbook for Jewish Living*

"A delightful and engaging story of growth into young adulthood and the challenges of faith. A wonderful opportunity for parents and children to explore together the meaning of the High Holy Days."

Rabbi Steven Wernick
Executive VP, United Synagogue of Conservative Judaism

"Finally, a book that is 'teachy' without being preachy. Dori Weinstein knows and respects her audience. By writing enjoyable, credible and intelligent fiction, she shows that learning and fun are not mutually exclusive. In fact, the subject of this book is one that parents and children can have a substantive discussion about together."

Rabbi Hayim Herring, Ph.D.
President and CEO, Herring Consulting Network
Author of *Tomorrow's Synagogue Today*

"In *YaYa & YoYo*, Jewish children will find fictional characters who inhabit the same world, use the same words, and face the same woes as they do. Dori Weinstein's first book is a testament to her love of Judaism, family, and teaching!"

Sari Steinberg
Author of *...And Then There Were Dinosaurs*
and *King Solomon Figures It Out*

Shaking in the Shack

Joel Silver (YoYo) loves to be a comedian and to play practical jokes. However, when he, his twin sister Ellie (YaYa) and the rest of their fifth-grade Hebrew School class find something surprising in the synagogue's sukkah just before the holiday of Sukkot, it's no laughing matter. Where did the mysterious four-legged visitor come from? What will become of it? Their unexpected adventure brings Joel and Ellie face to face with the importance of shelter and caring for those in need.

Praise for *Shaking in the Shack*
(YaYa & YoYo, Book 2)

"This is a lighthearted romp for middle readers with some substantial messages subtly worked into the fun. Recommended for ages 8-12."

Jewish Book Council

"Presented seamlessly within the story, Weinstein includes lots of information about the customs of Sukkot. Practical joker Joel and more serious Ellie are believable, likeable characters. Fans of Sliding into the New Year and readers just making the acquaintance of the Silver family will enjoy this peek into one family's unusual Sukkot. Highly recommended.

Association of Jewish Libraries

"Embedded within this fun and entertaining book are important messages that kids and adults will appreciate. Weinstein weaves in the Jewish teachings of helping the poor, extending hospitality, and even caring for animals. Kudos to Weinstein for writing a book that will inspire, teach, and help kids react to the realities in the world around them."

Rabbi Harold Kravitz
Senior Rabbi, Adath Jeshurun Congregation
Minnetonka, Minnesota
Past Board Chair of *MAZON: A Jewish Response to Hunger*

"In this enjoyable second volume in the *YaYa & YoYo* children's book series, Dori Weinstein does a beautiful job of teaching Jewish values, from respecting nature and animals, to caring for each other. Readers will enjoy the playful banter and antics of the close-knit and fun-loving Silver family, and will learn more about Judaism's rich history as we gather under the Sukkah together."

Gail Rosenblum
Columnist, Minneapolis Star Tribune
Author of *A Hundred Lives Since Then: Essays on Motherhood, Marriage, Mortality and More*

"*Shaking in the Shack* brings us another fun romp with YaYa and YoYo and the Silver family! Dori Weinstein portrays the holiday of Sukkot as a joyful celebration of family, friends, and caring for others. The relatable and likable characters demonstrate healthy, positive relationships among friends, siblings, and between adults and children. The threads from the first book are a nice link, and book two also stands well on its own. Packed with positive messages, *Shaking in the Shack* is a great addition to Jewish middle-grade literature."

Amy Ariel
Jewish educator and Author of *Friends Forever*

"*Shaking in the Shack* is another winner from Dori Weinstein! Like her first book, the story unfolds so naturally, you don't realize how much you're absorbing about Jewish culture and practice. Dori perfectly captures the tween voice with YaYa and YoYo."

Beth Grafman
Former Librarian
Solomon Schechter School of Westchester
White Plains, New York

About the Author

Dori Weinstein is an award-winning author who grew up in Queens, New York. She is a graduate of Binghamton University (SUNY Binghamton) and Teachers College, Columbia University. Dori taught in public schools in New York City as well as at the Talmud Torah Day School in St. Paul, Minnesota. Dori enjoys visiting schools around the country where she teaches about Jewish books, writing, and publishing. She also teaches Hebrew music to preschoolers while continuing to create more adventures in the YaYa & YoYo series. Dori lives in Minneapolis with her husband Gary and their three children (when they're home, which is not very often).

Visit Dori on Facebook, Twitter, and on her website at www.yayayoyo.com.